"Daniel…"

He threw another half-dozen rocks into the churning river before he acknowledged Kimberly's presence.

Dusting off his hands, his gaze met hers. "Can we not talk about this, Kimberly? I just—I just can't. When I'm with you, I want to tell you…everything. Every last detail."

Setting his jaw, he started back up the trail, determination in every line and crease of his face.

"I promised to protect that young girl all those years ago and I intend to keep that promise, at least until I'm released from it. And nothing—not all the sweetest kisses in the world—is going to change that fact, even though I wish they could."

Dear Reader,

Each year, thousands of girls and women across the US struggle with a bleeding disorder that they may not even realize they have. For women with bleeding disorders, it takes an average of sixteen years to get an accurate diagnosis, according to the National Hemophilia Association on their Victory for Women website.

Bleeding disorders are frequently underdiagnosed, but they can have deadly complications. For more information, check out victoryforwomen.org.

Like Marissa in *Man of His Word*, my daughter has a rare, mysterious bleeding disorder that doctors have struggled to diagnose and treat.

Whether it's a bleeding disorder, a food allergy or any other life-threatening condition, such an issue affects an entire family.

Like Kimberly, I've struggled myself with how to let go while trying to protect my daughter, something every mother must learn. And like Kimberly and Marissa, we are blessed to have a strong "Daniel" in our lives—my husband and my daughter's dad, who keeps us grounded and always has our backs.

Hope you enjoy Kimberly and Daniel's story!

Cynthia

HEARTWARMING

Man of His Word

—

Cynthia Reese

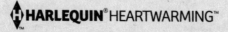

Recycling programs
for this product may
not exist in your area.

ISBN-13: 978-0-373-36721-4

Man of His Word

Printed in U.S.A.

Cynthia Reese lives with her husband and their daughter in south Georgia, along with their two dogs, three cats and however many strays show up for morning muster. She has been scribbling since she was knee-high to a grasshopper and reading even before that. A former journalist, teacher and college English instructor, she also enjoys cooking, traveling and photography when she gets the chance.

Books by Cynthia Reese

Harlequin Heartwarming

Seeds of Trust
A Place to Call Home
What the Heart Wants

Harlequin Superromance

The Baby Wait
For The Sake Of The Children

Visit the Author Profile page
at Harlequin.com for more titles.

To my sister, my best friend in the entire world

And in memory of Andrew...I'll say it like I mean it.

This book is owed in huge part to my smashing editors Kathryn Lye and Victoria Curran.

Another huge debt goes to my Heartwarming Sister Karen Rock, who patiently brainstormed with me.

Thanks, too, goes to Sgt. Tommy Windham and all the firefighters at the City of Dublin, Georgia's Fire Department. They very patiently helped me learn how real-life firefighters are NOT like firefighters on TV. In addition, I owe technical expertise to John Lentini, of Scientific Fire Analysis. All mistakes are mine!

This book was the product of the sacrifices of many: my critique partner, Tawna Fenske, as well as to my beta reader, Jessica Brown—and not least, my daughter and my husband.

CHAPTER ONE

KIMBERLY SLOWED THE car down to a crawl as she inched past the driveway. She didn't take her eyes from the dented mailbox that was in the shape of a chicken—a *chicken*, of all things. Even though she squinted, she couldn't make out a number or a name.

"Hey, Mom! There! This is it! See the number?"

Marissa's finger was trembling with excitement as she guided Kimberly's attention to a house number on the mailbox post itself, almost obscured by the thigh-high Bahia grass that had overtaken the shoulder of the narrow country road.

There it was—3332. Marissa was right. Relief sluiced over her. They had found it—*she* had found it, no thanks to the rather vague directions she'd been given. She gave her daughter a high five that smacked loudly within the confines of the car.

Kimberly glanced at the rearview mirror

and saw it was clear behind her, then reversed the car a few feet in order to make the turn into the drive.

No house was visible. She wound along a rutted dirt track between pastures dotted with cows.

"Hey, Mom, are those *chickens*?" Marissa asked, pointing at the field on the other side of the road.

"I think—" Kimberly squinted. Yes. There was a whole pasture, empty of everything except a huge flock of rust-colored birds streaming out from some sort of shed. As she drove past, she could see the chickens, cheek to jowl, pecking and scratching. "Yep. Those are chickens, city girl."

"I just didn't expect to see them like *that*, roaming around like cows," Marissa said. "How do they keep them from flying away? Or wandering off? I thought chickens stayed in a pen."

Marissa didn't sound as though she really needed an answer, so Kimberly turned her attention to the road ahead.

Now the chickens gave way to corn, slightly wilted from the hot late-May sun. The corn, in turn, gave way to a field of leafy green bushes—bush beans, maybe—that extended as far as the open pasture until it ended in a grove of thick dark trees.

The car dipped suddenly into a mud puddle, jouncing both her and Marissa. It was proof of their stretched, taut nerves that neither noted the big bump.

Then one last curve revealed a farmhouse. The house was green, with a steeply inclined metal roof a shade darker. The porch was wide with big curving beds of marigolds flanking the front steps.

Kimberly put the car in Park and glanced Marissa's way. Her daughter was twining one long red-gold strand of hair around her index finger, her lips compressed in concentration as she scrutinized the house.

"Do you think anybody's home?" Marissa asked.

"The captain at the fire station said this would be where we'd find the fire chief," Kimberly pointed out.

"I don't know what I was expecting," Marissa said. "It's not as if they're going to put on a welcome party for us, right, Mom?"

"Honey, there's no need to be nervous." Kimberly's stomach, full of butterflies, belied her statement. She *was* nervous. But she shouldn't let Marissa's nerves be fueled by her own neurotic thoughts. "It isn't as though we're meeting your biological mother or father. This is just the guy who…"

She trailed off. In the silence that followed, she heard a low "roo-roo-roo," the deep bark of what sounded like a decidedly large dog suddenly awakened from a midmorning nap.

"This is the guy who found me after my biological mom dumped me." Marissa's words were harsh and judgmental as only an eleven-year-old fixated on fairness and rules could be.

"Now, Marissa—" But before Kimberly could launch into her she-would-have-kept-you-if-she-could-have speech, a woman hurried around the side of the house, a large chocolate-brown dog at her heels.

"Hello, there!" she said as she wiped her hands on the dish towel she still held. The woman must have been in her sixties, but had a youthful appearance despite her salt-and-pepper hair, which was pulled back in a bun. Maybe it was the way she bounced as she walked, or the wide, welcoming smile on her face. "Can I help you? Are you lost?"

Kimberly had rolled down the window by now. "Uh, yes—I mean, no, I don't think we're lost. The captain on duty at the fire station told us we could find the chief here? That he was off today?"

"Daniel?" A frown marred the woman's smooth, tanned face. "Yes. He's here. I'm afraid he's still picking butter beans for me on the back side of the property, but I can call him for you. It will be a little while, though."

"Would you?" The doubt and anxiety that gnawed at Kimberly eased a little. "I would appreciate it. I'm Kimberly Singleton, and this is my daughter, Marissa."

"Okay, let me just…" The woman started to leave, then turned back. "Would you—would you care to get out? Stretch your legs a bit?"

"Sure, that would be great!"

"Absolutely. Make yourself at home. Y'all can wait on the porch if you'd like, and I'll bring you out some lemonade. Come on, Rufus! They don't want a big smelly dog jumping on them. C'mon, boy!"

Rufus hesitated, his tail flicking, then he obediently trailed the woman back around the house.

On the porch swing, Marissa extended one flip-flop-clad foot and grimaced at her pale white leg. "Mom, I'm still not tanned. I'll bet I could get a tan superquick in a tanning bed. When we get back home, can you please, please, please—"

"No. You are the color nature intended you to be, and I don't want to invite skin cancer on top of everything else you have going on. We don't know anything—"

"About my biological family's medical history. I know." Marissa's voice dwindled from a surge of anger to a tiny little whimper of self-pity. She jerked the swing with some violent rocking moves until she caught Kimberly's warning look and settled into a more sedate gliding motion. "You think that's his wife?" she asked.

"Maybe. I mean, I would think the chief would be older than the captain, and the captain was a bit older than me."

Just then, the lady of the house opened the front door and brought out a big tray of lemonade and glasses. "Here you go." She set the tray down on a table by the front window and with a tug pulled it close to them. "I talked to Daniel, and he said he'd be up here in about five minutes or so. And excuse me, I should have introduced myself—I'm Colleen Monroe. And I'm usually not this— Oh, was that a timer going off? My lunch is on the stove and a cake's in the oven—I need to check it, and then I'll be right back."

In a flash, she was gone. Marissa didn't have to be encouraged any further to serve herself a tall glass of the lemonade. She poured a generous serving from a fat-bellied pitcher into the two ice-filled glasses and handed one to Kimberly.

"Mmm…this is good, Mom! Why doesn't our lemonade taste like this?" Marissa smacked her lips appreciatively.

"Because we use a mix?" The lemonade *was* good—not too sweet, not too tart, perfectly chilled. It tasted of fresh lemons.

A tall rangy man about Kimberly's age in a dusty white T-shirt rounded the house. His hair was dark and rumpled, a hint of stubble along his jaw, his skin tanned, and he looked all sinew and bone and muscle in just the right proportions. The chief's son, perhaps?

"Hey. I'm Daniel Monroe. Ma said you were looking for me?"

Kimberly scrambled up in surprise. This was the fire chief? Had to be about her age, maybe very late thirties.

"Uh, yes. I'm Kimberly Singleton. And this is my daughter, Marissa." She swept her hand toward Marissa while nudging her to stand up with a carefully placed tap to the ankle. Likewise, Marissa rose to her feet.

Daniel Monroe's face continued to show polite curiosity, salted with a little apprehension in eyes that were the exact color of the summer sky. "Yes?"

"Well, we're sorry to bother you on your day off, but we're hoping you can give us some information. My daughter, Marissa…"

This was harder than she'd thought. She hadn't rehearsed it, and maybe she should have. She swallowed, feeling Marissa's growing anxiety emanating in waves beside her. "She was left as a newborn at your fire station. And I believe you were the one who found her?"

It was as though she had sucker punched Daniel Monroe. He rocked back on his heels and regarded first her and then Marissa for a long, long moment.

"So. You kept your name." The man's words, directed at Marissa, were tinged with wonder. It was an odd reaction that Kimberly had not at all expected.

Marissa shrugged her shoulders, then hunched them with the shyness that made her so often close up around strangers, or whenever she found herself the center of attention. She appeared, to Kimberly at least, as though she wanted to fall through the porch floor, not daring to meet the eyes of the fire chief—her rescuer. "My mom named me," she mumbled.

"The bracelet…" Kimberly's words trailed off. She dug the tiny baby bracelet out of her pocket and handed it to the chief.

He turned it over in his big sturdy hands, the delicate filigree of the bracelet so out of scale in comparison. Did his fingers shake? Or was that a figment of Kimberly's imagination? "I was afraid they wouldn't get it to you. To whoever adopted her—Marissa, I mean." He nodded in Marissa's direction, then handed the bracelet back to Kimberly. "Yeah. That's the one."

"We were hoping you could give us some information," Kimberly said.

She held her breath. Finally, finally, they were close to getting answers that could help Marissa's doctors—why had Kimberly put this off? Why had she been so afraid to make this trip?

Daniel didn't reply at first. Instead, he crossed the short distance to a chair and pulled it around to face the swing and the table. "Why don't we all have a seat?" he suggested, before he collapsed into the chair as though his legs wouldn't hold him any longer. "I've been picking beans since sunup, and I'm worn out. I see Ma got y'all some of her famous lemonade."

Kimberly and Marissa sat back down as well, the swing rocking under them. "It's very good, Chief Monroe," Kimberly told him. "Please give your mother my compliments."

But she couldn't ease back in the swing, not even if Daniel Monroe had sagged back against his chair and was downing a glass of lemonade.

He might have all the time in the world, but she didn't.

He placed the glass on the table with a thud. "Call me Daniel. I'm so new at the job that when I hear Chief, I think of my old boss, who recently retired, and when I hear Chief Monroe, I think they're talking about my dad. He was chief for years, but that…"

Daniel paused, his face shutting down for a moment. It left Kimberly pondering whether his father had pulled some strings to get his son the job. That would explain why Daniel was relatively young and yet had such a position of responsibility.

But he still hadn't offered any details about finding Marissa. Instead, he sat there, looking at them, his foot tapping restlessly on the porch floor, a pensive expression on his face.

"What—" Kimberly started to ask, but Marissa jumped in.

She blurted out, "So you found me? Where she dumped me?"

Kimberly winced. "She didn't—"

Marissa started to roll her eyes, then stopped because she must have been sure Kimberly would nail her on it. "Mom, you can dress it up any way you want, but the facts are the facts—she dumped me. She didn't want me, and she dumped me."

Daniel frowned. It erased the boyishness Kimberly had seen earlier in his face. "She brought you to a place where you'd be safe. She thought that's what she was doing—that fire stations were safe havens for newborns."

"You talked with her, then?" Excitement bubbled up in Kimberly as she leaned toward Daniel, nearly knocking over her half-empty lemonade glass. She hadn't dared to hope for anything as promising as this. All the court documents showed was that the baby had been left at the fire station.

"Yes." Daniel's response was clipped. "Briefly."

"You knew my birth mother?" Despite her

earlier hostility, Marissa leaned forward, as well. Gone was her fading-into-the-woodwork reaction, and Kimberly realized for the first time how deeply Marissa wanted to know about the woman—girl, really—who had brought her into the world.

"No. I didn't know her. I guess you could say I met her. That would be accurate."

"And she just drove up and handed me to you and left?" Marissa asked.

"No. Not exactly."

Even Kimberly found herself more than a little exasperated with Daniel's cagey answers. *Am I going to have to drag it out of him bit by bit? I only have the summer! I have to find this woman, have to know if she can tell us anything that will help Marissa.* "What can you tell us?" she asked.

He closed his eyes. For a few beats, he said nothing, only sat there, his arms folded across his chest.

Kimberly fought the urge to strangle him in frustration at his long silence. Finally he opened his eyes and gazed at her with a directness that jolted her. He compressed his lips and gave her a small, almost undetectable nod.

But his next words?

"Not much. I can't tell you much at all."

Then her heart did a double beat as he leaned forward and asked, "But how about I show you?"

CHAPTER TWO

DANIEL PARKED HIS pickup in the slot marked Chief and glanced in the rearview mirror. Yep. There was the little Toyota, with the mom and the daughter, pulling up behind him. They'd tailgated him the whole ride back into town from the farm.

He rubbed at a head that ached from too little sleep and too much sun. Between the new job and harvest time just gearing up, he felt as if he'd been run ragged.

And now this.

Blowing out a long breath, he opened the door. Gravel crunched under his foot, and behind him he heard the flags clanking against the pole. Wind was coming in from the west today, hot and dry. Unbidden, he found himself hoping there'd be no car fires on the interstate with such a stiff breeze.

Slamming the door, he saw that the girl and the woman had gotten out, as well. What was the mom's name? Kimberly? Yeah, Kimberly.

She wasn't what he'd expected. He didn't know what he'd expected. Adoptive parents didn't have to look like their kids.

And Kimberly and Marissa didn't match at all. Marissa had taken after Miriam, who'd been tall and had given Marissa her strawberry blond hair. Kimberly was slimmer and darker and much more petite. And she looked almost too young to be Marissa's mother.

But like Miriam, Kimberly possessed courage of a sort. Miriam had ginned up the courage and the fortitude to escape a dangerous situation, and he figured Kimberly had shown a similar bravery to tackle the red tape required to adopt a baby.

"So it was here?" Kimberly asked him.

Daniel tore his mind away from the razor-sharp memories of that day—ten years ago? No, eleven. Almost twelve, actually, this coming July Fourth.

"Yes." He found himself guarding his words. What could he tell them? What should he? Legally, he was in a bind, because Miriam was covered under Georgia's safe-haven law. But more than that, he remembered the girl's abject terror of her boyfriend's parents finding out about Marissa.

He'd given Miriam his word. And it was up to him to keep it.

Beckoning for them to follow him, he walked out to the patch of lawn between the firehouse and the street. One of the crew had just mowed the grass, and it smelled fresh and green. Unlike that summer day, there was no redolent smell of charcoal and sizzling burgers from a July Fourth cookout by the crew, no shrieks from kids playing tag under sprinklers on the side yard.

"She pulled up here," Daniel told them. "She was driving an old four-door. I was standing…" He pivoted, replaying the day in his head. "There, leaned against the side of the building. Everybody else had gone inside to eat."

It was all fresh—the grief he'd felt over his dad not being with them on that day, the fact that he had angered and worried Ma with his sudden move to follow in his father's footsteps as a firefighter, the last time his father had held his hand—his dad swathed in bandages, a mummy of a man in the burn unit.

Take care of your brothers and your sisters and Ma.

Keep your word, Danny, keep your word, no matter the cost.

The last words his father had spoken to him, an entreaty wrung out of a man in agony, a man needing assurance that his eldest son would take his place as the family's leader.

And Daniel had promised his father that he would.

On that July Fourth, he'd been bent on escaping the day's festivities, and that was why he'd been the one to see Miriam.

"What…sort of car?" Kimberly asked, behind him.

The question pulled him away from his own tangled emotions of that day and into the present. "You know, it was *old*. Like a 1970s Nova? I remember it had about four different colors of paint on it."

Daniel turned back to face Marissa. Yes, she had Miriam's red-gold hair, and it looked as though she was well on her way to achieving her biological mother's height. Funny how they both twirled their long strawberry blond hair around their index fingers.

Funny how he could remember that small habit of Miriam's at all.

"Is that why she dump—" Marissa broke off, apparently taking in the same look of exasperation that Daniel saw on Kimberly's face.

"Is that why she gave me up? Because she was poor?" Her words trembled with emotion.

"She gave you up because she cared about you. Because she couldn't figure out a way to keep you safe and still keep you, so she decided that keeping you safe was the better choice." Daniel fought a strange sense of protectiveness for Miriam, as though even the little he'd shared somehow violated his promise to her. "I honestly don't know if she was rich or poor or even if the car was hers. All I can say for a fact is that you were born here, in this spot, on July 4, 2003."

"I was born here? Right here? I thought..."

"You were born on the Fourth, right?" Now Daniel worried that maybe they'd gotten confused, that maybe this wasn't the same Marissa after all. No. No she was definitely Miriam's child.

"Yeah. I mean, yes, sir. People call me a firecracker baby. Because of my hair and being born on the Fourth and all..." Her face wrinkled as she said this, and her fingers settled for a moment on her hair and again twisted a strand of it. She didn't sound too enthused about the moniker.

Kimberly spoke up. "I didn't know she was born here, either. The court papers said Marissa's birth mother had tried to surrender her here at the fire station, and you were the firefighter who'd helped her. So…what can you tell us?" Kimberly asked. "What all do you remember? About that day?"

This Daniel could do. He smiled. "I was out here, minding my own business, and then this car comes roaring up, and I go to check it out…" He closed his eyes. The memory was still so sharp he could smell the charcoal. "And there you were, Marissa. Busy getting born, all on your own. You didn't even wait for the EMTs, and they were inside." He jabbed a finger over his shoulder to indicate the firehouse.

Again memories flooded him: the sweet weight of Marissa in his arms, the goofy feeling that swamped him as he held her.

The agony of having to turn her over to the child-welfare folks. At the hospital, he'd asked if he could keep her for a while, just in case Miriam changed her mind and came back for her daughter, but they said no, certainly not.

The "certainly not" had stuck in his craw. Miriam had trusted him. Why couldn't they?

But there were laws and regulations and he knew that he really couldn't raise Marissa on his own. So he'd made them promise that she would be placed in a good home.

Daniel had kissed the top of Marissa's little red head and handed her over, and that was the last time he'd seen her.

Until now.

And the mom they'd picked out for Marissa did look like a pretty good mom. Kimberly *was* pretty, and seemed caring. He noticed the furrow in her brow as she fretted silently over Marissa. She was worried. But she wasn't saying anything, just giving Marissa time to absorb what Daniel had told her.

"Really? You remember?" Marissa asked. Again, there was a tremor in her voice.

"As if it was yesterday."

He tore his gaze away from the girl's face, her expression so unreadable that he couldn't be sure if what he was saying was helping or hurting. Daniel turned to look at Kimberly.

Now, *she* was an open book. Her eyes, that curious blue, were bright with unshed tears. Her throat was working, and he could tell she was moved by the moment.

Had to be hard, helping her adopted daughter revisit the day she came into the world. Did Kimberly envy that mother? Envy the chance to have given birth to Marissa herself? Or was she afraid that Marissa would leave her in search of her birth mom?

"I have a picture," he said, his voice husky.

"A picture?" The words exploded from both Marissa and Kimberly. They stared at each other, their eyes wide with excitement.

"Can we see it?" Kimberly asked.

"Yeah. Sure. Come on. It's in my office."

Inside, Marissa glanced around the tiny office, shifting her weight from one foot to the other. Kimberly was more patient, and he noticed how she laid a light hand on her daughter's shoulder. Its fluttering movement seemed to comfort the clearly anxious Marissa.

He grabbed up the photo of him and Marissa and extended it to her. "See? I told you that you were tiny."

She stared down. "Oh." Disappointment was plain on her face. "I thought…I thought it would be of me and my birth mom."

But Kimberly had taken the photo from Marissa and was staring down at it. She traced her finger over the image, her mouth softly parted. A tear snaked down her cheek, and Daniel liked the way she let it be.

She looked up at Daniel. "This is you. With Marissa."

"Yeah. The guys took it. Right before I had to hand her over. DFCS said they'd find her a good home. Looks as if they did. I mean, I asked if I could keep you," he blurted out to Marissa, "but I mean, who was I kidding. I was a twenty-five-year-old unmarried guy, a rookie firefighter. Who was gonna trust me with a kid, huh?"

Marissa's eyebrows skyrocketed. "My mom was twenty-five when she adopted me. And she was single."

Something about that twisted in him. He shot a questioning look toward Kimberly, and she nodded. "Yeah, but, Marissa, at first I was just a foster parent. Besides, I'd already gone through all the foster-care paperwork and the classes, and they'd done a home study. Plus... you were listed as a special-needs baby. They needed somebody who would take you, no questions asked."

"Yeah. I forgot about all that." She leaned over her mother's shoulder and studied the photo. "Hey, I was kinda cute. I thought babies were ugly."

"You were beautiful. Tiny. But beautiful. Except..." Daniel scratched his head as he re-called the bruises he'd left on her pale pink skin. Other bruises, that the EMTs shrugged off, had started popping up, as well. Part of the birthing process, they'd assured him.

Just then the "ennnh" of the fire alarm's buzzer reverberated through the building, and the radio crackled to life. He listened, took in the bare facts: multicar accident on the interstate, gas-tank leak, trapped driver.

"Sorry," he told Kimberly and Marissa. "This will have to wait."

And then he was out the door, trying to focus on the fire call, the person trapped in the vehicle, that dry westerly breeze that could make fires on the interstate get out of hand with hair-raising speed.

But as he pulled on the last of his turnout gear and swung into the station's extended cab pickup with his captain at the wheel, he caught sight of Kimberly and Marissa's faces.

His gaze fixed on their expressions as Dave, his captain, peeled out behind the fire engine.

Marissa's was typical tweenager, like his nieces and nephews, her eyes alive with curiosity and excitement.

Kimberly? Her fingers went to her mouth, her brow creased ever so slightly and her eyes were dark with worry as they locked with his. She knew the life. The risks. The fact that even with routine calls, there were never any guarantees.

He didn't know how Kimberly knew, but her eyes held that same look that Ma's had every time his dad had left the table to answer a call.

And he didn't know how he felt about having someone he'd barely met worrying that much about him.

CHAPTER THREE

"You're sure you don't mind waiting?" Kimberly asked Marissa as they sat on the front bench in front of the fire station. They'd passed some of the time in the chief's office, but the cramped confines had seemed to make Marissa more restless, so Kimberly had suggested a change of scene. "The secretary said that it could take a while."

"I wish I could have gone with them!" Marissa enthused. "You know, see them cut the car up. Mrs. Karen—" she jabbed a finger back toward the station and the secretary's office "—she said they had to use the Jaws of Life. Man, wouldn't that be cool, Mom? To see them save somebody's life?"

Kimberly shuddered. She'd already picked up enough of the garbled radio traffic to understand that the woman driver was in critical condition and that the extrication was taking longer than Daniel had anticipated.

No, when she thought about the accident, all

Kimberly could picture was Marissa trapped in that car, critically injured, dying—it could have been them on that very interstate. She shook herself and purposefully focused her mind away from the grim vision and onto appreciating her good fortune.

Maybe they should leave and come back. Daniel would likely be tired and not in the mood for pesky questions when he returned. And wouldn't he have loads of paperwork? She needed him to be as cooperative as possible so that she could pick up any facts that might lead her to Marissa's birth mother. It was important.

No. She thought again about that woman trapped in the car. It was *critical* to find Marissa's birth mother.

"Maybe I could be a firefighter, huh, Mom?" Beside her, Marissa bounced with excitement. "It's a rush, don't you think? I mean, you're sitting here, or maybe washing the truck, and then, boom! You've got to fight a fire or get somebody out of a building—"

Kimberly didn't say the first thing that popped into her mind as Marissa burbled on. She didn't point out, not even gently, that there was no way a doctor would ever approve Marissa for a job as risky as a firefighter...or a police officer or a soldier or astronaut—any of the adrenaline-buzzing careers that Marissa gravitated toward. Maybe her daughter said she wanted to be those things because Kimberly had pointed out that they just weren't possible—and not because she was a girl, but because…

The rumble of the fire engine around the curve tugged her thoughts back to Daniel.

He did look weary when he slid out of the cab of the truck. His face was smeared with soot, his turnout jacket loosened to reveal a grimy white T-shirt.

"You're still here," he observed as his boots hit the concrete driveway.

"Yeah, you said— We waited." Now Kimberly was doubly uncertain about her decision. "But we can come back. I expect you're tired and you—"

"Hey, Chief! Did you save her?" Marissa interjected. "Is she okay? The woman in the car?"

"They airlifted her to Macon. I think she's got a good shot." Daniel's face brightened as he shifted to face Marissa.

"That is so cool! I wish I could have been there!"

"You sound like my niece. She's determined

to be a firefighter when she grows up. Gives my mother a heart attack every time she mentions it."

Kimberly couldn't help but admire the way Daniel was so patient and careful with Marissa. Maybe the fact that he had a niece explained it? Or maybe...maybe he still felt a connection with the baby girl he'd saved all those years ago?

"Should we come back?" Kimberly asked him, trying to gauge his willingness to talk with them.

He shook his head. "No. No, you've waited all this time. But can I have a few minutes to grab a shower? You wouldn't want to be cooped up with me in my condition right now."

Marissa spoke up again. "Can I help your firefighters some way? I mean, you've got to get things cleaned or organized or... something, right?"

Daniel chuckled, and Kimberly tried not to roll her eyes. This was the same girl who thought unloading the dishwasher every morning was equivalent to torture.

"Sure." He called over his shoulder to a firefighter—a woman, Kimberly noted. "Bobbi, show this probie how to check the hoses."

"You got it, Chief," Bobbi told him.

Then he turned to Kimberly. "Five minutes? You can wait in my office if you'd like."

It was more like ten minutes when he joined Kimberly. His hair was damp and curling, a droplet of water still clinging to the lock that brushed his forehead, but he looked less tired and more refreshed.

"Now, where were we? Oh, yeah, the picture." He picked up the photo, which Kimberly had placed on his desk after his hasty departure.

"Can I—can I get a copy of this?" Kimberly asked him. "It's a gorgeous photo. I'd love to have one, that is, if you don't mind."

"Sure." He nodded, and the droplet of water on his dark hair flew off. "I can scan it and email it to you, or I can go over to Walmart and get a copy made. How long are you going to be in town?"

"Er…that depends. We're trying to track down Marissa's birth mother. So if we can find her and talk with her, then we'll probably be leaving fairly soon."

"Oh, no. You…" Daniel worked his mouth, as if he was choosing his words carefully.

"I mean, you can tell us, right? Where to find her?" Kimberly scooted to the edge of the hard plastic chair, her stomach full of fluttering anxiety.

"She's been in touch with you?" Daniel asked instead of giving her the positive answer she had been hoping for.

"No. We knew about this place...and you..." She swept a hand to encompass the fire station. "And it was the only real clue we had, so we started here."

"I'm afraid this is a dead end, then," Daniel told her. "I can't tell you any more than I already have. I did tell you that I didn't know your daughter's birth mother. Didn't I?"

"You said that, but... I mean, if you thought back, you could remember details. And surely she mentioned her name." Kimberly hated the way her voice went up a half octave, that she was practically begging.

Daniel did a double take. His next words were loaded with patient forbearance that somehow managed to irk Kimberly even more than if he'd snapped at her. "Look, I know you've come all this way—I guess it's a long way?"

"Atlanta. We live in Sandy Springs, actually."

"Yeah, that's, what? Two and a half, three hours?" At her nod, he went on, "Yeah, a bit of a road trip. Like I was saying, you've come all this way, but I don't think I can help you. I've pretty much told you what I can."

"No. No, I'm sure there's more," Kimberly insisted. "Like what she looked like, or how you remembered what sort of car she was driving, and maybe she told you something that would help us locate her? And her parents? I mean, she was sixteen, she had to have parents—" Kimberly's throat, thick with emotion, closed up on her and she couldn't go on.

Daniel rubbed his mouth. He fingered the photo of him and Marissa as an infant. Kimberly could see him weigh a decision in his mind.

"Kimberly—may I call you Kimberly?" When she nodded, he continued, "I realize the not knowing is probably tough on the both of you. But have you really thought through whether this is a good idea?"

Now Kimberly's alarm turned to anger. "A good idea? My daughter desperately needs to find out about her birth mother—and anything she can about her medical history. She has a—a—" Again she choked on her words. She worked through her emotions, trying not to be the stereotypical hysterical female that would be all too easy for Daniel to dismiss.

Daniel sat back in his chair, his eyes focused on her with unwavering attention. Sounds of the firefighters working to restore equipment filtered into his office, but he said nothing while he waited on her to compose herself. She appreciated that. He didn't rush her. She was sure he had loads to do, and this was his day off, after all, but she could sense no impatience on his part.

"So…I take it," he said finally, "this isn't just idle curiosity, this reason you're searching for Marissa's birth mother? Because, I have to tell you, state law says her birth mother should remain anonymous. That's the deal—healthy baby surrendered in a safe and approved way in exchange for anonymity and no child-endangerment charges."

Kimberly let out a breath. Did he need a good reason to give her the information? Well, she had a jam-up one.

"No, it's not just idle curiosity. Not at all," she said. "Marissa has a life-threatening bleeding disorder, and her hem/onc—her hematologist-oncologist team in Atlanta—need to know everything they can. So please, please, any scrap you could give us, any way that we could track down her birth mother… It could mean the difference between life or death for Marissa."

CHAPTER FOUR

DANIEL SUPPRESSED AN inward groan at Kimberly's revelation. For a moment, he looked past her out the half pane of glass in his office door to the open back door and the yard beyond.

There was Marissa, wrangling fire hoses with Bobbi. She looked strong and healthy and practically glowed with enthusiasm and energy.

This kid's sick?

"You don't mean… Like what? Leukemia or something?" he asked.

Kimberly shook her head. "No, not a blood disorder. A *bleeding* disorder. Her blood doesn't clot properly. Well, it doesn't *stay* clotted properly."

He tried to work out what she was saying. "But I thought—call me a doofus—but I thought only boys could get hemophilia."

Kimberly rewarded him with a patient smile. "No, not at all. I mean—not to get too technical, but there's more than one sort of bleeding disorder. Girls can get certain kinds, too. And Marissa is one of the unlucky ones."

He leaned back in his chair, considering this new information and how it impacted his promise to Miriam.

Miriam.

He was flooded with an image of her little finger winding around his over the white sheet of her hospital bed, after he'd refused to bust her out of the hospital so she could run away...

"Daniel, you've got to promise," she'd said. "Pinkie promise. You can't tell anybody here who I am. Not anybody, because then he'll find her, and he...he can't." The girl's eyes had flooded with tears. "He just can't. I want her safe, and away from him, and the only way is if they don't know who I am. So...pinkie promise?"

At the time, he'd thought it a sad testimony that a girl who'd given birth was still young enough to use the phrase *pinkie promise* and believe in its power. He'd been inclined to not make that promise...until she'd blurted out the whole story, and until he'd clapped eyes on Uriel Hostetler.

And then he'd promised. Not a pinkie promise. A solemn oath...

"Are you listening to a word I'm saying? You look as though you're a million miles away!"

Kimberly's accusation hit the nail on the head. "I'm sorry. I was just… She looks so healthy."

Kimberly craned her head around in the direction he'd been staring and caught sight of Marissa. Her anger at him crumpled—he could see it in the way her eyes welled up with tears, which she blinked back.

"She does, doesn't she?" Kimberly whispered. "You've got to help us."

Daniel stood, stared out his office window at the cars going past. Listened for a moment to the cheerful ribbing between the firefighters.

It was that ribbing that made him decide. All that protected those men was their training and their promises to each other. After all was said and done, that was what a man was: his promise.

Daniel turned back to face her. She deserved that, at least. "Look…I want to."

"I hear a *but*."

He nodded. "You hear right. I'm in a jam. Legally, I can't. Like I said, it's a violation of the law for me to tell you anything that could identify her. Not just the laws that protect patient privacy—but the safe-haven law, too. The birth mother has to waive that right."

Whatever softness had been in Kimberly's face hardened with frustration. "But that's the point! I'm sure she would if she knew we needed her help. I'm not asking for anything else, only her medical history."

But so fast that he almost missed it, he saw Kimberly slide her middle finger across her index finger. He gave her a pointed look. "Really? Because somehow I don't believe that."

Kimberly's face pinked. He found himself liking the way *she* found it difficult to lie. "It's all *I* want. I can't say the same for Marissa. I'm not sure what she would want to know about her birth mother."

Daniel rubbed his jaw. The weariness of the day was catching up with him. Tomorrow he'd be back on schedule, back to figuring out exactly what being chief meant after his sudden promotion. He didn't think he had the energy to sort out the ethical conundrum of Kimberly's request. He'd made a promise, and besides that, the law said he couldn't give her the answers she wanted.

"Isn't there some other way to find out the information that you need? I mean, this is the age of genetic testing, where they can do anything in the lab. What could her family history tell you that the tests can't?"

"That's just it—that genetic testing." Kimberly scooched up to the edge of the chair, eager to plead her case. "This bleeding disorder is a mystery. It's so rare, Daniel. The doctors don't know for sure what it is. They've run almost every test there is out there, and there's...well, nothing. Apart from one other test—one level of her blood. It's called a PAI-1 test—"

"Pie? Like an apple pie?" He couldn't stop the chuckle that sprang to his lips. "Sorry. I didn't mean to laugh—"

She grinned back at him, and Daniel realized how much sunshine her smile brought into the room. It was a beautiful smile.

"No, I said the exact same thing when I first heard it. It stands for plasminogen activator inhibitor—*P-A-I*. It's a... Well, okay—" Now Kimberly stood, too, her body restless as she began to pace in front of his desk. "Your blood is like a jigsaw puzzle. It's got lots of different pieces that have to fall into place if it's going to clot—and stay clotted. If one of those pieces is missing or doesn't work right, well..."

"And Marissa is missing this PAI-1?"

"They don't know. Her hem/onc says the test isn't conclusive, but it's his best guess. The only way that they can conclusively diagnose it is through a DNA test or through a family history."

"So you *can* do a DNA test, then." A huge wave of relief swept over Daniel. He had an out.

"Oh, we could." Kimberly's mouth twisted. "But the only labs that can do the DNA testing are in Europe...and our insurance won't cover it. I've begged them...and they refuse."

The relief turned sour in his stomach. "That's...that's too bad."

"Besides that, her doctors say that inherited bleeding disorders are variable. Some are severe, some not so much. But if there's a family history...well, you can predict the course of it better. You know, like how she'd respond to surgery or trauma. I— Her doctors don't *know*."

She was fighting like all get-out not to cry, and he was impressed by that. Her grief and worry skewered Daniel, much as his mother's had in the days following his father's injury and death. And he understood then how Kimberly had known to worry about that car accident on the interstate. She'd imagined the worst a thousand times already.

But he'd given away his promise. And it had been for a very good reason, or at least he'd thought so at the time.

He walked around the desk and let himself be bold enough to give her the briefest touch on her upper arm. The contact felt more intimate than he'd meant it to, maybe because the warm silkiness of her skin tempted his fingertips to linger.

But she didn't protest. She stared up at him, her lips parted in an unspoken plea.

"I am sorry," Daniel told her. "I can't."

Kimberly whirled away from him and was halfway to the door before she accused over her shoulder, "You mean, you *won't*."

With that, she yanked open the door, intent on leaving.

Then she paused. Took a deep breath that he could see move through her slim body. Stared at him with those pleading eyes again.

"We're staying at the La Quinta near the interstate. Room 209. If you change your mind."

Then she was out the door and across the firehouse to retrieve Marissa.

Marissa, the baby he'd already said goodbye to once before.

Daniel collapsed into the office chair in front of his desk and picked up the photo of him and Marissa. In his mind's eye, he could see the bruises flowering against her pale baby skin, and he knew those memories gave credence to what Kimberly had told him.

With fingers that shook ever so slightly, he slid the photo out of the frame and watched as a slip of paper fluttered onto his lap.

The handwriting in the ballpoint ink was shaky, but still held a sixteen-year-old's flourishes, the hearts over the *i*'s, the loopy *M*.

Miriam Graber—born on September 19, 1986.

She'd added a phone number and an address, but Daniel had discovered that both were bogus when he'd called to check on her. So maybe the birth date was, too.

Still.

A quick online search would probably turn up a short list of possible Miriams. And if she'd gone back to her family—who'd been bent on returning to the Indiana Amish community where they'd come from—it couldn't be *that* hard to find her. There had to be some roll or register or paperwork somewhere. Census records, maybe? And now that she was an adult, maybe even voter registration lists?

He could do it.

Daniel stared from the paper to his computer. Considered.

Then he folded the paper and put it back behind the photo and the photo back in the frame.

Because there was nothing that said he had to do it right now.

CHAPTER FIVE

KIMBERLY'S HEAD ACHED as the hotel room's television blared out canned laughter from cartoon reruns that Marissa had watched a thousand times before. *Yeah, it would be great if our problems could be solved in a half hour minus commercials.*

She stared down at the list she was trying to make and attempted to focus on it.

People who might know something:
EMTs who responded
Police who responded
Emergency room staff
Newspaper reporter
Former fire chief
The person who took the picture of Daniel and Marissa

Daniel. He knew something. He was hiding some key piece of information.

The laughter blared out again. Marissa

slurped loudly from the fast-food drink she still had from lunch and completely demolished whatever little focus Kimberly had managed to muster.

Kimberly whipped her head around, ready to snap at her daughter to turn the television down and throw the cup away already when she took in Marissa's expression as the girl seemed to gaze at some point in the distance.

Marissa was stretched out, belly flat on the turned-back duvet, her chin propped on one hand and the empty cup in her other. Her eyes were wistful. Sad. She wasn't paying the slightest bit of attention to the TV.

Kimberly pushed her chair back from the unsteady laminate table and crossed the room to switch off the television. Marissa didn't even complain.

When she sat down beside her, Marissa jumped slightly. "Oh, sorry!" she mumbled. "I was thinking."

"I can see that. What's on your mind?"

"I just… Well, I just thought I'd *know* by now. You know. *Why.*"

The whole search for a family medical history had been a Pandora's box, as far as Kimberly could see it. She'd waited as long as she could, fought the insurance company on appeal after appeal. But when that didn't pan out, she knew she had to try to find another way to get that diagnosis.

Finding that diagnosis meant finding the girl who had given up Marissa. The prospect had filled Marissa with all sorts of conflicting emotions that Kimberly wished she could spare her daughter.

She squeezed Marissa's arm gently. "I know, honey. I thought so, too."

"We're never gonna find her, are we?" Marissa flopped over and stared up at the ceiling. "And the doctors are just gonna keep poking me and doing test after test after test and you're never gonna know what's wrong with me. And…I'm never gonna know *why.*"

Kimberly's throat closed up. She could barely breathe, much less swallow past the lump that had formed there.

Be the parent. Be the grown-up.

"Chin up," she told Marissa in what she hoped was a brighter voice than she felt. "We're not out of hope yet. I'm making a list of everybody who might know something."

Marissa giggled, her nose wrinkling and her eyes crinkling up. "You and your lists."

"Don't poke fun. They work."

"So let's get started, then. Go bang on some

doors. Anything is better than being holed up in this dump." Marissa exploded off the bed and started a search for her shoes. A loud dull *thunk* resounded from the bed's wooden toe-kick. "Ow! I stubbed my toe!"

"What? Is it—" Kimberly forced herself to stay calm. "Are you hurt?" She tried to ask this casually, as if she was a normal mom with a normal kid.

"Yes, I'm hurt! It hurts really bad—" Marissa hopped on one leg back to the bed, where she examined her toe. Kimberly could see no sign of injury.

The bruise would come later. And it would tell the story.

"Relax, Mom. It's okay. Nobody ever died from a stubbed toe, it just hurts. Normal kid hurt, okay? No need to get all worked up. Why do they put that under there anyway?"

"To make it easier to clean up—if it's blocked off, nobody can put anything under the bed," Kimberly told her. She rose. "I don't know if we can find anyone—"

"You mean, like a body? That would be creepy, wouldn't it? Finding a body under the bed?" She shuddered dramatically.

Kimberly succumbed to the temptation of a heavenward gaze and shook her head. "I think they had in mind something more like dust bunnies or an absentminded eleven-year-old's flip-flops. Like I was saying, it's almost five o'clock, so I'm not sure what we can get accomplished today. Are you ready for some dinner somewhere?"

"I *so* can't believe I'm asking this." Marissa shook her head in doleful disbelief. "And if you put this on Facebook, I will deny it to my dying day. But can we go somewhere that's *not* fast food? I miss real food. I miss you making me eat my vegetables. Can we go somewhere with some broccoli or something so that I can eat it and gag, and then enjoy a hamburger again?"

Marissa's crooked little grin warmed Kimberly.

"Sure. Open that drawer there and hand me the phone book—"

But her request was interrupted by a knock on the door. They exchanged glances. Marissa held up her hands and in playful mock seriousness pronounced, "I didn't do nothin'."

Kimberly stepped to the door and stared through the peephole.

Daniel.

With shaking fingers, she unbolted the security lock and swung the door wide to allow the fire chief entry. "Daniel! I—I honestly wasn't expecting you. Uh, come in!"

He didn't budge from the threshold. Instead, he rested one hand on the doorjamb and shuffled a work-boot-clad foot before he said, "Actually...I just came by to— Uh, I was wondering. Would you two care for some supper?"

Kimberly was gobsmacked by the invitation. Was this his way of gearing up to tell them who Marissa's birth mother was? Her thoughts were so weighed down with a blur of questions and pulsating hope that she couldn't even give him an answer.

"Is it fast food?" Marissa blurted into the silence.

Regret etched his features. His rangy frame began turning away, as if they'd said no. "Uh, no. I wasn't thinking of something quick. Sorry, I guess I didn't consider what a kid might like to eat. I'll leave you two to your—"

"I'm in!" Marissa bounced off the bed, the total antithesis of the pensive child she'd been a few minutes before. "Mom? You need your purse?"

CHAPTER SIX

FOR THE FIRST few minutes in the truck, silence reigned. Yes, Daniel had switched off the radio as it blared a staticky sports talk show when they'd driven out of the parking lot, but after that, he didn't offer much in the way of small talk.

The way he drove, his strong hands lightly gripping the steering wheel at precisely ten o'clock and two o'clock, his eyes flicking between the rearview mirror and the road ahead, the speedometer never straying above the posted speed limit, didn't encourage Kimberly to attempt any conversation.

Marissa, she noted wryly, didn't break the silence, either, despite her enthusiastic acceptance of Daniel's invitation. Something about wheels turning on a vehicle signaled her to slap her earbuds in and listen to whatever was on her iPod. And as soon as she had slid into the crew cab seat of Daniel's pristine truck, she'd done just that.

So Kimberly occupied herself with absorbing the sights. The town was small by Atlanta standards, but it was busy. The four-lane they were on, while not exactly choked with traffic, still held a good number of impatient five-o'clock drivers.

She watched as they passed by a host of fast-food joints and several casual dining choices—a steak house, a buffet-style restaurant, a Mexican place, something that looked like a mom-and-pop Italian pizzeria. Strip malls gave way to the downtown, its buildings showing signs of a recent facelift and heavy on planters filled with bright annuals, stores with colorful awnings and sidewalks with strips of deep redbrick.

When Daniel passed up the two downtown restaurants shoehorned among jewelry stores, boutiques and a bakery, something niggled in the back of her mind.

That something went to full-alert status as he made a turn onto a familiar-looking highway heading out of town.

"Where are we going?" she asked.

It took him a minute to respond, almost as if he didn't register what she'd asked at first. "Oh! Didn't I say? Sorry. Out to the farm. Is that okay? We're having supper out there, and I thought…since it was Marissa…"

A peek over her shoulder netted Kimberly a quick averted glance from Marissa, but not before she had seen a flash of telltale curiosity. So. Marissa had been listening in on the conversation despite the earbuds.

Kimberly swiveled a bit in her seat to face Daniel. "Your mom won't mind? We don't want to intrude—"

He took a hand off the steering wheel, waved it to dismiss her concern. "No, Ma was all for it. And so was everybody else."

"Everybody else?" Exactly what was she walking into? Kimberly didn't mind standing up in front of thirty students to hammer the intricacies of English grammar into their heads, but she'd never been great at social gatherings.

She'd been a shy child who'd grown into a shy teenager, much to the disappointment of her social extrovert of a mother. Between working an unending series of low-paying jobs as a waitress or bartender and blowing off steam with her current group of party-hardy friends, her mother had pretty much left Kimberly to her own devices.

Daniel seemed to thaw a bit. His eyes, that

amazing sky blue, crinkled at the corners, his mouth curved up and his whole demeanor lightened. "I gotta warn you, it's a brood of us. Ma had six of us, three boys and three girls, and so the house is always rocking. I hope you don't mind kids, because there's probably a half dozen around all the time."

"Yours?" Was he married? She realized she was disappointed—and that she'd already checked out his ringless third finger without even being aware she had.

"Oh, no. My sisters' kids—let's see, there's Taylor and Sean and the twins, and Cassandra, and—"

He kept reeling off names, and every additional one made her palms grow even damper. This sounded more like a family reunion than supper—and it turned her stomach into the headquarters for a butterfly convention.

Those butterflies were in mad midflutter when Daniel turned onto the bumpy driveway to the farmhouse. As he drove past the chickens, she shook off her anxiety to blurt out, "Why do you use a whole pasture for a single flock of chickens?"

"Well, it fertilizes the pasture. And then our cows eat the grass, and they fertilize it some more, and then we rotate out our crops.

We try to do everything pretty much organic here—better for the land. My dad…my dad was a big believer in being a good steward to the land. It's how he would have wanted us to continue."

His hands tightened on the steering wheel, and his face became closed off. Kimberly wasn't exactly sure what to say—it was obvious from Daniel's tone and use of the past tense that the one person who wouldn't be here was his father.

They had that in common, then…although Daniel's father probably wasn't a ne'er-do-well who spent more time in jail than on the streets like her dad, who had finally died in a prison knife fight. No, Kimberly decided as she slid out of the truck onto the carefully tended lawn—Daniel's family seemed to be a different kettle of fish altogether.

They had parked around back, and Kimberly could see that the lawn around the back deck and tall white privacy fence was filled with cars and trucks—had to be nearly a dozen. Children scampered around the deck in swimsuits and shorts. A loud screech followed a sudden splash of water.

"Sean Robert Anderson! You are dead! D-E-A-D, do you hear me?" a woman yelled.

"Because now that I'm good and wet, there's no reason for me not to jump in and drown you, now, is there?"

A smaller splash signaled someone had gone in after the unfortunate soon-to-be-deceased Sean Robert.

"Wait, no— Aunt Cara, it was an accident. I swear— No, not the tickles, not—"

Laughter spilled out over the fence with its carefully tended rosebushes—not just from the boy and his aunt, but other people, too. For a moment, Kimberly was frozen in place by a potent mix of feeling wistful and bashful.

Daniel had gone on ahead, but must have sensed that she was no longer beside him. He turned, grinned and crooked his finger. "C'mon. I promise. They're loud, but they don't bite."

Her breath caught in her throat at the way he'd beckoned her to come. Silly. But for a moment, she wished that he was more than just a polite guy with a secret or two to hide.

A screen door squawked open at the back of the house, off the deck. "Daniel? Did she and the girl come?"

It was Daniel's mother, wearing an apron, her face flushed from the heat of the kitchen. Around her still more kids spilled out.

"I wanna see the baby! Can I see her?" a towheaded boy of about six asked.

Another, an older sister by the resemblance, rolled her eyes. "Logan, it's not a baby. She's my age. Uncle Daniel *found* her when she was a baby."

Logan looked disappointed, then confused. "So why didn't he keep her?"

By now, Daniel's mother had cut the distance to Kimberly and Marissa in half. Kimberly's feet started moving to the woman of their own volition—she found it impossible to resist her warm, welcoming smile and the twinkle in her eyes.

"It's good to see you again!" his mother said in way of greeting, as if they were long-lost family members, not perfect strangers. "Thank you so much for coming out to eat with us— it's not fancy, now, just plain fixin's. And be sure to call me Ma, everybody does. If you call me anything else, I might not answer."

"Thank you." Kimberly's tongue couldn't wrap itself around any other words, but it didn't matter, because in all the noise and laughter, Colleen Monroe didn't seem to notice. She just put one arm around Kimberly shoulders, and the other around Marissa's, and guided them to the deck.

"Hey, there," Logan's big sister said to Marissa. "I'm Taylor. You bring a swimsuit? No? Well, we look about the same size, and I've got a spare. What do you have on that iPod? Want to see my playlists?"

And with that, Marissa would have been gone without so much as a backward glance if Ma hadn't hollered after her, "Marissa, honey, you have any food allergies?"

Taylor rolled her eyes again. "Ma! Just because I have food allergies doesn't mean you have to—"

"I will always ask, young lady. And besides, I saw the medical ID bracelet on Marissa's wrist. I want my food to be safe for everybody."

But there was no sting in those words—in either of their responses. It wasn't the vicious power struggle that Kimberly remembered between her and her mother, and she'd never really known her grandparents.

Marissa shook her head. "No. No food allergies."

"Great! Y'all go on, have a good time." Ma turned again to Kimberly. "Don't mind me asking Marissa instead of you, but around here, we're trying to get Taylor to be the one in charge of her food allergies—peanuts and corn, of all things."

"Oh, no, that's okay. Personal responsibility about your health is a really big thing for me," Kimberly said as she followed Ma into the kitchen.

If outside was noisy, in the kitchen it was pure bedlam. Every counter was full of in-progress meal prep, with two women working alongside still more kids. They greeted her with distracted but warm hellos and introductions, and then someone pressed a bunch of carrots and a peeler in her hands. Before she knew it, Kimberly had forgotten to be shy and had fallen right into working beside them.

And she loved it. Here, she felt respect and family love radiate out and wash over her. The teasing, the joshing, the inside jokes—things she swore normally would have made her feel more alien instead made her feel as though she could fade securely into the background and absorb it all just by osmosis.

As she was finishing up the carrots and turning to ask if they should be sliced, diced or shredded, she felt a tug on her pants. She looked down to see the towheaded boy staring up at her.

"You're pretty," he said. "Are you gonna

be Uncle Daniel's girlfriend? Because his last one wasn't nearly so pretty as you."

"Uh, Logan, I, uh—"

"Nope, I'm *Landon*, can't you tell? I'm bigger than Logan. 'Cause I was first, so that means I'm oldest. So are you? Uncle Daniel's girlfriend?"

Thoroughly flummoxed by how identical the boy was to his brother and by his question, which had been issued in a rare moment of quiet in the kitchen, Kimberly stared around for help. DeeDee, the little boy's mom, had stepped out to check on the meat on the grill. The other women could barely smother their amusement. To her chagrin, she saw Daniel himself had come in. He leaned against the doorjamb, an amused smile playing on his lips as he waited for her answer.

She stuttered it out. "No, no, I'm not, Landon. Your uncle is just a… Well, he's a…"

What was Daniel to her? She locked eyes with him, feeling a strange buzz of connection. Already he was more than the stranger she'd met that morning. He'd been the man who'd saved her daughter, and didn't that mean he was more to them than some random Joe Blow?

Daniel took pity on her. "I hope she and

Marissa will be my friends, Landon. Wouldn't that be good? To have a new friend?"

"She'd be better as a girlfriend. Mama said you needed a girlfriend, and so I figured maybe you were gonna mind her, you know, like you say I need to mind Mama?"

Just then, Landon's mother stepped back inside with a platter full of grilled pork chops, her face beet-red. "Landon Anderson! If you're going to 'mind' me, then maybe you should do a better job listening when I tell you to lay off the personal questions!"

"It wasn't personal, Mama! It wasn't about the bathroom or how much she weighs or—"

"Come on, bud." Daniel held out his arms. "I think it's time we hightailed it out of here— what do you say about a ride on my shoulders? Let's go find out what your uncle Rob and uncle Andrew are up to, huh, buddy?"

"Daniel! You're encouraging him!" DeeDee protested. "How will he ever learn what's appropriate if all of y'all keep laughing it up about how cute he is when he gets too personal?"

"I'll have a serious heart-to-heart with him, Scout's honor. We'll do the whole boundaries deal." By that time, Daniel had swung the kid up on his shoulders and the kitchen rang with Landon's giggles of delight.

Something about the sight melted Kimberly's heart. Maybe it was because she'd never had anyone do that for Marissa. Maybe any handsome guy with any cute kid would have made any single mom's insides quiver.

Or maybe it was the way he held her gaze just a tenth of a second longer and added in an offhand manner, "I'll keep an eye out for Marissa, too."

Whatever it was, Kimberly had to remind herself that the only reason they were here, in the midst of everything she couldn't give Marissa, was that Daniel, handsome or not, was holding out about Marissa's birth mom.

And that didn't square with the man strolling out the back door, a little boy securely on his shoulders.

CHAPTER SEVEN

THE LAST DISH was washed, the grill cleaned, the scraps fed to Rufus and even Landon and Logan were splayed out on the floor asleep in the living room. Daniel looked around for Kimberly, sure she'd want to head home.

Maegan caught his gaze and whispered over the sleeping baby in her arms, "I think she went to check on Taylor and Marissa."

Daniel couldn't help but reach out to stroke baby Sophie's plump cheek. Just as his fingers drew closer, Maegan swatted him away. "Don't even think about it. It took me a half hour to get my niece asleep, and if you wake her up, she can be *your* niece again."

"She *is* my niece."

"Funny, ha-ha, you always seem to forget that when she's cranky and crying, big brother." But there was no real reproach in Maegan's voice, just her usual teasing.

"I guess I'd better see if Kimberly is ready to go. I got sidetracked with the dynamic duo..." He trailed off and pivoted toward the back of the house.

"Hey, Daniel...I really like her," Maegan called after him in a hoarse whisper.

"Sophie?" he asked.

"No, you big lug. Kimberly. And Marissa. I'm glad you brought them out here."

Daniel nodded, but he wasn't convinced that it had been his smartest move. He'd viewed it as a consolation prize, a way to give them something when he couldn't break the promise he'd made so many years ago. Now he worried that it would be harder than ever to keep that promise.

He found Kimberly standing stock-still in front of a bedroom door, the door slightly ajar. Tweenage-girl voices came filtering through it. When Kimberly spotted him, she blushed but held up a finger to her lips.

"—and I thought I had it bad," Marissa was saying. "You mean you never get to eat a Big Mac?"

"Nope. High fructose corn syrup in the ketchup and the bun. But I get to drink the coffee, so whenever I go with friends, I get me a coffee and sip on it."

"Wow! You get coffee? My mom would never let me drink coffee. It's always, 'Marissa, remember your bleeding disorder,' or 'Be careful, Marissa,' or...I dunno. She doesn't *mean* to be a pain, but man, is she ever a helicopter mom. That could be her motto, you know? I am Helicopter Mom. Feel my rotor wash."

"But you've got that cool medical ID bracelet... Wow! I've got to get my mom to order one like that. Where'd you say you got it? Mine's all clunky, like something a fifty-year-old man would wear with pants up to his armpits and a sweater vest," Taylor declared.

That, along with the rotor-wash comment, was the last straw for Daniel. He felt a mix of laughter and shame at eavesdropping pulse through him, and he tugged Kimberly by the arm and headed down the hall and out the door to the side porch.

"Do you do that a lot?" he asked. "Listen in at keyholes?"

"No. And I got my just desserts, let me tell you. Feel my rotor wash?" She laughed and wiped her eyes with the back of her hand.

"You know, the two of us are smack-dab in the middle of middle-aged, if those girls think fifty is ancient." Daniel sank down into the swing and let out a belly laugh.

Kimberly collapsed beside him, closer than

she'd been all night. He could feel the silky strands of her hair brush against his arm, smell the scent of strawberries clinging to her as she chuckled along with him.

She lolled her head back on the swing and stared up at the porch ceiling. Her laughter petered out into a rueful sigh.

"I only want to keep her safe, you know? Safe and healthy. But...if I make sure she survives to be a grown-up, will her love for me survive, too?" Kimberly's words vibrated with a regret and uncertainty that pulled at Daniel. With a team under his command, and the memory of the awful fire that had claimed his father and critically injured several other firefighters, he understood Kimberly's dilemma perfectly.

He didn't even realize that he'd clasped her hand in his until he felt her twine her fingers more tightly into his grip. But he couldn't pull away. Her hand in his fit too neatly, too right.

"It's a tough job. I'm sort of in the same boat, what with keeping my guys fit and healthy and safe. They don't see the need for the exercise program I've insisted on, or the regular home-cooked meals. You know the number one killer of firefighters in the line of duty? Heart attacks. Not burns, not smoke inhalation, not heat stroke. Heart attacks. Every time I see a fast-food sack in one of my guys' hands, I can almost picture him keeling over in the middle of a structure fire."

"But they respect you. I could tell that. Today. They listened to you, they didn't argue." Something in the way Kimberly said it made Daniel sure that she didn't enjoy the same rapport with Marissa. "So how do you keep them safe and not make them hate you?"

"Ultimately it's easier with guys who need a paycheck," Daniel admitted. "With kids… Honestly? I don't know. When I was Taylor and Marissa's age, I thought I was ten feet tall and bulletproof, too. Still, even with kids… I mean, she's almost twelve, right? So you can ease up. She knows, Kimberly. She gets it, even if you don't think so. I see that in Taylor. She may carp and complain, but when someone offers her something to eat, she's the first one to say, 'No label? No, thank you.'"

Kimberly snuggled deeper into the cushions of the swing—and tighter against Daniel—as she slipped off her shoes and tucked one foot under her. Daniel's breath caught in his throat as he noticed the petite perfection of that foot, with the pale pink polish on the toes. Inwardly, he shook himself.

This woman would be gone by tomorrow. What they had here was some sort of fake chemistry, some tenuous bond because of their link to Marissa. It wasn't real. And even if it was…

Kimberly yawned. In a drowsy, distracted way, she said, "It's hard to believe, isn't it, that Marissa is just four years younger than her birth mother when she gave birth to her?"

Daniel's body stiffened. It was as if a page to a fire had sounded, her words zapping through him and setting every nerve on high alert. How to answer that? Was this Kimberly's sneaky way of worming more information out of him?

"What do you know about her birth mother?" Daniel asked in way of a reply.

"Well…not much," Kimberly said. "I have a copy of the police report. And when DFCS gave me custody of Marissa, they provided me with their own incident report. Maybe the social worker shouldn't have, I don't know, but it gave me the bare outlines of the events. Although…I didn't know Marissa was actually born at the fire station until you told me."

Again, Daniel was taken back to that day, to that one peaceful, amazing moment when, amid the chaos, he'd held the baby snugly against his chest, astonished that any mother could willingly let anything that perfect go.

Miriam's pleas came back to him… *She's not safe, Daniel! She's not safe! He'll kill her! I know it!*

He had turned out to be the baby's grandfather—Uriel Hostetler. And though Daniel had at first thought Miriam was overly dramatic, the minute he'd spied Hostetler in the hospital's waiting room, he had to admit he'd never known anyone to have eyes as cold as the tall, hulking man in broadcloth and suspenders. With a flowing head of golden hair and a full beard to match, he'd resembled nothing so much as a lion on the prowl for a hapless gazelle.

Standing in that waiting room, Hostetler had lorded over the entourage that had accompanied him—over Miriam's own parents, who seemed henpecked and browbeaten and in no way capable of offering the support and protection Miriam so badly needed.

Hostetler had turned out to be the baby's grandfather, and the leader—some might say tyrant—over the small Amish community that had relocated here.

Daniel had known lots of people of the Amish and Mennonite faith—good, honest folks who worked hard and showed compassion and mercy in their everyday lives.

Uriel Hostetler? He didn't deserve to be named in the same class of people.

Kimberly's next question, not to mention the gentle squeeze to his fingers, brought Daniel back to his present dilemma.

"So? Are you ready to tell me?" she asked. Her eyes were huge and seemingly bottomless, filled with hope and pleading as she gazed up at him. "About Marissa's birth mother? It's not idle curiosity, I promise. And you of all people—I mean, you understand how it is to have a child in the family with health issues. I have to know. I have to help Marissa."

A wrenching pain tore through Daniel's very soul. It would be so easy to say the two words Kimberly desperately wanted—needed—to hear. They were on the tip of his tongue, a nanosecond, a very exhalation away from being uttered.

Miriam's face floated through his memory, eyes that had pleaded as much as Kimberly's. She'd trusted him with the most important secret of her life and her baby's, and had come to that fire station in need of sanctuary.

"Kimberly…I can't. Legally. Ethically. I can't. I am so sorry."

Her pleading eyes turned stony. She leaped up from the swing as though the seat cushions had suddenly ignited beneath her.

"Ethically? You have the nerve to talk to me about ethics? When my daughter's health— her life—is at stake?"

He rose and tried to take her hands in his, but she shook him off. "Kimberly, you have to see things from my position. There's a reason that we have safe-haven laws. It's to protect the babies. Without a safe haven to turn to, Marissa might not have even been alive if—"

"And she might not *stay* alive if you don't help me! Don't you get that, Daniel? What if someone held back information on, I don't know…a fire, and how bad it was. Maybe it was started with hazardous materials that could kill your—"

He cut her off midsentence. "I get it. I get why you need to know. But can't you get why *I* can't tell you? Just for two seconds, see it from where I'm standing. I'm bound, Kimberly. Legally. The State of Georgia says I can't."

Why did he even try to make her to understand? To approve, even? She was never going to.

Sure enough, Kimberly shook her head in disgust and grimaced. "I think I'd like for you to take us back to our hotel now. No. I know I would."

With that, she strode across the creaking porch boards and slipped in the house without so much as a backward glance.

CHAPTER EIGHT

KIMBERLY RUBBED HER eyes and started over with the pocket calculator. A few keystrokes later and the grim truth emerged. The red-alert figure the calculator had coughed up had not been a mistake. Her checking account really *was* running on fumes.

Medical bills. And now this trip, which had taken longer and required more money than she'd bargained for. The gas, the rooms, even in a no-frills interstate landing spot, the fast-food meals...

Kimberly allowed herself the luxury of remembering the meal at Daniel's the night before. Not only had it been free, but it had also been delicious: grilled pork chops done to a turn, homemade baked beans, coleslaw, potato salad and homemade strawberry shortcake. Most of it had come from the family's farm—she would have paid a fortune for the same meal done at a farm-to-table restaurant in Atlanta.

More than that…it had been the way it was served. Kimberly's main memory of baked beans was cold out of a can for dinner, liberated with a manual can opener while her mother was out working—or partying. Sometimes it had been hard to tell the difference, really.

"What's the point of going blind studying? Have fun while you still can, honey bunch," her mom would tell her, trying to pry her loose from her work. "None of those books will do you good when you get out in the real world. Life's a grind and then you die."

How crazy was it that Kimberly had envied the friends who had parents who went nuts over a B on a report card? Or who actually came home and cooked dinner? And when Marissa had dropped into her life like the miracle she was, Kimberly had been determined that the little girl would know stability and routine and dinner on the table every night.

The Monroes, though… She hadn't known families like that actually existed. They'd laughed and teased and joked…and she could see hints of deeper emotions, too. The care they took with Taylor, the way they looked over each of those kids. And Ma… Oh, Ma, how she ruled over the whole brood with such a gentle but firm spirit.

To have a family like that. To belong.

Because honestly, Kimberly had never felt like she belonged to anybody except for Marissa, and lately, what with all the emotional upheaval, sometimes Marissa didn't seem to want to belong to her.

Last night had been a beautiful reprieve. She hadn't even realized how much she had been starved for the rowdy good humor of a large family. But, and now she glanced back down at the LED numbers on her calculator, she couldn't afford to linger too much longer.

A day longer, maybe two, was really all she could afford. Back in Atlanta, she had bills to pay, and school would be starting soon enough—the first week of August. If she wanted to save money and time enough to make the trek out to Indiana to have Marissa seen by the world-renowned specialist on PAI-1, Kimberly couldn't waste seventy dollars a night on a hotel room in a town with no real answers.

If only Daniel would tell me what he knows...

She closed the checkbook and pulled out her list of people to talk to. She would start with the police officer listed on the incident report.

Galvanized by the hard look at her finances and priorities, Kimberly called out to a sleeping Marissa, "Hey, sleepyhead! Time to get up, okay? We need to start seeing some folks."

Kimberly rooted around in her bag. Yes, there it was, the folder with the incident report and the scant information she had about Marissa's birth. And the responding officer, Timothy Clarke. With any luck, Officer Clarke would still be working for the police department, and maybe he could help her— or at least point in the direction of someone who could.

Which was more than Daniel was willing to do.

Be fair. He's an honorable man. He doesn't want to break the law.

But if the spirit of the law had been to protect children, then surely, to help Marissa, bending it would be okay.

"Fifteen more minutes. Please, Mom, please." Marissa burrowed deeper into the covers. "I. Am. So. Tired."

"Yeah, well, you played hard yesterday. And we stayed out too late."

The memory of Daniel beside her on that swing, his hand in hers, the night air soft and velvety around them, suddenly swamped Kimberly. To shake off the unsettling feeling, she needed to get moving. And to get moving, she had to get Marissa vertical. With her free hand, she yanked at the thin coverlet.

With reflexes like a cat, Marissa yanked back. "Mo-om. Lemme stay here, please? I'll lock the door. I won't go anywhere. I'll just sleep. For a month. Or maybe two."

"No, I am not about to leave you here by yourself in a strange hotel room in a strange city."

Marissa opened one eye. "Well, okay. Let me go hang out with Taylor. That was fun yesterday. She's cool."

Kimberly dropped to the bed, confused. "Marissa, this isn't a fun-and-games vacation. This is… I thought you wanted to be with me when I talked to these people."

"Well, of *course*, I want to know. But I… Can't you go and tell me about it? You know, later? And I wouldn't have to, er, actually, *be* there?"

This last phrase, she uttered in a small voice. Her knuckles were white against the coverlet. She bit her bottom lip and closed her eyes, but Kimberly could see that she wasn't really sleepy anymore.

No. She was…apprehensive. Yesterday had been tough for Marissa, maybe tougher than even Kimberly had realized. Was she putting her daughter through too much too soon?

If she'd had anybody to leave Marissa with back home, Kimberly would have made this trip alone. But she really didn't. Most of Marissa's friends were off at camp or on vacation, and the ones who weren't… Well, their parents weren't Kimberly's pick of the litter. Her own mother? That certainly hadn't been a possibility.

And Marissa had been okay with the plan, even a little excited. Still…

"I'm sorry, honey. We barely know the Monroes. I can't invite us out there—"

Marissa rolled her eyes. "They're practically *family*, Mom. I mean, Daniel *found* me. And Taylor wanted me to spend the night last night, or at least come out today."

"Look, it's great that you bonded with Taylor—you and she have a lot in common, what with her own health issues—"

"Mom! Not everything is about medical stuff. I like Taylor because she's funny and cool and they've got a *pool*, which is way more fun than having to follow you around all day while you do your Nancy Drew thing. Me and Taylor, we're not like a pair of old ladies, trading doctor stories."

"The answer is no. You know my rule. The mom has to call me. It can't be something—"

"Kids cook up." Marissa finished Kimberly's standard speech on the subject. "Oh, all right, you *win*! *Again!*" Then with ill grace she slung herself out of the bed and slammed the bathroom door.

Kimberly sighed and rubbed her temples. Already she could foresee that the day would be a tough one. She knew, from long experience, that Marissa would stew for at least an hour, but then eventually, if she left her alone, her fair-to-partly-cloudy child would come around.

This is for her, Kimberly told herself. *It's not as if I have any other options. And I certainly won't trouble Daniel Monroe again!*

THE POLICE STATION was smaller than Kimberly had expected, its cramped reception area bare and sterile looking and awash in fluorescent light. At the front desk, glass separated her from a police officer with a phone jammed to his ear and a harassed expression on his face.

It seemed that each moment one phone call ended, another button would light up, and the officer would shrug apologetically and take yet another call.

There was nowhere to sit, so Marissa passed the time by leaning against the wall and playing a game on her phone that beeped and pinged. Kimberly tried to rehearse what she'd say if she got the chance to talk to Officer Clarke.

Finally the man on the other side of the glass plunked down the phone and smiled. "Can I help you?" he asked.

Kimberly took a huge breath and started in on her story.

"Wait, wait, you mean Lieutenant Clarke? He oversees our detective division. He's out on a case now, but I can call him."

"Yes, that would be great!" Kimberly told him.

"If you were by yourself, I could let you back there to wait for him…but, uh, policy says we can't allow minors," the officer told her. He gazed pointedly past Kimberly's shoulder at Marissa.

Marissa murmured in a singsong voice, "Told you I should have spent the day at Taylor's."

Kimberly managed a smile. "Thank you, sir. It won't be too long, will it? We don't mind waiting here? Do we, Marissa?"

The officer nodded. "I'll call now, and then I'll let you know."

The wait stretched out. Kimberly shifted from foot to foot, wondering why on earth the police department didn't spring for chairs in the waiting room.

As she pulled out her cell phone to check the time, it buzzed in her hand. She didn't recognize the number, but the area code was the local one.

"Hello?" she asked.

"Is this Kimberly? Marissa's mom?"

"Yes, and this is…?"

"Oh, I'm sorry! This is Ma, honey. Colleen Monroe. We were wondering if Marissa could spend the day with us. She'd mentioned to Taylor that you two would be in town for a few more days."

"Hmm." Kimberly shot a look toward Marissa. She had an expression of patient endurance on her face. The earlier sullenness was gone. She seemed engrossed in her game, not even bothering to eavesdrop. "That's very thoughtful of you—"

"I don't want to interfere with your time together. I mean, it is your vacation."

"No, ma'am, it's not exactly a vacation. It's—" What had Daniel told his family? Anything? Nothing?

"Then, if it's business, why not bring her on out? She's welcome to hang out with us at our pool. Daniel's sisters are both out of town today, and I've got the babies here, but it's just them, and Taylor's going stir-crazy not having anyone her own age."

"I would, but I'm waiting on someone that I hope to meet with, and I can't leave at the moment."

"Not a problem. Daniel said he and one of his firefighters needed to pick up some vegetables out here on the farm for the station's kitchen. If it's okay with you, I'll tell him to swing by your hotel and bring Marissa."

"Er—" At the mention of Daniel's name, Kimberly's skin prickled. "We're not at the hotel. The person I need to meet works at the police station, a Lieutenant Clarke."

"Timmy? My goodness. Timmy and Daniel go way back—they were in high school together. And they won't let young people in the back of the station, so it's just as well that I send Daniel by to pick her up."

"Oh, that sounds like too much of a bother—"

"No trouble at all. He'll see you in a jiff."

And with that, Ma rang off.

Kimberly tossed the phone back in her purse. She must have made some sort of noise because Marissa surfaced from her game.

"What is it, Mom? Something wrong?"

"No, it's… Ma has invited you out to swim."

"Cool beans! So I can go?"

"I guess. Don't let it become a habit, okay? We don't want to wear out our welcome. Daniel and someone else are supposed to come by and—"

The connecting door to the back of the station swung open. A tall red-haired man with an overwhelming amount of freckles and dressed in khakis and a knit golf shirt smiled at them. "I'm Lieutenant Tim Clarke. I understand you're waiting on me?"

"Yes! I'm Kimberly—"

The man waved a freckled arm. "Yep. Daniel's filled me in."

"Daniel?" Kimberly stared past the lanky redhead to the man behind him.

Lt. Clarke slapped Daniel on the shoulder. "Yep. He said I should help you if I could. Hey, why don't the two of us grab a cup of coffee at the diner across the street?"

Daniel and the lieutenant came out to join them in the reception area, the door locking shut behind them. Daniel smiled warmly at Marissa, but was it a little forced when he turned to Kimberly?

"Marissa, I've got orders from Ma to ferry you out to the farm. Ready to roll? Bobbi's waiting for us in the truck. You remember her, right?"

And with nothing more than a casual wave goodbye to Kimberly, Marissa trooped out the open door that Daniel held for her.

He must have sensed Kimberly's momentary panic, because he stopped, gave her a nod and said, "She couldn't be in better hands. Ma raised six of us to be tax-paying productive citizens, and all in one piece. She's got this. But you can call anytime—me or Ma—if you're worried."

Kimberly drew in a calming breath and reminded herself not to be a complete mess when it came to Marissa. "Thanks, I appreciate you taking her out there and, er, giving Lieutenant Clarke here my bona fides. As for Marissa—" Kimberly even managed a joke "—relax, Daniel. That's the breeze outside you feel, not my rotor wash."

He chuckled. "I like that. Gotta go grab

these veggies if I'm going to con some of my firefighters to help me cook them and actually eat them."

With that, he was gone, and suddenly the space reverted back to its bare sterility.

She shook herself to get rid of the empty feeling that washed over her. Well, she wasn't here for Daniel. She was here on a mission. She was here for Marissa. She turned to the detective. "How about that cup of coffee, Lieutenant?" she asked.

CHAPTER NINE

ON THE WAY across the street, the first thing the detective did was release Kimberly from using his title and last name. "Ma practically raised me, so any friend of Daniel's is welcome to dispense with the formalities."

They walked into the diner, and Tim hustled her back to a booth at the end. The waitress immediately brought two cups and a hot carafe of coffee.

"Morning, Tim… Ma'am, Tim here likes his coffee fully leaded and black as night, that okay with you? Or do you want something else?"

"That's fine," Kimberly said. "The sugar's here on the table. Can I have some cream, though?"

"Coming right up." The waitress glanced Tim's way. "Same as usual, even though it's a tad early for lunch?"

"Yep. Eat when you can, that's my motto. Oh, my usual is the steak, mashed potatoes and gravy with a side of green beans and extra mushrooms. You want that? Or…what else, Vera? Y'all still got breakfast?"

"Actually…" Kimberly remembered that grim encounter with her checkbook balance this morning. She couldn't afford two breakfasts in one day. "The coffee will be fine."

A moment later, Vera brought a pitcher of cream to go with the sugar packets Kimberly had waiting by her cup. Tim had begun quaffing down his coffee, seemingly immune to its scalding temperature.

"Daniel said Marissa had some health issues, and you were trying to get the birth mom's identity?" Tim asked, setting his mug down. "You know I can't give you that information. State law and all."

"Right." Kimberly didn't look up from stirring her coffee. She wanted to frame her words exactly right. "But what *can* you tell me? Anything? Can you…can you tell me if anybody was with her? If she told you about any health problems?"

Tim frowned, a line forming on his freckled forehead. "Let's see…she was by herself. I was the first officer on the scene. I got there as they were loading her into the ambulance.

Man, that was a scene! You know she nearly died, right?"

Kimberly's heart skipped a beat. "No. How?"

"Some sort of hemorrhage. They didn't catch it at first, but they couldn't stop the bleeding. I know I closed out my case after my boss told me to count it as a safe-haven surrender and the birth mother was flown out to Macon—that's the nearest trauma center."

Kimberly placed her coffee mug down on the laminate to hide the way her fingers trembled. Finally, a clue about Marissa's family medical history. Hemorrhaging during childbirth *could* have been caused by PAI-1 deficiency, or any number of possibilities. "But she survived?"

Tim blinked. He sagged back into the booth. "That's—that's something I don't know. I guess I *assumed* she did. I mean, I know she made it to Macon. But honestly, I couldn't tell you. She had no charges pending against her once my superiors told me to count it as a safe-haven surrender." He grinned and ducked his head. "We, um, were more interested in how the baby was doing, to be truthful. Man, it's amazing how that baby's all grown-up now."

Kimberly fought back conflicting emotions: fear that her assumption all this time that Marissa's birth mother was still alive and could give them the answers they needed was wrong; the familiar frustration that finding her wasn't as easy as a quick check of the records; and a surge of appreciation that, even before she'd come into Marissa's life, her daughter had people looking out for her.

Someone, somewhere, knows something. And if I can't talk to the birth mom, I could track down her parents or the birth father or even his parents.

Vera plunked down a huge platter of steak the size of a small continent with a mountain range of potatoes and green beans beside it. "There ya go. And here's your bill, just like you like it. More coffee?"

"Thanks, Vera. Why don't you leave the carafe?"

She put her free hand on her hip. "Now, Tim, you know I can't do that. His Highness back there doesn't like it."

Tim craned his head to peer around Vera and apparently spotted whoever His Highness was, and shrugged. "Well, it was worth a try. Fill her up, then."

Coffee refreshed in both mugs, and Vera

once again gone, Tim tucked into his food. "Sure you don't want something?"

The smells wafting from his side of the table tempted Kimberly mightily, but she fought back. "No, thanks, I'm fine. You were saying that you got there just as the mother was put on the ambulance."

"Yeah. I was new on the job then, and grateful to my bones that I didn't have to catch that baby! No offense, but it was better all around that Daniel was the one. I mean, I was a town kid. Daniel grew up on a farm, and he's always been good in a crisis. Me? I would have dropped her on her head, probably."

Kimberly smiled at his self-deprecation and shook her head. "All the excitement was over, then? When you got there?"

He forked up another bite of potatoes and considered. "Yeah, pretty much. Baby was safe, mom was safe, all I had to do was take care of the car and follow them to the hospital to get the paperwork filled out."

"Take care of the car?"

"Well, it had to be towed, right? It couldn't be left on the lawn of the fire station. So I alerted the tow company on call and waited for them to come, then headed on to the hospital. By then, the mother had taken a turn for the worse, and she wasn't saying much to anybody anyway, except Daniel, so I hung around to wait for her to be airlifted out."

"Wait…you said 'except Daniel.' What do you mean? Did—did you or Daniel know her? I mean, before that day?"

"Not me. Never seen her before in my life. And I don't know if Daniel had, either. But she took a shine to him. One of the EMT guys told me later that she didn't want to say a word to anybody except to him."

A slow boil, as hot as the coffee she'd downed, fired up within Kimberly. Daniel knew who this girl was. He'd at least befriended her. She'd trusted him, and she'd probably told him enough details that he could help Kimberly track her down.

She recalled how carefully he'd phrased his words: what *could* he tell her. Could. Not would.

And apparently Daniel had a very narrow definition of *could*.

She put aside her anger at Daniel and shifted her focus to the conversation at hand. If Daniel wouldn't help her, maybe Tim would be more forthcoming. "The car… Daniel said it was old."

"Had about a half-dozen different paint colors on it, looked like something from a demolition derby," Tim agreed, chuckling. "Tow-truck guy gave me trouble about towing it, because the vehicle didn't belong to her, so he knew he wasn't going to get any money out of the deal."

Now Kimberly was confused. "She stole the car? But you said there were no charges pending?"

"Er, no felonies. Traffic tickets aren't something we arrest you for. You can either show up in court or call back and pay your fine. And the owner of the car showed up and said he'd given her permission to use it, so it didn't get towed after all. Boy, was that tow-truck driver steamed!"

"Which tow-truck company? Do you remember?"

Tim grinned. "Now you're thinking like a detective. Are you sure you're not on the job?"

She felt her face grow hot at the compliment. "No, I'm a teacher. But thanks."

"As for the tow-truck company..." His face took on a serious expression. "I don't know that I can tell you that. Daniel reminded me that we can't identify this girl to you. And he's right. She's protected under safe-haven laws." He brightened. "But...since you're a junior detective anyway, I can tell you that there aren't too many towing companies in this town, *and* the guy's still in business. What's more, he's still as grouchy as he was that same day."

Kimberly laughed. The triumph at this clue was tinged with frustration, though. *This* was what she'd hoped Daniel would do—lay down a trail of bread crumbs for her, even if he couldn't reveal the girl's identity. "All I have to do is hunt down Mr. Grouch Towing?"

"Good name for him, that's for sure."

By now, Tim's steak was half-gone and his mashed potatoes were history. Kimberly had the feeling that once that plate was empty, this interview was over.

"You mentioned the EMTs... Could you tell me who they were?"

"Sure. I'll even call the guy for you, give him a heads-up. He's Randy Paxton. The other guy with him—Gene... Now, what was Gene's last name? Higgins, that was it. He dropped dead of a heart attack, oh, about three or four years ago." Tim glanced down ruefully at his plate. "And if I keep eating this way, I'm probably not long behind him."

"I don't know. You look pretty healthy."

"What? You think all cops have the dough-nut belly?" There was that self-deprecating twinkle in his eye again. "I'm hurt."

"This Randy Paxton—when can I talk to him?"

"Give me some time to call him. He's still an EMT, but he's the county's EMT director now, so he's always hopping." Tim flipped out his notebook. "What's your number? I'll call you as soon as I talk to him."

She gave it to him. "Do you think he'd be free sometime today? Because we have to head back to Atlanta very soon."

"I can try. But I warn you, he's always swamped. I can definitely promise you Mon-day morning, first thing. That's the best time to catch him. Say, Daniel knows him better than I do, even—you could get him to call for you, as well."

Somehow Kimberly had her doubts that Daniel would go out of his way to help her. He could have told her what Tim had, or even offered to point her in the right direction. But he hadn't.

And…he'd made it his business to fill Tim in on what she wanted, reminding the detective about safe-haven laws. What would Tim have told her if Daniel hadn't warned him?

That's not fair. Tim's a police officer, so he'd know what the law required. And Daniel did offer some information.

Still, as she made her way to the cash register and paid for her coffee, Kimberly realized that, even with Tim's bread crumbs, the information she'd gleaned was not nearly enough.

And her time and her money were going fast.

CHAPTER TEN

DANIEL HEFTED THE crate of beans onto the back of the truck alongside a companion crate of squash. The guys at the station would give him some kind of trouble when he asked for volunteers to shell the butter beans. They might walk through a burning building, but gardening and preserving and cooking? They'd howl.

"Daniel…" Ma had that look on her face, the one that meant a lecture was headed his way.

"I know, I know, I should have remembered these this morning and not wasted time—"

"No, I know you're busy. You've got a lot of responsibility on you right now. You're like your father, you know." Her blue eyes suddenly filled with tears, and she swiped at them. Sniffling, she cleared her throat. "He'd be so proud of you, Daniel. So proud."

The image of his dad in the burn unit came back fresh and strong. The feel of his gauze-wrapped hand in Daniel's, the barely audible commands.

Take care of your brothers and your sisters and Ma.

Keep your word, Danny, keep your word, no matter the cost.

He stared out across the yard to see Marissa chasing after one of the twins—Logan, Daniel thought. She tickled the kid, let him go, then chased after him again as he shouted, "Again, 'Rissa! Again!"

Could Daniel keep his word to Miriam? Was he really protecting her secrets?

And at what cost to Marissa and Kimberly?

Kimberly had not looked pleased to see him this morning. Their set-to last night was still fresh in his memory. He understood why she was going after this information, but couldn't she have some mercy on him and not put him in such a difficult situation? He wanted to keep his word, even if he'd given it as a wet-behind-the-ears rookie who hadn't thought of the implications.

"She's something, isn't she?" Ma commented.

He could tell that she, too, was eyeing Marissa. "Yeah. She's a great kid. Fits right in with our bunch."

"That's what I was going to say. Daniel, you can't let that woman pay for a hotel room when I have empty beds at this house. Now that Andrew and Rob have flown the coop, it's just me and you and Maegan here. We have five bedrooms here—five!"

"Ma, we don't really know them—"

She tapped him on the arm. "Don't give me that. If nothing else after raising six kids, I'm an excellent judge of character, Daniel Monroe. And you are, too. You would have never asked me to have them out here last night if you hadn't thought them good people."

That was true enough. For some reason, within five minutes of meeting Kimberly, he'd felt as if he'd known her for years. It had to be a trick of the mind, because of his connection to Marissa. But how could a few panic-filled moments of chaos translate into this bond that vibrated between Kimberly and him? She hadn't been the one who'd given birth to that baby after all.

No, that had been Miriam, and the one thing he owed her was his word.

His mother wasn't letting her idea go. "Well? Are you going to ask Kimberly, or should I?

"I don't think they're planning on staying long—"

"I like her," Ma said firmly. "I like her, and I like Marissa, and you can tell a lot about a woman from the way her children act. I like the fact that she's a careful mother who's trying to help her daughter. If it were DeeDee in some strange town hundreds of miles from home, with Taylor, wouldn't you want someone—"

"Ma!" He threw up his hands. "All right, okay. You win. If it were any of my sisters, I'd want to know that someone decent at least offered. I'll ask her. Today. You're one in a million, you know that? There's not a stray you can ever turn down, is there?"

"And there's nothing wrong with that, Daniel. Not a thing."

"Where'd Bobbi get off to? We've got beans to shell and squash to wash and slice, and if I hang around here, you'll hornswoggle me into doing something else against my better judgment."

Right on cue, Bobbi strolled out of the back door, her hands full of foil-wrapped care packages. "Ma, that is the absolute best apple cake! I swear, I could eat half of it all by myself."

"You've been eating cake?" Daniel gave her a mock fierce look. "While I've been slogging away loading beans? Beans that I picked yesterday, mind you!"

She licked an errant bit of cake and apple filling off her fingertips. "I saved some for you, don't worry. And besides, you had help with those beans. Logan said he picked all of them but two."

"Tell you what, I'll let you pick beans with a six-year-old boy and see if that's easier than doing it by yourself—"

Ma interrupted. "Bobbi, it was good to see you again. Don't be a stranger, and bring that fellow of yours out as well, okay?"

"If there's any more apple cake in the offing, you can bet I will," Bobbi told her.

"There'll be no more cake until these beans are shelled," Daniel said. "That's orders from the chief." He slammed the tailgate of the truck shut.

Bobbi tucked Ma's various home-cooked goodies into the cab of the truck. "Yeah, and I know how to wield a fire ax if you get between me and the rest of that cake, buddy boy."

Ma laughed and headed toward the house. She stopped as Daniel slid into the driver's seat of the pickup. "Don't forget, Daniel. You need to ask Kimberly."

His momentary lightheartedness evaporated. Now the question of the promise to Miriam niggled at him.

It had been hard enough to keep his mouth shut when Kimberly and Marissa were staying at the hotel.

How could he resist Kimberly's pleas if she was under the same roof 24/7?

KIMBERLY STEPPED GINGERLY through a maze of bent fenders, rusted-out bumpers and even a grease-covered engine block halfheartedly covered in a blue tarp. She knocked on the jamb of the big sliding metal door that was ajar just wide enough for her to slip through sideways.

"Hello? Mr. Hicks? Anybody here?"

Her words fell unanswered into the dim interior of the shop. Unease rattled through her. Hicks's Towing Yard was on the outskirts of town, and it looked as though the owner supplemented his towing business with a junkyard.

But she'd tried the other two tow companies. Both had been friendly and helpful—something that, based on Tim's broad hint, told her they were telling the truth when they said they hadn't responded to a call on the Fourth of July twelve years ago.

From behind a stack of car doors came a low guttural growl. Kimberly's heart thudded in her chest, and she pivoted slowly around. Junkyards meant junkyard dogs—was she about to have her throat ripped out?

"Nice doggy," she said in a shaky voice. "Nice doggy."

The growl came again, this time louder. Her knees nearly turned to water. Usually she wasn't afraid of strange dogs—but usually their owners were nearby.

"Mr. Hicks?" she called out again. "Mr. Hicks! Anybody!"

"Well, don't get your knickers in a knot." The surly reply couldn't have sounded sweeter than a lullaby. "A body's got to have a chance to get to you."

A slight man in a grease-stained uniform appeared from behind a pile of doors. The uniform shirt opened over a T-shirt equally smudged with grime, and the warm summer breeze made the man's wild, unkempt white hair stand up straight.

The growl sounded again, followed by a protesting bark so deep it evoked images of wild animals. "Uh, uh, can you call off your dog?"

"My dog? What dog?"

Now the barking grew louder, more fierce, and Hicks frowned. "Oh, that," he muttered.

He pushed by her and slapped hard on the frame of the door. The dog's bark squawked in midroar and fell silent. Hicks came back outside. "Don't fool with a real dog. Takes too much money to feed 'em. You come to pick up a car what got towed?"

"Er, no." This fellow certainly fit the bill as the grouchiest tow-truck operator in town. But Kimberly wasn't at all certain he'd have maintained records of vehicles he'd towed five minutes ago, much less more than a decade past. "My name is Kimberly Singleton. Do you have a minute?"

"You ain't from the government, or one of them *po*litical surveyors, are ya?" Hicks asked. He squinted at her with suspicion. "'Cause I don't have a minute for the likes of that."

"No, sir," she replied. With a rush, she leaped into her story.

"Huh. Don't that beat all." Hicks looked intrigued. "Adopted, you say?"

"Yes, sir. And I'm trying—"

"My daddy, he was adopted. Put him in the *Market Bulletin*, they did. His, what you call 'em? Birth parents?"

"I beg your pardon?"

"Birth parents, right?"

"Oh, yes! But I don't think I understood about your father—"

"Right. They put him in the *Market Bulletin*. This was back in the Depression, where nobody had two dimes to rub together, but my grandpa didn't cotton to seeing nobody writ up like hogs for sale. So he rode out and adopted him. You did that?"

"Well, yes, in a manner of— You mean, your father was advertised in the classifieds?" Kimberly didn't even bother to hide her astonishment.

"Sure. Like you would a puppy. Free to a good home. He carried that advertisement with him for years in his wallet—still got it probably. He's eighty-five now. Lives with me."

"That's…that's amazing. Listen, you probably won't even remember this, but the day my daughter was born—"

"That'd be your *adopted* daughter?"

"Yes, yes, my adopted daughter." Funny how she always had to be reminded that she hadn't given birth to Marissa—either by people or the blank spaces on seemingly endless forms requesting biological family medical history, where all she could enter was "unknown."

Hicks leaned against the rusty corrugated

siding on the shop building. "She was born around these here parts?"

"At the fire station in town."

"That new chief, Daniel Monroe? You been to see him? He's been out here, him and that brother of his, the fire marshal? Came to tell me my place is a fire hazard." He let out a rheumy *har-har-har*, and spat in disgust in a stand of weeds. "Tell me something I don't know. What did they think a junkyard was gonna look like?" Now he fixed her with a watery blue eye. "So? What did he say?"

"He—he didn't have much information that he could give me," she admitted.

"Figures. Them Monroes, they a clannish bunch. And they tend to have a lot of rigid ideas about couldas and shouldas. Like you said, he *couldn't* give you no information." He made air quotes around the *couldn't*.

"Them Monroes, they're sticklers. Bet he knows more'n he's telling you."

"I expect so," Kimberly agreed. She swallowed back the anger that she'd pushed down earlier during her conversation with Tim. "But could you?"

"Lay it on me. I've got a pretty good memory."

So she did.

Hicks scratched his whiskered face with grime-encrusted fingernails. "July Fourth? I remember that. Called me out there for no good reason, and I didn't even get a red cent for my trouble. That Tim Clarke was the fellow—not a bad sort. Let a guy have a heads-up, pretty fair on making sure the call list was rotated out, you know? But back then, he was wet behind the ears, didn't know enough to call the owner first. So I go, and then I have to wait and wait, 'cause the owner, he says he's gonna show up, but he sure takes his sweet time."

"Do you remember who the owner was?" Kimberly's pulse quickened. This could be it, maybe the parents' name or the birth father's.

"Why, sure. It was Thornton Cross. He was stingier than I am, and that's saying something. Car wasn't worth towing, if you ask me. Heap of scrap metal."

"Thornton Cross? Is he— Does he still live around here?"

"Died four, no, five years ago. Big stroke, but at least he didn't linger."

"Oh." The anticipation whooshed out of Kimberly in a wave of disappointment.

"But if you were thinking he was something to that baby of yours, well, that wouldn't be the case at all. Thornton's a confirmed bachelor. No woman in her right mind would take on that cussed skinflint. Back then he had to be, hmm, sixty-five or seventy, and he'd never been married. No kids. Lived out near the Mennonites, retired military. Army, I think. Raised llamas, of all things. What on earth anybody'd want with a llama…" The man shook his head in befuddled wonderment.

"But he let the birth mother use his car? That doesn't… With what you've told me about him…"

Hicks shrugged his bony shoulders. "If they offered him enough money, I expect he'd do just about anything. I am sorry I couldn't be of more help. But you go on back to that fire station. Make that Monroe boy tell you the truth. They got all that in their files, I'll bet. I just bet they do."

CHAPTER ELEVEN

KIMBERLY DID NOT, after all, go back to the fire station. For one thing, she couldn't face it if Daniel once again refused to tell her anything more. Hicks was probably right; Daniel knew more than he was telling her.

But she needed some sort of leverage to pry the info out of Daniel, and if a mystery bleeding disorder wasn't a big enough crowbar, then she would have to look harder for one that would work.

On a whim, she pulled into the hospital parking lot. The building looked modern, as though it had recently been plopped down in the open field where it stood. But there had to be records, right?

It took forever for Kimberly to finally be shuffled over to the medical records section, and another half of a forever to explain her dilemma.

The fresh-out-of-college young woman behind the computer frowned and handed back

Kimberly's paperwork without so much as a good glance at it. "I don't know. You don't—you don't have a name. I mean, of the birth mother. And you're not, um, related to her. So I can't *legally* give you any information—even if I could find it."

"But I *am* related to my daughter. I'm her mother—her guardian. And am I not entitled to any medical records you have regarding her?"

The girl played with one of her dangly dream-catcher-style earrings. "Well, I dunno. I still don't have a *name*."

Kimberly sucked in a deep breath. "Is there anyone else here who might be able to help?"

The clerk sighed. She picked up the phone as if it weighed two tons. "Pauline?" she chirped. "I've got a *situation* here. Can you come?"

For a few minutes, after the clerk shot down a couple of Kimberly's attempts at small talk, the two of them stared at each other uneasily.

This Pauline person had to be the girl's supervisor, and probably would prove to be equally unhelpful. Kimberly glanced at her watch and saw with a start that it was well past lunch. No wonder her stomach was rumbling.

The door opened and a petite older woman in a tight hot pink sleeveless sweater and floral skirt swept into the office.

"Well, hey, sugar, what's doin'?" she asked the clerk with a wide grin.

"I'm sorry to bother you, Pauline, but—"

"Never you mind, my butt was gettin' plumb numb from sittin' in that office chair. What's up?"

In halting terms, the clerk began relaying Kimberly's request. Several times, Kimberly had to jump in and correct a few points, but Pauline remained patient.

The woman leaned against the Formica desk, one manicured hand with rings on every finger propping her up, her dark eyes bright and birdlike. "So let me get this straight. Your daughter was born here—well, not here, but at the fire station—and you want her medical records?"

"Yes. It sounds so simple when you put it like that."

Pauline cocked her peroxide-blond bouffant hairdo to one side. "Honey, never make it harder'n you have to. Most things are simple when you boil 'em down to their basics. Now, you got a birth certificate?"

"Yes. And the original paperwork from the

adoption—" Kimberly spread out the paperwork that the clerk had earlier rebuffed.

Pauline peered at the forms. "Just so. Okay, then, now all we've got to do is figure out a way to find your daughter in this here system. It's all on the cloud now. Makes it harder for an old dog like me to keep up, but I do. Kayla, you scooch over so I can use your computer."

The clerk rose from her desk in the same slow way she'd picked up the phone. "Pauline, if it's going to take you a while, I'm going for a coffee, all right?"

"Sure, sweet pea. We'll be fine, won't we?" Pauline winked at Kimberly, her fingers flying over the keyboard. The door closed without a reply from Kayla.

"Thank you. I felt as though I was banging my head against a wall," Kimberly told Pauline.

"These girls. They just in it for a paycheck, you ask me. They don't look at it for what it is—a little mystery to be solved, every single time. You make it fun, you don't mind coming to work. But these girls, they're all about their cell phones and their social media. Now, mind you, I'm into that, too, but when I'm at work, I'm at *work*." Pauline frowned, bent closer to the screen and squinted. "Huh."

Kimberly's heart skipped a beat. "Did you find something?"

"Not quite yet. But I'm close! It won't get away from ol' Pauline!" The magenta-tipped fingers clacked over the keyboard at an even more furious pace. She frowned again. "Nope, no, you don't hide from me."

She tapped a few more keys.

This query must have yielded a more satisfactory response. Pauline sat back and grinned smugly. "There you are. Told you you couldn't hide from ol' Pauline. I know where all the bodies are buried, I do." She took one long fingernail and tapped on the screen. "Okay, honey, here's what I've found. We've got records of one baby Jane Doe born on July 4, 2003 and brought into the hospital. That'd be the one, right?"

"Yes! Yes, that has to be!"

"Uh-huh, it does, because the only *other* babies we had in the hospital that day were boys. And they all had proper names. But this little girl, we got her. She's right here." Pauline beamed again.

"Can I get a copy?"

"Sure. Only one problem. This here is in our archived records, and all we got in that stupid cloud is an abstract. I can print this much off for you, but I'm gonna have to request that they pull the actual file. It's in a stack for scanning in, but it's not been done yet."

"Oh. Well…how long will that take?"

Pauline wrinkled her nose. "Usually we tell you to allow a week."

"A week! I'm only in town for today, maybe tomorrow. I guess…I was hoping to get it in hand, not have to wait on the hospital to mail it. But…"

Pauline rubbed at her mouth, her lipstick staining her finger the exact shade as her nail polish. "They sure don't like to get in a hurry with these older files. I'd do it myself, but it's in a shed outside the building, and we have to ask the maintenance guys to go in and move the boxes and pull the right one. Then they bring us the box and we pull the file."

Her bright eyes moved across the words on the computer screen. "Say, I remember this. My friend Gail was the charge nurse in the ER that day. I think it was that day. Back then, we didn't get many babies delivered here—it's only been in recent years that we started back with our OB department. Malpractice, you know. Hard to get an OB to stay in a small town like ours when they've got so much malpractice insurance to pay for. Yeah. The baby at the fire station. I do remember that, and it *was* Gail. You hold on."

She pulled out an old-fashioned flip phone from her pocket and punched a number. "Gaily-o! What's doin'?" Pauline listened for a few seconds, making a series of affirmative yeahs and well-I'll-be responses. Then a break came in the conversation, and she said, "Look here, sugar, I got one from the old way-back-when file. You remember that baby that got left at the fire station? Yeah, on July Fourth, remember? And that Monroe boy was the one who delivered it? Yeah, yeah. That one. Well, her mama is here—no, no, not the birth mama, but the one who took that kid in. And she's trying to find out…"

Kimberly bit the inside of her cheek as she listened to Pauline recount the story, making it sound as dramatic as a soap opera. It was all she could do not to leap across the desk and grab the phone. This woman—this Gail—had been there. She'd seen the birth mother. She could help Kimberly.

Pauline talked for another eon and then hung up the phone. "Well, now, sweet pea. She wants to talk to you, see that baby all grown-up!"

"Really? She remembers, then?"

"Why, shoot fire, I reckon she does! And now I don't feel so bad about making you wait a few days for those medical records. You and Gail can get together and you can ask her every little thing that's on your mind. She's retired now. Off RV'ing with her hubby. They been gone to the Grand Canyon with all their grandkids, and she's about stir-crazy, I'll bet."

"Oh. So she's not in town?" Crushing disappointment ate at Kimberly.

"No, they're on their way back. She'll be in town the middle of next week, either Wednesday or Thursday. She said, if you could give her till Thursday afternoon, at least, so she'd have a day or so to catch her breath, and she can put body and soul back together. Those grandbabies, they are something else."

Kimberly thought about her dwindling checking account. She had a weekend ahead of her, plus the majority of the week if she waited for Gail to return. Could she go home? Try doing this by phone or by email?

No. She'd tried that before—people tended to be more open when you were face-to-face with them.

It couldn't be helped. She'd find the money somewhere to stay the extra two nights. This was a chance that couldn't be wasted. This woman could tell her—could remember the day that Marissa was born.

"And hold on! That ain't all that's in my bag of tricks!" Pauline peremptorily lifted a finger. She picked up the office phone and buzzed a number. "Well, Gerald, as I live and breathe, I'm glad *you* were the one who answered." She winked again at Kimberly as her voice bubbled over with flirtation. "I got this teensy, tiny little favor I need, and you are just the man to do it. This poor woman here, she needs her daughter's medical records. Her baby girl is real sick, and we treated her when she was just a baby, just a day old." Pauline listened for a few moments. "I know, that lumbago of yours, it's something awful. But I know what'll put it to rights, sugar. Oh, Gerald!" She tittered. "You're truly wicked, you know? And me a happily married woman! But if Joe Bob ever does me wrong, you're at the top of my list. No, no, sugar, what I was thinking was one of my famous upside-down pineapple cakes. Wouldn't that lumbago of yours perk right up with a bite of my luscious, hot-from-the-oven upside-down pineapple cake? Why, sure! No, I don't mind, not a bit. So you'll do it? For me? And for this poor woman? You are a good man, even if you *are* wicked."

She dropped the phone back into its cradle and dusted her hands. "That's done. He'll get it for me by Wednesday morning, how about that?"

"I am sorry you're going to the trouble of baking a cake for him—"

Pauline waved her hand in dismissal. "Sugar, that's a boxed cake mix and a can of sliced pineapple. I've got to make one for my young-at-heart group Wednesday evening, so I might as well make two while the oven's hot. Nobody need know it's an old boxed cake, now, do they?" She winked a third time. "Not when it's my *special* recipe."

Kimberly couldn't help but burst out laughing. She'd bet that people would eat saltine crackers with gusto if Pauline handed them out with her particular flirtatious sass. "I don't know how to thank you—"

"Thank me? Honey, this is my job. I am the Queen Bee of Information, and that's information with a capital *I*. If I don't know it, then I need to find out who does. It helps in this job to be a hopeless busybody with a nose for news. So all you need to do is tell me, when you can, the end of the story. That's all."

"I will. I will indeed. So Wednesday? And I ask for you?"

"That's right." Pauline made an okay sign with her magenta-tipped thumb and forefinger. "Just ask for ol' Pauline."

MARISSA FELT THE water slide like silk across her back as she made another slow lap to the end of the pool. She and Taylor had been in the water for over an hour, and she was tired from all the racing they'd done earlier. Still, if she said she was tired, maybe they'd make her get out.

Coming to a rest against the lip of the pool, she shaded her eyes and stared at the covered back porch. Ma had been shelling peas earlier, but now she'd gone back inside. Wow. Marissa's own mother would have never dreamed of leaving kids unattended in a pool, even though her friends' parents did it all the time.

Yeah. More proof that her mom was *weird*.

Taylor glided up beside her. "I've been thinking," she said.

"Uh-huh?" Marissa switched her focus to Taylor, noticing the serious expression on the girl's face.

"About your birth mom. Well, your birth *dad*. Is it okay to talk about it? Because if it's not, then that's cool. Sometimes I just get so freaked out when people bug me about my food allergies. Ya know, I wanna be *normal*."

"Don't I know it," Marissa agreed. "When my mom tells people I have a bleeding disorder, they're certain I'm going to bleed to death from a paper cut. But at least your parents don't hover. I mean, look, nobody's out here watching us. And my mom would have a duck if she knew that."

Taylor shrugged. "It's because I've taken swim classes for forever. I got certified as a junior lifeguard last summer—all of us do when we turn ten or eleven. It's expected of all the Monroe kids. And there's two of us, so Ma doesn't worry so much. I still can't swim by myself, which is why I am *so* glad you came."

Marissa paddled her legs and, in the most casual tone she could muster, said, "It's okay. I mean, talking about my adoption. It's no big. What were you thinking?"

"Well, it just sort of occurred to me when we were changing. You *look* like us. You know, like a Monroe. I mean, *technically*, I'm an Anderson, because my mom married an Anderson, but everybody says I'm Monroe through and through. See? The cleft in the chin? That's from the Monroe side. And your eyes? Ours are all either blue or green, just like yours. I'll bet you're double-jointed, too." She stretched out her elbow and pivoted it into a twisty contortion.

Marissa frowned and imitated the move. "Sure, I can do that. Can't everybody do that?"

"Uh-uh. My dad can't. He says it grosses him out when Mama does it. But all of us Monroe kids can."

Marissa let Taylor's words sink in. She treaded water for a minute or so in silence and stroked the cleft in her chin that she'd always thought made her look more like a boy than a girl. But Taylor was pretty, and she had one. Maybe cleft chins weren't so bad.

A strand of her hair floated across the surface of the water, spoiling the fantasy. "Yeah, but my hair isn't like yours. I mean, it's this awful strawberry blond, and all of you have either dark hair or really blond hair."

Taylor frowned. Then her face cleared. She fired her index finger at Marissa as if it was a gun. "Gotta be from your birth mom. You inherited it from her. But I think you're mostly Monroe."

"So…" Marissa was still confused and

couldn't quite follow Taylor's line of thought. "How does that figure into my adoption?"

Taylor gaped at her and rolled her eyes. "Silly! Don't you get it? *Uncle Daniel* has got to be your birth dad!"

The breath went out of Marissa. She sagged against the pool wall. "You think so?"

"Yeah. It's the only explanation. Why else would that girl go to a fire station to have a baby? Probably it was like, I don't know, what do they call Romeo and Juliet? Star-crossed lovers? You know, where the parents say, you marry her over my dead body? I'll bet your birth mom was trying to get to Uncle Daniel so he could rescue her from her evil parents, but they caught up with her and made her give you up. Otherwise, you'd have stayed a Monroe."

Marissa could see more than a few holes in Taylor's story—like why Daniel hadn't kept her even if he couldn't marry the woman he loved.

But…

"You know, he said that he tried to keep me." Marissa recalled the wistfulness in Daniel's voice when he'd told her mom and her that. "And he was kind of bummed that my mom had been able to adopt me, and she was his same age."

"See? You *are* a Monroe. And that means we're *cousins*, cuz!"

In an instant they were hugging each other and shrieking so loudly that Ma came out on the porch. "Y'all okay?" she called.

Embarrassed, they shook their heads. "Yeah, we were just horsing around," Taylor said.

Ma shook her head. "You two look as if you're seeing each other again after years apart. Come on, out of that water. The twins will be up from their nap, and they'll want a snack, and I expect the pair of you could use some grub, too. How about some homemade ice cream?"

Taylor scrambled for the deck. "Last one in the house is a rotten egg, cuz!" she shouted over her shoulder.

"I'm no stinky egg!" Marissa cleared the poolside in one leap and grabbed for the towel. "'Cause I love me some ice cream, *cuz*!"

Somehow, it gave her a special thrill to use the word. Finally, she had people. Cousins. Family. And family that she liked, which was a definite plus-plus, in her view.

CHAPTER TWELVE

DANIEL DID A double take Monday morning when he pulled up at the county's Emergency Management Services headquarters. In front of the low, dun-colored building that housed not only the EMS, but also his brother Rob's hole-in-the-wall office, a familiar car was parked on the blacktop.

He squinted as he closed the truck door. Through the shimmering heat waves rolling off the asphalt, he made out a Fulton County tag.

Kimberly.

Daniel's heart sank.

He hadn't heard a peep from Kimberly over the weekend—he'd gone by the hotel room Friday to issue Ma's invitation, but they hadn't been there. Part of him had hoped they'd left town.

But they hadn't. They were still here, still digging. And he'd totally forgotten about Randy Paxton—he should have warned Randy the same way he'd warned Tim this morning. It had been sheer luck that he'd gotten to Tim before Kimberly had.

The door of the car swung open and one long leg extended out. His breath caught, and he tried to tell himself that he was simply glad that he still had a chance to protect Miriam.

"Kimberly?" He closed the gap between his truck and her car.

By the time he reached her she was out of the car, craning her head around to see who had called her name. The momentary flash of irritation on her face disappointed him in a way he couldn't quite fathom.

"Well. Aren't you here, there and everywhere?" she remarked in a flat tone.

"My brother Rob? The tall one? He's in charge of arson investigations. His office is here, and I have a meeting with him. What are you up to?"

She chuckled, and he felt his heart skip a beat as her expression lightened into amusement. "All of you Monroes are tall. I admit, it's hard for me to keep the rest of your brothers straight—you, I know. The others? Sort of a blur."

Again, delight surged through him. He stood out. In a good way, he hoped. "Won't be long, and you'll know us all better than we do ourselves. We're no mystery."

Her smile dimmed. "I'm afraid time is a luxury I don't have. If I'm going to save back money to make the trip out to Indiana, then I—"

"Indiana?" That was where Miriam's family had been from. Had Kimberly already uncovered her identity? He'd clobber Tim if he had—

"That's where a doctor who specializes in PAI-1 deficiency is. She's agreed to examine Marissa, see if they can determine without a genetic test if Marissa has the disorder. And anyway, this specialist knows all about bleeding disorders, so even if it's not PAI-1, maybe she can figure out what it is."

Relief pulsated through Daniel. He breathed out a sigh. Here was a lifeline for him, another reason why he didn't have to break his promise to Miriam. "So why not go there to start with?"

"They're not in network. And I have a ten-thousand-dollar deductible for out-of-network health care."

Daniel groaned. "Insurance companies."

"Me and you both," she agreed. "If they'd agree to give me a waiver for either the genetic testing or to see this doctor, that would be wonderful. But the testing and examinations are sure to mount up—even with in-network doctors here in Georgia, one blood test was nearly a thousand dollars. A thousand! I—I—" She blinked, and Daniel saw that her eyes were awash with tears. "I don't have that kind of money. This trip—" She waved her hand to encompass her surroundings. "It was a gamble. I hoped that we'd find something, anything…"

Daniel swallowed past a lump in his throat. He could provide that something. All he had to do was say the girl's name and the internet would probably take care of the rest.

But a promise was a promise. That was why you had to be careful what you *did* promise.

Silence stretched out between them. Then she twisted her mouth into a small smile. "Anyway, you asked why I was here. The EMS director? A Randy Paxton? Tim told me that he might be able to give me some information."

Daniel hoped he hid his dismay well. In as bright a voice as he could muster, he said, "Sure! He was there, same as me. Let me introduce you two—"

"Oh, no, there's no need for you to take that trouble—"

"No problem. His office is right inside." With a touch to her velvet-smooth arm, Daniel guided her toward the building. "Remember, I've got to see Rob anyway, and he's right down the hall."

"But—" She twisted around to look him in the eye as they moved through the glass door. "I wanted—"

You wanted to meet him all by yourself so you could sweet-talk him like you did Tim, Daniel thought grimly. *I made that mistake once already. I won't do it with an old softy like Randy. One blink of those long lashes of yours, and he'd melt into a soft puddle of sure-I-can-help-you.*

"Oh, by the way," he said, "Ma asked me to invite y'all out. To stay, I mean. And it is a waste for you to spend money on that hotel room—and no kitchen. She'd love to have you."

And there's an upside for me: I can keep tabs on exactly what you find out about Miriam. If nothing else, I can at least give the girl a heads-up that you're barreling her way.

Kimberly came to a standstill in the hall.

"Really?" Her lips parted in surprise. "Stay with her?"

"With us. I live there, too, you know. That wouldn't be a problem, would it?"

He was gratified by the surge of pink that flooded her cheeks. For a moment she was completely... What was the word Ma always used? Discombobulated? The tip of her tongue touched the center of her upper lip, and she dropped her gaze. All Daniel could see was the crown of her head, shining with those dark, silky curls. He fought the urge to lift her chin, to...

What? He had no business thinking these thoughts about *this* woman, of *all* women.

"No. Of course not. Why would it be?" she replied in a husky voice, still not meeting his eyes.

"Then after work, I'll go by and grab your gear, and we'll move you two in."

"I—I don't know what to say."

Say you'll stop chasing after Miriam. But he knew she couldn't do that, no more than he could break his promise. They each had obligations.

"It's our pleasure. And Ma— Well, she's—"

"Wonderful," Kimberly breathed, and at that exact moment looked up at him. The intensity of her voice and the shining emotion in her eyes vibrated through him. He imagined what it would be like for her to be saying that to him *about* him. "She's wonderful. You're lucky to have her."

"I know. After my dad… Well, I don't take a single day for granted."

A door opened and slammed in a distant part of the building. It broke the spell. "So, um, can you direct me to Randy's office?"

"Sure, let's go."

Daniel led the way, then poked his head into Randy's office. "Hey, Pax."

"Daniel! Good to see you—wait, you're not asking for me to apply for more grant money, are you?" Pax shifted back in his chair behind a desk piled high with files and ran a palm over a gleaming bald pate fringed with a dusting of salt-and-pepper hair. His white polyester uniform shirt strained over the spare tire he was always swearing he would work off. "Because my plate is full now, brother. Yeah, my plate runneth over."

"No, no. This isn't to do with county business." He opened the door wider and ushered Kimberly in ahead of him. "This is Kimberly Singleton—"

"Hey, Tim called about you. You're the one

with the little girl—that baby. You delivered her, didn't you, Daniel?"

"Yeah. I did." And in that moment, Marissa's chubby newborn face sprang in clear relief in his mind.

Kimberly stepped forward. "Tim and...uh, Daniel, too, thought maybe you could help? With remembering things about Marissa's birth mother?"

Pax looked past Kimberly to Daniel, who slowly shook his head and put a finger to his lips. In response, Pax scowled.

"If—if it's not too much trouble—" Kimberly stuttered, apparently thinking that Pax's frown had been meant for her.

"Nah, nah, not a bit. Whenever I see Daniel, it makes me think of that last firefighter's grant we applied for—forty pages of nitpicky stuff. And he could have done it himself—"

"Yeah, but you wear the grant coordinator's hat. Wouldn't want to horn in on your territory, bud," Daniel quipped. He was grateful that at least Pax was covering for him. Maybe that meant he'd be careful with what he told Kimberly?

"I know it was a safe-haven surrender," Daniel said carefully, "and that means you can't legally give her the girl's name or any, well, clearly identifying details."

Pax raised one fluffy white eyebrow. "And you think you need to remind me of that? I'm the one always after you firefighters to remember patient privacy rights." He shook his head and gave Kimberly a roll of his eyes. "Firefighters. A blabbety bunch."

Kimberly's laugh was dry and nearly devoid of mirth. "Funny. Daniel seems fairly closemouthed to me."

"Yeah, well, he's about the only one who remembers that even a fish wouldn't get in trouble if he'd keep his mouth shut. Sit down. I might not be able to tell you identifying details, but you must have a number of questions. Maybe I can help." Then he scowled at Daniel. "You staying? 'Cause if you are, you can start on this stack of paperwork for me." He jabbed a finger in the direction of a foot-high pile.

It was a clear warning to beat it. Daniel got the message, waved him off and made tracks. "Looks like you have this," he told Pax. "Uh, Kimberly, I'll call you? About moving your stuff?"

She blushed. "Yes. Thank you…and be sure to tell your mother thank you, as well."

He nodded, closed the door behind him and sagged against it for a moment. A near calamity averted. From now on, if he was going to protect Miriam, he needed to think like Kimberly and be one step ahead of her.

At least that would be an advantage of her sharing a roof with him. That, and enjoying the pink of her cheeks whenever she blushed.

He shook off that last thought and headed down the hall toward Rob's office.

It was smaller and more cramped than Randy's, but Rob didn't mind. Most of the time, he was out in the field. Daniel pushed the door open. "Hey, Rob Roy, how's it going?"

Rob looked up from his computer screen. "Have I told you lately how much I hate bureaucracy? I thought I'd have that report for you this morning, but I've got one piece of information I still need to get—and the DA is saying we have to issue a search warrant to shake it loose. So here I am, doing the DA's work for them, since they're too busy for a Podunk third-degree arson charge."

"You reckon they'll even take it to the grand jury?" Daniel collapsed into the folding chair by Rob's desk. "I mean, if they're not willing to help out now?"

"Oh, sure, I do all the grunt work, and

they get a slam-dunk indictment? You can bet they will. Plus, the woman has already pretty much confessed to me that she was the one who burned her boyfriend's car. Remind me to never fall in love—all that happens is you get your heart broken, and then you lose all logic and think you can get over a broken heart by setting fire to somebody else's belongings."

"So what do you need to finish the report?" Daniel asked.

"The boyfriend's financials. I have to show that he was current in his loan payments and his finances weren't in distress."

"Can't you ask him?"

"Ah, he's already forgiven Miss Matchbox Girl. I even think they're engaged now—she probably popped the question so he wouldn't testify against her."

"Wow. So how long will it take? The subpoena?"

Rob shrugged. "Don't know. Could be quick, if we get the right judge…and it could be a few days waiting for the right judge to come back from vacation. But, hey, maybe the boyfriend will wise up—hopefully before she burns down the house around him—and he'll give us what we need without a subpoena. Sorry you made the trip for nothing. I meant to call—"

"No, actually, Kimberly was here."

A slow grin kicked up the corners of Rob's mouth. "Now, what did I just tell you about falling in love?"

"I'm nowhere near falling in love," Daniel huffed. "It's only that Ma had asked me to ask Kimberly to stay with us while she was in town."

Rob's eyebrows waggled. "Ma did, huh?"

"You're cynical, you know that?"

"Me? No, cynical would be that you're moving Kimberly in to keep an eye on *her* little investigation. Me thinking you're doing it so you can put the moves on her, that's my born romantic side."

The fact Rob was too close to *both* sides of the truth made Daniel's conscience squirm. "I haven't been keeping tabs on what Kimberly's doing," he insisted. "Besides, she's wasting her time. Nobody can tell her anything anyway. The law says so."

"Dumb law in this case, if you ask me. What's so wrong with her knowing the family health history of her adopted daughter?"

"Well, nothing in theory, but if girls had to fill out a batch of paperwork before they could anonymously surrender a baby, you can bet we'd be back to finding dead newborns rather than just abandoned ones, like we did before this law went into effect. It's there for a reason, Rob. Like that subpoena. You wouldn't want just anybody poking into your finances for kicks, now, would you? But if law enforcement needs to, for some legal reason, they can. There's a remedy."

"Not for Kimberly, there's not. Ma was saying she has no way of knowing anything about the girl who gave birth to Marissa, and she needs to know because the kid's got this rare disease."

"She has options. They're not easy ones, that's all—or cheap." Was he trying to convince Rob? Or himself? Either way, it didn't seem to be working.

"So which is it?" With way too much casualness, his brother flicked through a stack of files. "Are you moving her into Ma's for romance or for spying? Or a little of both?" Now Rob looked up and winked.

Daniel shoved back the chair, ignoring the screeching it made against the hard tile floor, and stood abruptly. "It was all Ma's idea."

"Right. And that woman I'm investigating will never, ever again be tempted to solve problems with a pocket lighter and a can of lighter fluid. No, sir, officer, not on your life, officer—"

But Daniel let Rob's office door close behind him and cut off his brother's sarcastic humor before he'd have to hear any more.

CHAPTER THIRTEEN

KIMBERLY SLAMMED ONE drawer closed and yanked open another. It was here. It had to be here—

A rap on the door interrupted her frenzied search. Pushing her hair back from her eyes, she went to the door and peered through the peephole.

Daniel… Here already, and she wasn't even finished packing. She swung open the door. "Hi, there. I'm not ready—"

Daniel's glance zoomed past her. "Wow. That—that looks like an explosion in a Laundromat."

"Oh." Her face heated up the way it did whenever she was embarrassed. "I—I lost something, and I've been pulling everything out trying to find it."

"Can I help?"

She hesitated, then with a shrug of her shoulders stood back and let him in. "I sure haven't had any luck, and I can't leave without it. I can't believe I've lost it."

"What?"

"Marissa's bracelet—the bracelet her birth mother gave her." Her heart ached at the loss. How would she ever explain to Marissa that the one link she had to her birth mother was gone?

Daniel frowned. "Bracelet?"

"You know, the gold ID bracelet, the one with her name engraved on it. The one I showed you? Her birth mother gave it to her—well, that's what the social worker told me anyway."

The confusion on his face cleared. "Oh. That one. I thought, well… You'll want to find it, then."

"Yes. And I've looked everywhere. The last time I had it was when we went to the fire station. You know, we talked to you at the farm, and then we showed you the bracelet? And then you took us back to the station."

Daniel nodded. He slowly turned around the room and surveyed the mess. Kimberly was embarrassed all over again. She started stuffing things back into her and Marissa's suitcases, but he halted her with a wave of his hand.

"You checked your pocket?" he asked.

"Yeah, first thing I did. And my makeup bag, where I usually keep the jewelry I take with me on a trip. And Marissa's toiletries bag. When I couldn't find it, that's when I started tearing the place apart."

He closed his eyes and stood stock-still. Frustration rose within Kimberly. He was wasting time. How could a man who hardly knew her or her habits even presume to think he could imagine where she'd put a baby bracelet?

Then he nodded with a measure of satisfaction and opened his eyes again. "If it's not on the floor of the closet, then it's with your keys."

"What?" Kimberly gawked at him. "I checked the closet—what do you mean, my keys?"

"Yeah—what's the one thing you'd need right away? That you wouldn't want to leave in a strange hotel room? Your keys, right?"

And suddenly it came to her—the bracelet *was* with her keys. She sprang to the dresser where her purse was perched haphazardly amongst a pile of books and notepads she'd tossed out of her suitcase during the hunt. She stuck her fingers down deep into the pocket where she usually kept her keys…and felt the tiny links of the bracelet, trapped in the bottom crease.

Kimberly pulled it out and gasped. "How did you do that?" she asked. "I'd even forgotten."

Daniel shrugged. "It comes from being a firefighter, I guess. You have to find things, or people, in a hurry in the middle of zero visibility, when the roof may crash in on you at any minute. And anyway, that's where I would have put something that important to me."

"Thank you. If I'd lost this…" Kimberly clasped the bracelet in her hand. Swallowing hard, she opened her palm and stared at the shining gold nameplate. Simple and plain, the only decoration it had was the beautiful engraved script that spelled out Marissa's name. On the back, it had her date of birth and even her birth weight and length.

The birth mother had gone to extraordinary lengths to have this done and get the piece of jewelry to the social worker. Over the years, for Kimberly, the bracelet had come to symbolize all the love and affection the birth mother must have had for Marissa. She had to love her, to be thinking of her, to want her child to have something from her.

Something lasting, something that would never tarnish or turn.

And Kimberly had almost lost it. A careless tug of her keys might have yanked the bracelet free and landed it on the street. It would have likely ended up on a pawnshop shelf or been melted down for quick cash. She closed her fingers around it again. "Thank you. Oh, thank you, thank you, thank you."

Daniel seemed flummoxed by her gratitude, uncomfortable even. "It was nothing. Really. But I'm glad I could help."

"Oh, you did! And you can help me out by reminding me I'm putting it in the zipper compartment of my purse." Carefully she tucked the bracelet into a secure pocket. She looked up. "But—" Kimberly swept her hand around the room. "Now I've got to straighten everything and repack. And Marissa's not going to know what on earth has kept me."

"I don't pretend to know how to fold girl clothes to suit you, but…"

"Really, I mean, it's so late that I'll be charged another day anyway—"

"No." Daniel shook his head and shoved his fingers into the front pockets of his dark uniform pants. "I talked with Annie, the night clerk, and she said if you vacated the room by five-thirty, she'd put you down as a late checkout. She does that for the county sometimes when we have instructors come in for a training seminar. It lets them have the room to store their stuff so they don't have to pack it up that last morning."

Kimberly glanced at the bedside clock. "Oh, wow! Fifteen minutes! I'd better get a move on, because that's seventy dollars plus tax."

Now she began tossing things in the suitcases pell-mell, making circles around the room and the adjoining bathroom to be sure she hadn't left anything. It was the quickest, dirtiest packing job she'd ever done, and it felt even weirder to be doing it under the watchful eye of Daniel.

"I swear," she gasped as she sat on the overstuffed bag, "I never pack like this." She tried and failed to zip up the bag.

Daniel walked over to her. "Here. That's going to take a little more muscle, I think." He leaned down, and she caught a whiff of soap and water and a hint of lime. It made her think of beaches in the tropics. His hand closed over hers, and together, they zipped the bag shut.

For a moment she stood there, her back

against his chest, feeling the warmth of his body pour into hers, his breath on her cheek. She hadn't been this close to a man in a very long time—and it had been even longer since she'd actually wanted to be this close.

But just when she was summoning the nerve to turn into his embrace, he released her and stepped back, leaving her feeling cold and alone in the over-air-conditioned room.

With impeccable smoothness, he gripped the suitcase. "I'll take this one to the car for you. You can get that other one?"

"S-sure," Kimberly whispered.

Alone in the room, she sank to the bed and sat on it, the edge of the too-firm mattress biting into the backs of her thighs.

Maybe taking up Ma on her invitation was the wrong move. Maybe, if Daniel could make her feel weak in the knees by simply standing too close to her, she'd lose her focus in her hunt for Marissa's birth mother. Right now, single-mindedness was what she needed more than anything.

Single-mindedness would be hard to have with Daniel distracting her every other moment.

Logic fought back. It wasn't, she reminded herself, as if Daniel would always be around.

He had to work, after all, and she would use these precious few days to the max, so she'd be gone, as well. And having a home to stay in had even more advantages than saving on hotel bills; no, she'd have access to a kitchen, so they wouldn't have to spend money eating out, and maybe Ma would let her use the washer and dryer.

Plus, Marissa would be happier with space and kids her own age to hang out with.

Kimberly put her hand to her face, considering, and discovered that Daniel's scent still lingered on her palm. It buzzed through her, jangling her nerves.

Clomping footsteps on the breezeway outside grabbed her attention. Daniel's voice and a woman's filtered through the thin door to the unit. Kimberly popped up, surveyed the room and satisfied herself she'd left nothing behind.

She slung her purse over her shoulder and grabbed the remaining bag as Daniel tapped on the door.

Yes. For better or worse, she'd accept Ma's hospitality. She'd simply have to use good common sense.

Who knows? she thought to herself as she opened the door to find Daniel and presumably Annie waiting for her. *Maybe being around Daniel more will help me convince him to share whatever secrets he's keeping about Marissa's birth mother.*

THE ONLY LIGHT on in the house was the one over the kitchen sink when Daniel arrived back at Ma's later that night. He was careful not to slam his truck door, mindful of guests who were probably sleeping.

His breath caught as he realized he could form a clearer mental image of *Kimberly* sleeping than he should have been able to. He could picture her snuggled up in billowy white sheets, her dark curls spread out against the pillow.

This was exactly what he didn't need—and exactly why he'd made himself scarce and headed to town once he'd hoisted Kimberly and Marissa's luggage into two empty bedrooms. He'd wanted to avoid sharing supper with Kimberly after what had happened in that hotel room.

Nothing happened, he tried to convince himself.

Yeah, but you wanted it to.

Putting it out of his mind for about the ninety-ninth time, he crunched across the pea gravel Ma had spread out as a turnaround and mounted the steps.

A shadow moved on the back porch swing.

Daniel's pulse ratcheted up, slowed to a more reasonable pace, then sped up again when he realized it was Kimberly.

"Sorry if I scared you," she said. Her words were quiet, barely above a whisper, but her voice had such a crystal clear quality that he was sure he could hear it over a roaring structure fire.

"I wasn't expecting— I thought you'd be asleep." He came to a stop at the top of the steps and grabbed hold of the cap topping the deck post.

"Oh, so you *were* trying to avoid me?" she teased.

His silence was his confession. Daniel made a clumsy attempt to recover, saying, "I figured you'd want time to get settled in—and I did have that inspection to do."

That inspection wasn't due for another week, but he'd grabbed on to the excuse like a lifeline.

Because whenever she stared up into his eyes, he had to bite his tongue not to blurt out everything he knew about Miriam.

She patted the porch swing. "Want to know what Randy—excuse me, Pax—told me?"

He could hardly resist. His work boots echoed off the deck boards. The swing dipped a bit under his weight as he sat down on one end, and he had to shift toward her to equal out the load.

"Was he helpful?"

"Oh, he got your message loud and clear," Kimberly told him in a dry voice.

Daniel gave her a sharp glance. "What's that supposed to mean?"

"What is it that's so terrible you don't want me to know, Daniel? I mean, if you gave me the girl's name, I'd be gone, out of your hair."

Daniel swiped at his brow and pinched the bridge of his nose. He stared down at the scuffed toes of his work boots and saw that the deck boards needed a good staining before the fall. "I don't want you gone," he admitted, and he realized with a start that he meant that with every fiber of his being.

"Obviously not," she retorted, "because if you do, you're going about it in all the wrong ways. I don't need chapter and verse about Marissa's birth mother. I need to ask her one question. Or not even ask *her*—I'd settle for anyone who knew the answer to it."

"You say that now," Daniel muttered.

"What?"

"I *said*, you say that now. But if I did give you her name—mind you, I'm not saying I even know it—but if I did, then it would be something else you'd want to know. And then after you had that question answered, it would be just one more thing. I grew up with sisters. I know about how women's minds work."

"Well, I never!" Kimberly drew back as if she'd been stung. "That's a sexist remark if I ever heard one."

"Okay, fair enough. I know how *people's* minds work. Curiosity gets the better of us. Look, if I pay the money for Marissa to go to Indiana, would you take her?"

She chuckled. "And you said you didn't want me to leave."

Frustrated, he leaped from the swing, causing it to gyrate wildly. He reached out a hand to steady it, only to find his fingers gripping Kimberly's knee.

She put a hand over his and pulled him back down. "Don't march off. Talk to me. Surely if we discuss this, we can come up with some sort of resolution."

"I offered you one not thirty seconds ago," he growled. "And for the record, I'm not trying to run you off. I'm… I need to keep my word,

Kimberly. I made a promise to her. Okay? And a man is only as good as his word."

She let go of his hand. "So you *do* know more than you're telling."

"Of course I do, but I can't tell you. Don't you get it? This girl put her faith in the laws of the State of Georgia. It took a tremendous amount of courage to do what she did, and the only reason she could make that leap was to know—to absolutely *know*—that her identity would remain a secret. There are reasons that I can't tell you—good reasons. It's not... What's the word? You're the English teacher. When it's just your willfulness, the mood you happen to be in at the moment?"

"Caprice," Kimberly whispered.

"That's it. It's not caprice. I've told you what I can. I swear to you. And rest assured, it's killing me to know Marissa needs help and I can't give it to her. You realize that, right?" Now it was Daniel staring at Kimberly earnestly.

He was gratified to see her head dip a fraction of an inch. "I know you're a good man, and you don't want to break the law." Her concession was shot through with fatigue and resignation.

She stood up and without saying so much

as a good-night, crossed in front of him and made for the back door. As she put her hand to the knob, she stopped and turned back. "You'll be glad to know, then, that Pax didn't really tell me anything."

With that, she slipped inside and closed the door with a quiet thud.

CHAPTER FOURTEEN

IF KIMBERLY HAD thought that she'd avoid Daniel by getting up extra early for her breakfast, she'd been sorely mistaken. As she walked into Ma's kitchen, there he was, pouring a steaming mug of coffee.

The gray light of early morning shone through the window and lit his uniformed figure, touching the planes of his face. Even with something as simple as pouring coffee, Daniel Monroe was all concentration.

"Can I pour you one?" he asked, not turning to face her.

She jumped, unaware that *he'd* been aware of her presence. "You have ears like a cat," she observed.

"Need to, if you're fighting a fire."

"Is it..." She stretched out to accept the mug he'd poured for her. "Is it as dangerous as it seems? Firefighting, I mean?"

Daniel shrugged. He peeked into the toaster

oven. "I've got two pieces of raisin toast. Care for one? I can make some more."

"Sure. That would be good." Kimberly couldn't understand why his niceness made her feel embarrassed about the night before. She'd been right. Okay, so she'd been more than a little short on tact, but this was about her *daughter*.

Again, with that silent air of focus, he pulled the butter from the refrigerator and sliced two pats. She noticed how he put each one precisely in the center of the raisin bread.

"It's not if you know what you're doing," Daniel said suddenly.

His words bewildered her—but then she realized he was giving her a delayed response to her earlier question. "Firefighting?" she prompted.

"Yeah." He shut the toaster-oven door and propped himself against the kitchen counter. "If you're properly trained, and you have the right equipment, and everybody keeps their word and does what they need to do, then even in the worst fire, you'll get the job done safely."

"That's a lot of *ifs*." Kimberly slid down into a ladder-back chair at the kitchen table. "Any one of them can go wrong."

Daniel shrugged again. "The only thing you really have no control over is whether the firefighter beside you is going to keep his word, do what he says. I make sure my crews are trained and have the right equipment. That mitigates a lot of the risk. Besides, somebody's gotta do it. What are we supposed to do? Let a person's whole life burn down because somebody might get hurt? We can't let that happen."

Kimberly traced the lip of her mug, letting her finger linger over a tiny chip in the otherwise glossy finish. "Your attitude is kind of surprising. I mean…Pax said your dad died in a fire."

Daniel's scowl cut deeply into his face. He took a gulp of his coffee. "Pax says too much."

"It didn't happen that way?" She knew she was pushing too hard, but maybe if she understood Daniel—Pax had said she had to get to know him, to see what made him tick—then she could figure out how to convince him to tell her what he knew.

Daniel's jaw worked, the muscles taut. "Yes, my dad was killed in a fire. It was…" He trailed off.

"Don't say a freak accident. Because that

blows what you said a while ago about mitigating risk right out of the water."

"No, it most certainly wasn't a freak accident," he said grimly. He lifted an index finger. "One guy. One arrogant firefighter who thought he knew better. That's why my dad died."

Kimberly held her breath. She waited to see if he would tell her more.

Her patience paid off. He set the mug down with a thud, so hard that a rivulet of black coffee dribbled down the side. "He wasn't where he was supposed to be, that guy. And he didn't respond to my dad's radio calls to evacuate the structure. So my dad…my dad went back in to find him. See, that was my dad's promise, that he'd never leave a firefighter behind. And he kept his end of the bargain."

"What happened then?"

"The roof collapsed. My dad had pushed the other firefighter to safety, but a burning beam landed on him—Dad, I mean. So then the firefighter finally used his radio to call for help, and the crew managed to pull him out. But it was an arson fire—and the accelerant made the fire superhot. It was too much—even with his turnout gear, he suffered third-degree burns. He just… No one could have survived it."

"And the guy? The other firefighter?"

"Not a scratch on him." Daniel shook his head. "Not so much as a single scratch. And if he'd kept his word, been where he was supposed to be, done what he was supposed to do, Dad would still be here. And my mom? It nearly killed Ma. I thought for sure we'd have to bury her, too."

"I take it that firefighter doesn't work for you?"

"Are you kidding me?" Daniel pivoted around, ostensibly to check on the toast, but Kimberly could see his entire frame was rigid with disgust and that he was trying to hide his emotions. "He broke about a half-dozen regulations that day alone. He was gone. The county fired him, as they should have. The funny thing is, Dad had given him multiple chances to get things right—he'd really bent over backward for this guy, not wanting to fire him. But some people—they just don't think the rules apply to them, you know? They don't understand that rules and regulations are there to protect people, to keep people from getting hurt…or worse, killed, like my dad."

Another sliver of hope died within Kimberly as she heard this last bit. This was why Pax had said she needed to hear the story from Daniel himself.

No wonder he was so wedded to following the absolute letter of the law. With a memory like that, he'd never understand her need to bend the rules and regulations to help Marissa—even if that was exactly what *she* needed to save her daughter.

The rattle of the toaster rack pulled her back to the present. She couldn't give up. She had to believe that somewhere, someone besides Daniel knew at least enough of the story to give her the information that she needed.

Daniel brought the toast over to the table, cinnamon wafting up from the plates. "Need a refill?" he asked.

"No. I'm fine."

He poured himself another cup and sat down beside her. "What about you? Your folks?"

His question startled Kimberly. "I, uh, well, I certainly don't have any dramatic stories like you do," she said in an attempt to evade answering him.

"So you had the normal happy childhood, two parents, one-point-six siblings, the white picket fence, a dog and a cat?" he joked.

"Not…exactly," Kimberly replied. "I never

really knew my dad. And my mom...worked a lot."

"You didn't know your dad? What was up with that?"

Daniel's eyes were kind as he watched her over his slice of raisin toast. He'd been honest with her. The least she could do was be honest with him, she supposed.

"He wasn't any candidate for Father of the Year," she said. "He was in prison. For armed robbery. He and his buddies had pulled a string of stickups in convenience stores. And then... Well, not long before he was supposed to get out, he was killed in prison. Another prisoner took offense at something he said, which, according to my mother, was not unusual."

"Wow. That had to be tough on your mom. I know how it was with Ma, trying to hold the family together after Dad died. Being a single parent's no fun."

Kimberly's laugh was bitter. "You'd have to know my mom. She...doesn't take things seriously at all. It's all *que sera, sera* with her. It was me who worried. She'd come in, tell me she'd gotten fired from yet another waitressing job and say something like 'Sugar, it's not so bad. I can find another, easy. That was a crappy job anyway.' And then she'd go out and party away her last paycheck. But it was me who had to answer the door to the landlord when the rent was past due, and me who had to figure out how to cook on the gas stove in the dark when she let the lights get cut off. We hardly bothered turning the phone on even when we did have money because we moved so much and because even Mom knew it would get cut off again."

From Daniel's quick intake of breath and the pitying expression on his face, Kimberly knew she'd said more than she should have. "Look, don't get me wrong," she rushed on. "My mom has her good qualities. And she means well. It's just—inside, she's still sixteen. And she always will be. But, hey, I learned self-reliance and how to fend for myself and how *not* to be a mother."

"That you did. And you're a good mom, Kimberly." Daniel's mouth pursed in thought, and she saw him figuring out exactly what to say next. "I've never doubted that. You impress Ma, and that's no easy feat."

"Really? Impress Ma? Golly." Kimberly's cheeks flared with heat. "That means... I never knew families like yours existed, Daniel. Not outside of books or movies. I thought it was somebody's ideal. Do you realize how lucky you are? To be part of something so good? To be valued by a group of people you respect? To not...to not be alone?"

To her horror, her voice broke and tears spilled down her cheeks. She dashed them away. "Sorry. I'm not usually this mushy."

He caught her fingers in his and squeezed them. "You're not alone. You're a Monroe now...an honorary Monroe. And we've got your back. We Monroes, we always have each other's backs."

Kimberly couldn't help it. She let the tears flow in earnest, ignored the scrape of his chair as he pulled it closer to her and folded her into a reassuring embrace. This was not what had vibrated through her yesterday—no, having him hold her meant something much more than mere attraction.

Even though he wasn't helping her with her hunt, somehow, some way, she truly believed he meant what he said. He'd have her back when she needed it the most.

MARISSA DREW BACK into the shadows of the hall off the kitchen and listened to her mom cry. Grandma could be a twit, worse than any middle school brat, and Marissa knew how much grief her mom had had to take from *her.* But she had never realized how lonely her mom was.

Well, she never dates. And all she does is take you from one doctor to the next.

Through the sliver of space between the door hinges, Marissa took in how Daniel—her *dad*, if Taylor was right—was holding her mom. They looked good together. As if they belonged to one another.

If Daniel and her mom got together, then they could be a family. She and her mom could move down here, live near Taylor, be a Monroe.

You're a Monroe now, Daniel had told her mom.

So there it was, clear as daylight. Daniel was as good as admitting that he was Marissa's dad. Maybe he wasn't saying the exact words. But Taylor *had* to be right.

Marissa fingered the cleft in her chin. A Monroe. She was a Monroe.

Well, there was only one thing to do. She had to get her mom together with Daniel.

She smiled. *Looks as if my job's already half-done. All it will take is a nudge and a push. And then I can really be a Monroe.*

With that, she turned and lightly ran back up the stairs, avoiding every step that creaked, so she could text Taylor about their next project.

CHAPTER FIFTEEN

PAULINE'S OFFICE WAS a broom closet compared to the shiny front office where Kimberly had first met her, and that office couldn't have been mistaken for roomy in the slightest. For some reason, Kimberly had assumed that the woman who called herself the Queen Bee of Information would have a huge corner location, down the hall from the big cheese.

Pauline, who managed to dominate the small space despite her tiny stature, must have noticed Kimberly's surprise.

"Honey, the size of the office don't matter. It's the size of what you keep up here that counts." She tapped one long fire-engine-red nail to her temple—the nail perfectly matching her pencil skirt and red-and-white polka-dotted blouse. "If I start demanding a big ol' office, next thing you know, it's out the door for ol' Pauline. So give me any hole in the wall, long as it's got a window and a door and a computer, plus…" She waggled her key card. "I got better access to the entire campus than even the CEO. Now, *that's* what counts."

Kimberly chuckled. "That's true. And very wise. So…were you able to find the original file?"

Pauline grimaced. "Yep. But there's a hitch."

"What sort of hitch?"

"Well…before I get into that, were you able to talk with Gail? That nurse I told you about?"

Kimberly didn't want to waste time talking about Gail. She wanted the file. She wanted to tear through it and see if its contents could give her any medical history that might provide a clue about Marissa's bleeding or, if not that, then something that might point to her birth mother's identity.

"Yes, I did. I talked with her on the phone yesterday, and she asked me to wait until Friday to come over and talk." Kimberly hadn't understood why Gail was so insistent about wanting to wait.

Still, when you were asking people for a favor, you were beholden to their timetables. Plus, maybe the poor woman had needed that extra day to get over her trip to the Grand Canyon. "What was the hitch you found?" she prompted.

Pauline blew out a breath. "Privacy laws say I can't give you anything on the mother of the baby. And really, until I can definitively prove that your Marissa and this baby are one and the same, then I'm not supposed to give you anything out of this here file, either." Pauline patted a file laid square in the center of her otherwise pristine desk.

"But...but you said that was the only newborn baby girl in the hospital that day, and that she was a Jane Doe. It has to be Marissa." Kimberly eyed the cream-colored file folder as Pauline's restless scarlet nails drummed out a rhythm on it that sounded like a galloping horse.

"That's right." Pauline nodded in approval. "You have a really good memory. There *was* only one newborn girl here that day. But it's a question of legality. Unless I have a court order from a judge saying that your baby girl is *this* baby girl, then I can't provide *you* any information in here."

"A court order! From a judge! That...that sounds complicated. And as if it would take time." *And money*, Kimberly thought.

"Crazy, isn't it?" Pauline shook her head in disgust. "I know and you know that it's got to be the same baby. But a judge has to review it. I even sweet-talked our chief legal counsel about it—he happens to be a fan of my pecan pies. No dice."

"Oh, Pauline. Isn't there anything you can give me?"

"You? Nope, sweetie. Not right now. However…" Pauline grinned. "If, say, a doctor or nurse needed access to this, you know, to refresh their memories, now, *they* could have it. I could print them a thousand copies, no problem. And it's sort of a gray area, but it appears that, if even a retired nurse needed it—if she were, say, worried about a lawsuit or some sort of pending legal action, and if she had contributed to this here file—well, *she* could look at it. Couldn't really share anything—at least, she's not *supposed* to."

Kimberly caught her drift. "You mean Gail—"

"Funny you should mention Gail. Why, she asked me, all-of-a-sudden-like, if I'd fax her a copy of this. And of course I said, why, sure, honey, 'cause you have the right to access this file." Pauline winked broadly.

For a moment, hope surged in Kimberly. Then it sputtered out, leaving that same sour disappointment puddling in her stomach.

"But she won't be able to actually tell me anything."

"Well…she's not *supposed* to. Not until a judge okays it."

"Right, the judge. How do I go about that?"

"See, now…it just so happens that I know Judge Malloy here in town. He's the chief judge on the circuit, old as the hills, but sharp as a tack, I might add. And he happens to be a big fan of my *apple* pie."

Kimberly burst out laughing. "I think I need to add to your baking fund, as many cakes and pies as you seem to be making on our behalf."

Pauline waved a beringed hand. "Pshaw. There's a reason they call things easy as pie. It ain't rocket science. Now, it won't happen right away. I wrote him up a nice official memo—because that's how he likes these things—so it has to chug its way through the red tape. Well, now, that's a mixed metaphor, isn't it? Sounds like a train pushing through a red tape at the finish line of a foot race, doesn't it? Never you mind. What you want to know is how long. A few days—maybe a week or two. He's pretty quick on these things. I am sorry, Kimberly. If you'd been sent to me first instead of another person, well, I could have gotten forgiveness instead of permission, but Kayla, she's a mighty big stickler for doing things right, and she mentioned it to our boss."

"You have a boss?" The idea of Pauline being supervised by anybody was amazing to Kimberly.

"Why, sure. Everybody has a boss, honey. He don't tell me much what to do—he sets quite a store by my peach cobblers—but sometimes his boss muscle flares up, and he's got to feel all boss-like. So that's why all the lawyers got involved."

Kimberly sighed. For a moment, she remained glued to the chair, hoping against hope that Pauline would relent and maybe open that file and wander out of her office like in the movies.

But the movies weren't real life, and Pauline didn't budge.

Instead, she reached over and patted Kimberly's hand. "Sugar, I can tell you love that girl of yours and you want to help her out. And I've read this here file from top to bottom, back to front. It's your daughter. I feel that in my bones. Just give it a few days, go tomorrow and talk to Gail, see what she can tell you. Before you know it, I'll have my magic-wand powers restored to me courtesy of Judge Malloy and my best apple pie recipe. Shoot, I'll even use fresh apples, even if I do hate peeling the sorry things. I'll even make the piecrust from scratch. You *need* this information. You need to have it in your hands, and you need to have it so you don't have to explain how you got it. And I intend to get that for you."

Kimberly swallowed hard to speak past the lump in her throat. Still, she couldn't manage to. She felt as though she might cry from the frustration of it all. Maybe Gail could at least tell her something.

In the meantime, Ma had extended her hospitality to them, and they didn't have a hotel bill mounting up. But another two weeks? Would it be pushing it to ask Daniel's mother to stay for that long? And the start of school on August 1 was coming at Kimberly like a freight train. She needed to be home in Atlanta for preplanning the last week of July, so this extra two-week delay would eat into the time she and Marissa had to drive to Indiana to see the PAI-1 specialist.

And Daniel... Something about staying near him unsettled her. Every shred of common sense told her to avoid getting more involved with him, even though her heart told her differently. Sure, he'd been there for her—take the way he had held her yesterday. That hug had warmed her to the core.

But his embrace, though devoid of the chemistry that had so rattled her in the hotel room, had served to awaken a different sort of apprehension.

She could more easily shrug off physical attraction than the tug on her heart, the idea that with him she wasn't alone anymore. Because of that embrace, she'd fooled herself into thinking that Daniel would stand beside her in her fight for Marissa.

Of course he wasn't going to fight for Marissa.

He'd gotten to Tim and Pax and warned both of them. What his reasons really were, she didn't know, but it had been clear that he put Marissa's birth mother ahead of Marissa's own medical issues.

She met Pauline's eyes across the desk, that file folder sitting within easy reach, and felt in her bones she was right. This week or two offered more than a test of her patience. It held the threat of Daniel finding out what she was trying to do.

If he knew this Judge Malloy—and chances

were that he did—and he found out that Pauline had requested a court order allowing Kimberly to see the file...

She had no doubt that Daniel would do his level best to block it.

DANIEL HEARD THE heated voices even from the gravel turnaround as he slid out from behind the wheel of his pickup. At first, he thought one of them was Taylor, wound up like she usually got over something her mother had said to her. DeeDee had proved to be as stubborn a mom as she had been a little sister, but Taylor was every bit as unyielding.

Then Kimberly's voice rang out across the warm summer air, the tone sharp and steely and every bit as stubborn as DeeDee's with Taylor. "No, ma'am, you will not ride on that four-wheeler, and that's final."

"But Mo-om!"

"But nothing! We are three hours away from your doctors—"

"I'm sick of it! I'm sick of being smothered! I hate this! I hate *you*!"

The sound of running feet across the deck and the crunch of gravel should have prepared Daniel for Marissa's outbound status.

Still, he couldn't move fast enough from the path to prevent her from barreling into him.

Tears streaked her face, all splotchy and red and swollen, her eyes burning with frustration and anger. Daniel held her back at arm's length.

"I guess you're gonna say I need to go back and apologize," she mumbled, dropping her gaze to the gravel at their feet.

"I—" Daniel looked past her to see Kimberly staring anxiously at them from a distance. She started toward them, her steps unsure.

Daniel glanced back at Marissa, the cleft in her chin prominent as she jutted out a defiant jaw. It reminded him of Taylor and the battle royals he'd seen DeeDee go through. Maybe he could spare Kimberly this stress.

He waved off Kimberly, half surprised that she stopped in midstride. Though she wore a doubtful expression on her face, she didn't follow them as Daniel guided Marissa away from the house.

"What you need first is a little space," Daniel told her. "How about you tell me what all the fuss is about?"

So she did. As Daniel led the way across the pasture, Marissa's words tumbled out: how

Taylor had invited her to go four-wheeling, and how cool that would have been because she'd never been on a four-wheeler before, and how Taylor had said she was going to show her the creek and the old mill house.

"But then Mom made this awful stink about me and my stupid bleeding disorder and how if I got hurt— I hate her! She ruins *everything*!"

If he hadn't heard Taylor say the exact same thing about DeeDee, he might have been shocked. But Daniel recalled how, really, he'd said the same thing about his parents— he'd guess all middle school children said equally vehement things.

"Everything?" he quizzed with a grin. "There's nothing she gets right?"

By now, they had crossed three-quarters of the back pasture and halfway up its gentle incline. Marissa stopped, as if Daniel's half-jesting query was serious and she needed to think to get the true answer. She toed a tuft of grass with her flip-flop. A grasshopper leaped out and jounced off across the ankle-deep rye grass Daniel had planted earlier in the spring.

"She's not so bad," Marissa admitted grudgingly. "It's just—I want to be *normal*. And she gets all— I don't know. Smothery."

"Well, what do you expect? I mean, *smother* does contain the word *mother* after all," Daniel quipped. "I think it's in their job description."

Marissa laughed. Some of the tension went out of her. She took in her surroundings. "That's a cool tree," she said.

Daniel followed her gaze to the huge oak tree sprawled out on a rocky outcrop at the end of the pasture. "That? That's not just any tree. That's our thinking tree. It's all the Monroe kids' thinking tree."

"Yeah?"

He had her attention now. Maybe it was because she was an only child, but he could sense that she liked the idea of being part of a big family.

"Sure," he told her. "When I'd get mad with Ma—or she'd get frustrated with me—she'd tell me to go hang out in our thinking tree for a while. It always helped."

"But Ma's so great! She never gets mad!"

Daniel laughed. "Maybe not with you, but I sure seemed to be good at pushing her buttons. I had a special talent for it when I was your age."

They walked on until the oak tree's low gnarled branches were within reach. A welcome breeze fluttered through the leaves, and a startled bird flew off. Daniel held one of the smaller branches—still as big as his forearm—and gestured for Marissa to go first.

He followed behind into the cool dimness the canopy of branches offered. Looking up, he saw that the rope ladder was still in good shape. Instantly, he was taken back to an age where a few minutes spent in this tree could put the world to rights.

Back then, his problems had seemed huge—too many boring chores, his allowance gone to pay for a windshield smashed from one of his errant knuckleballs, not being allowed to go to Tim's end-of-school spend-the-night camping trip because he'd messed up his English grade, a travel game lost because he'd walked in the winning run.

Somehow, this big old tree had managed to put life in perspective, to shrink his problems down to size. Maybe it was because it was so solid and unchanging, and as a boy he couldn't remember it *not* being here. Maybe Ma had been right and time alone had been the cure.

Marissa hadn't waited for an invitation. Already she was scrambling up the rope ladder—not very elegantly, Daniel noted from the ladder's precipitous swaying.

"Hey, don't you know how to climb a rope ladder?" he asked.

She stopped and stared down at him, her face coloring. "This is the first time I've ever tried."

"Good gracious. Kids need to climb— builds your strength, keeps your core strong. Too much screen time for you, kiddo." Daniel shook his head. "Okay, go slower," he advised, "and keep your arms in close. That will make it easier on you. And watch out for rope burns on your palms. If you don't, you'll wind up with a nice set of blisters tomorrow."

He waited for her to reach the platform his dad had helped him and his brothers build years ago before he followed her up. As he cleared the break in the railing at the head of the ladder, he heard her utter a short, derisive chuckle.

"Seriously?" she asked him. She jabbed a thumb at a hand-painted no-girls-allowed sign hanging from a short length of rope on a limb.

"Yeah, my sisters had the same response you did. They ignored it, so I guess you can, too. Chalk it up to us being the age where we thought all girls had cooties that were as contagious as chicken pox." Daniel settled on the wide plank boards that formed the tree house's floor and leaned against the trunk.

He drew in a breath, felt his lungs—his whole being—expand to fill this private space. It felt as though he'd taken off a pair of too-tight shoes and was able at last to wriggle his toes.

Oh, he or Rob or Andrew would check on the tree house every spring to be sure it was structurally safe with no rotting wood, but this was the first time in a long time Daniel had come up here just to sit.

Not much had changed since the last time he'd come here as a boy. He could still see the green metal roof of the farmhouse glinting through the oak tree's leaves, and the fields, with their neat rows that followed the contours of the earth, stretched out as far as the eye could see.

"Wow, this is so neat!" Marissa whispered. "You can see for miles—I can see the horses way out on the edge of the pasture."

She didn't seem nearly as upset as she had a few minutes earlier. Daniel was glad that the leafy branches were performing their usual magic on tweenage ruffled feathers.

"You know how to ride?" he asked her idly as he let a ladybug crawl onto his finger.

Marissa scowled. "My mom would have a duck if I asked."

What does *this kid get to do? Kimberly might as well have her swaddled in bubble wrap.* "We've got some really safe horses—old and gentle. My sister Maegan's an equine therapist—she uses horses to do physical therapy with all sorts of kids. I'll bet if Maegan and I talk to your mom, she might let you ride while you're here. All of the Monroe kids ride, have since we're old enough to sit up straight."

Marissa turned to face him. Her expression was filled with longing and hope that he could see she was trying to tamp down. "All the Monroe kids? You think she'd let me?"

"Sure. Your mom wants to keep you safe, Marissa. I know it seems hard and unfair. But she does love you."

"It *isn't* fair. Sometimes…"

"What?" he prompted. The ladybug spread its scarlet wings and flew off his finger. "Sometimes what?"

"If we just *knew*, you know? What was

wrong with me? Maybe then the doctors could tell her what was safe for me, how to *fix* me. That's why we came down here. My mom said if we could find my birth mom, maybe she has the same thing I do, and she could tell us how bad it was, how much we really have to worry."

Daniel's stomach tightened. It was even harder to stonewall Marissa than it was Kimberly—harder because whenever he looked at Marissa, he remembered seeing those same eyes staring at him when they were a scant few minutes old.

"What do the doctors say?" he asked as a way to move the subject away from Miriam.

Marissa retrieved a fallen branch from the floor of the tree house and broke off the tip. She stripped it of its dried leaves, then tried to force it into a circle. "That they don't know. That there's something wrong. That I could die—but then again, maybe I won't. It's all 'maybe this' and 'maybe that.' They're clueless. I mean, they're great and all, but they don't have a clue. Last time we were there, my main hem/onc literally sat down in front of me, stared at me for a minute, scratched his head and said, 'Marissa, you're a mystery.'"

"That's got to be frustrating."

"My mom… Wow!" The branch in Marissa's hands reached the limits of its elasticity and snapped in two. The break was sudden and jarring in the silence, and it startled another bird from its nest in noisy protest. "She blew her stack when we got out of that doctor's office. I mean, she pays these huge bills for all these tests, and she sees them draw vial after vial of blood—we stopped counting after a hundred vials, but it's gotta be getting close to two hundred—and she hates it that they can't figure this out. She hates it for me, you know? And any time I have to have surgery or a procedure—even if it's something really simple—I have to be put to sleep, and that *really* freaks her out."

"I'll bet" was all Daniel could manage to say. His guilt magnified and it felt like tentacles were squeezing him.

Marissa's face brightened. "But we're close! Mom told me when she got in from town that the hospital here is going to give her the medical files—you know, of when I was born. And that maybe they'll have my birth mother's name in them."

"What?" Daniel's guilt evaporated into alarm. "They're giving her the files?"

"Yeah. Well, not right away. She said a

judge has to give them permission, but that she has a lady helping her."

Twin feelings of anxiety and inexplicable relief curled through Daniel. Did it count as a betrayal to Miriam if her identity was revealed through some other source?

Yes. I promised her to do everything I could to keep her safe—and something in that file might reveal who she is.

Daniel shifted, then asked in what he hoped was a casual tone, "So…you happen to remember if your mom mentioned the judge's name?"

"Malloy?" Marissa frowned. She closed her eyes, pondered on it for a moment. "Yeah, that's it. Judge Malloy. You know him?"

Shoot. That old soft touch. He'd give Kimberly the moon if she asked. To Marissa, he replied, "I do. He was a good friend of my dad's."

"You can talk to him?"

"I don't know." Daniel felt himself squirming inside. *Please don't ask me to put a word in on your behalf. I can't do that* and *keep my promise to Miriam.*

She kicked off her flip-flops and stretched out onto the boards along the far rail. "I guess…I guess you're not supposed to talk to a judge, huh?"

"What, you mean to ask him to decide one way or the other?" When she nodded, he sighed. "In this case, I don't think I can ask him to open those files for your mom, Marissa."

She bit her bottom lip, twirled her strawberry hair around her finger—so like Miriam. "Yeah, it was a dumb idea. But fingers crossed, right?"

"Fingers crossed," he repeated, but didn't add that, for Miriam's sake, his fingers were crossed for the opposite result.

CHAPTER SIXTEEN

KIMBERLY HAD WATCHED with a mix of relief and envy as Daniel and Marissa strolled across the pasture, their heads together in conversation. People had warned her that once Marissa hit those middle school years, she'd be harder to talk to—and Kimberly had known their warnings were true.

How many times had parents sat across from her in a parent-teacher conference and agonized over the fact that all they could wring out of their kids were monosyllabic grunts?

She knew Marissa chafed against all her rules—but they weren't *her* rules alone. Marissa had heard the doctors warn her about injuries. She knew the drill.

Feeling at loose ends, she wandered back into the house, where Ma was busy shelling yet another pan of butter beans.

"Where's another dishpan, and I'll give that a whirl?" Kimberly offered. "I'm a city girl, but maybe you can teach me how to shell beans."

Ma chuckled. "You must be a city girl, to be offering to help with butter beans." She stopped and rubbed the tip of her thumb. "Ah, but it makes my thumbnail ache. If it were just me, I'd settle for field peas instead— easier to shell than these blasted beans. But the boys like butter beans better. If they're willing to pick them, then I'm willing to shell. If you're really itching to help, look in the laundry room and you'll find another metal dishpan on the shelf."

Kimberly did as she was told. The laundry room, off the kitchen, was more of a sewing/craft/all-purpose room, with neat, organized areas for different activities. She found the pan on the shelves above the freezer, beside a carton of quart canning jars and a huge old pressure cooker.

As she was pulling out the pan, a piece of brightly colored cardboard fluttered out. She bent down to retrieve it.

It was a baseball card—and not any base-ball card, but one with a very young Daniel staring back at her. She flipped the card over, saw that he'd been the pitcher of a minor league team—and from the stats, a pretty good one at that.

Kimberly stared at it. Daniel? A baseball player?

"Kimberly? Need some help in there?" Ma called. "You mightn't be able to find it in all my jumbled mess in there."

Guiltily Kimberly grabbed the pan. She started to stick the card back where she found it, then decided to take it with her as she returned to the kitchen.

"I'm sorry," she told Ma. "I got distracted. I found this."

"What on earth?" Ma took the card and sighed. "My land. No, that doesn't belong in there. Looks as if Landon and Logan have been playing scavenger hunt again—this should have been safe in my photo album. Gracious, but doesn't Daniel look young!"

"Is that…real?" Kimberly settled into the chair alongside Ma and helped herself to a heap of butter beans. She worked at the bean, trying to figure out how Ma could zip through them so quickly.

"Try flipping the bean over— That's right, jab that thumbnail right along the back spine. You've got the hang of it now," Ma encouraged.

As Kimberly tackled another bean with a tad more confidence, Ma went back to her study of the baseball card. "Oh, yes, he really was a professional baseball player. A good one, too. They were just about to call him up to the majors when his dad died. I still remember…" Ma's eyes grew wet and she set aside the card. It took her a few butter beans, their hulls thumping against the interior of the white plastic bucket, before she could continue in a husky voice, "Daniel was on the road when the accident happened. He drove in from… Gosh, I forget where, but I think it was somewhere in Maryland. I remember he drove all night to get here, and I was so scared I'd lose both him and his dad on the same day."

"But he…he made it?"

Ma nodded. "I think that was what his dad was hanging on for. He wanted to talk to Daniel before… Well, before he died. After that, it wasn't long at all, which, I guess, was a mercy. He was in some kind of awful pain, I tell you. Morphine didn't even begin to touch it."

"And Daniel gave it up? His baseball career?" Kimberly marveled at that. She wondered how a man could turn his back on the promise of fame and fortune. "When he was so close to making it in major league baseball?"

"I couldn't talk him out of it. He was determined to stay close to home, watch out for me. Said he'd promised his dad to take care of us, and that he couldn't do that if he were on the road. When he hung up his glove and bat, he hung it up. Swapped it for turnout gear and his dad's ax, and that was that."

The rhythmic thump of empty butter-bean shells as they hit the bucket was the only sound for a long moment. Kimberly turned over Ma's words in her mind as she shelled. Finally, she managed to say, "He takes his promises seriously, doesn't he?"

Ma's mouth curved into a small bittersweet smile as she nodded. "Yes, he does. That was his father's doing. He always set a store by integrity, my husband did. A man's word is who he is and it's all he's got, he'd say. I can't say I'm sorry to see Daniel take after his father, but…sometimes I think he takes it a little too much to heart. I wonder if his dad would have really wanted him to quit baseball. He never missed a game when Daniel was in high school, you know? And he saw a lot of his college games. Despite being chief and all that responsibility he had on his shoulders. He always made it a priority, said that he'd promised Daniel that he would be there."

"Sounds like Daniel got that from his dad, then, all his promise keeping."

"You can take it to the bank, Daniel's word, that I'll grant you."

The back door opened, and Kimberly heard Marissa's breathless laughter at something Daniel was saying. No sign of her earlier truculent rebellion could be detected in the sounds coming from her daughter.

Again that twin feeling of relief and envy coursed through Kimberly at Daniel's ability to jolly Marissa out of her sour mood. She squashed down the envy and wrote it off as being a holdover from her long years as a single mom. She needed to let go. She should be grateful Daniel was giving her a hand, not envious at his ability to soothe Marissa.

Marissa bounced into the kitchen and slid into the chair beside Kimberly. Without missing a beat, she started shelling beans—and more expertly than Kimberly. "Mom, you're slow!"

"I'm learning. I see you've had practice," Kimberly observed.

Daniel had followed Marissa in, and now

he was bending over to brush his mother's cheek with a kiss. "I see you've got everybody in on the act, Ma. I hope since I picked 'em, I don't have to shell 'em." His head swiveled toward Kimberly, and for a split second she thought he intended to give her a peck on the cheek, too.

To her disappointment, he pulled back—maybe it had all been wishful thinking on her part. Instead, he dropped into the chair across from her. "Thumbs sore yet?" he asked, teasing.

"Not yet, but I can see how they will be."

"Before we all got big enough to help, Ma had to do it practically by herself, and one summer she shelled so many that she lost a thumbnail."

"Eww!" Marissa wrinkled her nose. She tossed aside the butter bean she was shelling. "That's it, I'm done. No butter bean's worth that. Now, if it were Krispy Kreme doughnuts, *that* would be worth a thumbnail."

Ma laughed. "It was only part of my nail, but it did end my shelling days for a while. That's when Daniel's dad decided that, small fry or not, all the kids were big enough to grab a pan and shell."

"Remember Maegan?" Daniel ran a hand

through his dark hair as he leaned back in his chair. "She had that toy dishpan of hers, no bigger than a cereal bowl, and she'd say that she was done helping when she finished the beans in her pan." His eyes twinkled.

"What I remember is how your dad sent you and Andrew and Rob out to pick butter beans while I was supervising the shelling, and you scamps filled buckets half-full with my empty hulls to get out of picking, because your dad had rashly said you could go swimming after you'd each picked a bucket."

"Oh! Don't remind me! Worst trouble I ever got into. That was one of the few times Dad tore up my tail—I didn't think I was going to be able to sit down for a week." Daniel looked over at Marissa. "Hey, 'Rissa, if you're not going to help your mother out, how about you swap places with me?"

"No problem. I've shelled two pans already today, and I don't even like butter beans— well, unless Ma cooks them." Marissa surrendered her seat to Daniel.

Kimberly cursed her pulse as it kicked up a fuss at Daniel's proximity. His big hands nearly touched hers as they reached into the dishpan for a bean to shell.

He spotted the baseball card where Ma had

laid it on the table. "Man, that old thing. Look at all that hair. Ma, I'll bet you were itching to get the shears after me when I sent you that card in the mail."

"I was itching to have you close enough that I *could* get the shears after you—back then you were going from pillar to post." She must have thought about how he might interpret her words and her face softened. "But I knew you were doing what you wanted, Daniel. You really loved baseball."

Something—pain? Irritation? Whatever the emotion was, it flickered across Daniel's face so quickly that Kimberly couldn't decipher it. In its place was his usual cool, collected demeanor. "A boy's game. Only think, I'd be nursing a blown-out shoulder and boring y'all with tales of my twenty seconds in the big leagues if I'd stayed."

Marissa's eyes rounded. She picked up the card. "Wow! You were a professional baseball player?"

"It's not as glamorous as it sounds," he said. The empty hull in his hand hit the bucket with a little too much force and bounced back out. "Besides, I was just good enough to make the minors. I didn't really have what it took to make a career in the majors."

Ma's mouth compressed, and she appeared on the brink of disagreeing. Kimberly watched the struggle on her face, but in the end, she said nothing.

"So they fired you?" Marissa asked, with all the graceless tact of a soon-to-be twelve-year-old. Kimberly shot her a warning glance that Marissa didn't even seem to notice.

He shook his head. "No…my dad died. And, well…"

"You came home to be fire chief like him," she suggested.

"It didn't happen quite that fast. I came home to—" Daniel met Kimberly's eyes over the shared dishpan "—keep a promise."

She shivered. To have a man who was that serious about keeping his promises…

Sometimes that would be heaven. After a lifetime of her mom never keeping her word, and her dad never being around to even try, Kimberly would love to have someone she could count on, especially to help raise Marissa.

But if Daniel could give up a chance at major league baseball to keep one of the promises he'd made, then Kimberly didn't have a prayer of convincing him to break the promise he'd made to Marissa's birth mom.

DANIEL FIDGETED IN the anteroom outside the county commission's board office. The door was closed, and the small dusty room where he sat on the lone hard bench was deserted.

He glanced at his watch, checked his phone for messages. Nothing. His radio hadn't squawked, either.

The quiet unsettled him.

For days now, the only calls the fire department had been getting were minor ones—a barbecue grill forgotten and aflame, a few grass fires on the interstate's median because it was still so dry, a kitchen grease fire that the wife had put out with her home fire extinguisher by the time her rattled husband, who'd caused the fire to begin with, had hung up with 911. Shoot, the department had even rescued a literal cat from a literal tree.

Call Daniel superstitious, but a lull never boded well. For one thing, it made the entire crew anxious and antsy. He'd kept them busy with cleaning and scrubbing and even some painting—the fire station had never looked so good. They'd had plenty of time to cook the produce Ma had been sending, plus exercise as a group.

Still, they were keyed up, and Daniel knew why. So many times such quiet was an omen of a big, deadly fire. It took him back to the tales they told of the fire that had taken his dad's life: a quiet, restless early summer that exploded with a raging warehouse fire.

He shook himself and stared at the closed meeting-room door, willing it to open. All he had to do was give a five-minute presentation on the current state of the department's budget, and then he was free to get back to his real job. He wanted to fight fires, not wrangle with the county commissioners.

The door did not open. For the dozenth time, Daniel stared down at the papers in his hand. This time, he couldn't concentrate on the words and figures. Instead, he found his mind wandering back to the day before, the conversation with Marissa.

Maybe he could call Miriam—if he could track her down. She'd been pretty determined to leave her family and its twisted version of Amish faith behind, so there was a chance she'd embraced technology and the modern way of life and the internet would turn her up.

Then again, she'd been equally determined to hide from Uriel Hostetler, the so-called religious leader and Marissa's birth grandfather. Old Uriel had wanted different things for his son, things that didn't include an unwanted pregnancy, especially with a girl who didn't fit into Uriel's plans for his boy. Uriel had been grooming his son to take his place. Those plans had been put in jeopardy by the baby—what congregation would follow a boy with such a grievous sin in his past?

Miriam had been certain that he would kill her and the baby to hide his son's moral lapse.

And after Daniel had met the man—and his weak-willed son—he could see why Miriam was afraid. She had no one to protect her, not even her own parents, who were so cowed by Hostetler.

Surely, though, there was a middle ground. Maybe Miriam could write out her medical history, give Kimberly just the facts she needed to keep Marissa safe.

Would it be enough, though? Or would Kimberly pick at that frayed edge of secrecy until she'd unraveled the whole story? That seemed more in keeping with her tenacious nature. She'd never let it alone.

A hinge squeaked, and Daniel's eyes shot to the meeting-room door—but no, it had been the connecting door to the courthouse's central hall. In walked the stooped figure of none other than Judge Stanley Malloy.

"Daniel, my boy! You're the fellow I was looking for."

Daniel's mouth went dry. What did the judge want with him? Did it have anything to do with Kimberly's request for medical records?

"What can I do for you?" Daniel asked. He scooted over and made space on the bench for the judge, who thumped across the room with a walking stick for added stability.

The thin old man, in a brown suit and tie and cream shirt, resembled a heap of dried fall leaves that could be blown away with a stiff gust of wind. He had to be in his early eighties, but despite the cane, he seemed as spry and sharp as ever, with no date for a retirement in sight.

Now he settled beside Daniel, mopping his pink pate with an actual linen handkerchief. "Whew! It's hot out there, and none too cool in here. Trying to save money, I guess."

"Are you waiting on the commissioners, too? They've been in an executive session for the past half hour—swore it would only take five minutes and for me to wait." Daniel heard his tone slide into the slightest edge of grumbling territory.

"No, no. I called over to the fire department to ask you to come by, and they said you were here in the courthouse at the county meeting. I was hoping to catch you before you left." The judge planted his walking stick between his shiny brown oxfords and clasped the gleaming clear glass ball on top with both of his gnarled hands.

Daniel shifted on his end of the bench. "Here I am," he said. "A captive audience, at least until that door opens."

"I suspect we'll have more than enough time, from the sound of their raised voices," the judge told him wryly. "It's about that child."

Daniel's stomach knotted even more tightly. "Child?"

"The girl you delivered, what, eleven years ago? Nearly twelve now. It was on the Fourth of July, wasn't it?"

"Yes, sir. Funny, it doesn't seem as though it's been that long. I guess the hospital asked you to take a look at it?"

Judge Malloy winked. "*Pauline* did, and brought the request to my office herself, along with one of her apple pies. It was, if I do say so myself, one of her better ones. This time she went all out and used fresh apples. She doesn't think I can tell the difference, but I can."

Daniel couldn't help but chuckle, though he did so with a sinking heart. Pauline's apple pie *and* a case involving a kid? Malloy had probably already signed the order and was just talking to him as a courtesy.

Now the judge's eyes dimmed. "I remember that Fourth of July. I was out by the pool—it was one of Margery's last summers. I didn't have her with me too much longer. Cancer. A terrible thief." He shook his head and returned to his narrative. "She came to me and said you were at the door. I had no clue what you wanted."

"I sure appreciated your help that day, Judge. The hospital—the hospital was all set to turn her and the baby over to Uriel Hostetler... Well, her parents, but—"

The judge nodded. "Yes, if they'd released her to her parents, it was the same as putting her in Hostetler's not-so-tender hands. That man. If he'd been here a little longer, I believe I would have had the pleasure of putting him behind bars, where he deserved to be. No, Daniel, I was glad to do my part to help that girl, and luckily you were right. The law *was* on her side."

"So are you going to do it? Release those medical records?"

Judge Malloy didn't seem in any hurry to answer the question. He pursed his lips, drew his brows together. His fingers smoothed over the glass knob on the walking stick again.

Watching him, Daniel had a fanciful wish that the clear globe would be a crystal ball, where the answers to his dilemma would magically appear.

"Daniel, I've reviewed Marissa's records, and I believe they can be released without revealing Miriam's identity. There's nothing in them that leads back to her. I've read them very closely. Frankly, I'm surprised that Ms. Singleton doesn't already have a copy—surely this hospital forwarded the case file up to the hospital in Atlanta when they airlifted the baby."

A whoosh of relief rushed through Daniel. Kimberly could have the records and Miriam would still be safe.

"That's great, sir! I know Kimberly will—"

The judge cleared his throat, an awful phlegmy sound that he followed with an apologetic glance in Daniel's direction. "Ahem, allergies. All this Bahia grass. No, as I was saying, the records don't reveal Miriam's name. They don't reveal very much at all, in fact. Maybe it was because it was a holiday. Maybe it was the ER doctor on duty. Whatever the reason, those records are extremely… scant."

"Oh. So…"

"Ms. Singleton won't find many answers in them, Daniel. She's going to follow up with a petition to have the birth mother's records opened up, I would bet you anything. It's what I would do, and she seems, from the conversation I had with her on the phone, like a very intelligent, tenacious young woman."

Daniel closed his eyes and sank back against the bench's unforgiving back. The judge was accurate in his assessment of Kimberly. "Sir…"

"Perhaps this is, hmm…unconventional, a judge talking with someone in an unofficial capacity about a case before him. But this particular request—to release Miriam's records—hasn't come before me yet, and *you* were the one who had the strongest connection with Miriam." Judge Malloy fixed Daniel with a piercing stare.

"You want me to… What, sir?" Daniel couldn't contain his agitation any longer. He leaped up from the bench and started pacing.

"I'm considering this in my mind. It's been many, many years, so has the threat to Miriam's life been reduced? Is Uriel Hostetler even still alive? What harm would occur if I were to release those medical records?"

"But doesn't the patient privacy law..." Daniel trailed off. "And the safe-haven law, too? Isn't she protected based on those two laws?"

"Ahem." The judge rubbed his mouth in thought. "It's a gray area indeed, with no real precedent on the state level. The law concerning patient privacy does have some flexibility built into it for just these situations, on a sort of need-to-know basis if it involves a life-or-death matter. The safe-haven law... Well, I expect that any decision of mine to release the birth mother's records could well end up before the state's supreme court for a decision, if the hospital chose to fight it—or the birth mother."

Daniel wondered if perhaps that was the judge's biggest concern, that one of his last cases could be dragged out and eventually overturned on appeal, as he was nearing what had to be the end of his career.

Then Judge Malloy shrugged his shoulders. "That's well and good—the appeals process can do what it wants. That's what they're there for. But I have to decide the question to begin with. Daniel—*you* remember this girl. And you know the Singleton woman's situation. Is she…exaggerating her adopted daughter's illness?"

"Exaggerating?" Daniel froze midpace. Here was his out. If he told the judge that Kimberly was a drama queen, someone who was simply chasing a diagnosis, he had no doubt that Judge Malloy would deny Kimberly and that would be that.

All he needed to say was that Kimberly was so overprotective that the kid had never been allowed to climb a rope ladder. Boom. Case closed.

He couldn't do that, though. Kimberly had her reasons for being so cautious. He needed to tell the truth—and yet still convince the judge to continue to protect Miriam.

"Well?" the judge prompted.

"Kimberly *is* a very protective sort," Daniel allowed. "But I think she's got reason to be. Of course, I haven't talked to any doctors, but Marissa herself has told me about how puzzled her doctors are."

"Hmm. And your judgment of Ms. Singleton? Is she astute? Does she seem to be the overreactive type? Or can she, say, read the body language fairly well of a doctor? Understand what a person is trying to tell her?"

For some reason, the first thing that came to Daniel's mind was how he had almost given Kimberly a peck on the cheek the day before when he'd walked in the kitchen. He hadn't thought about it—it had seemed like the most natural thing in the world to bend down and brush her cheek, flushed with the warmth of supper cooking on the stove.

And Kimberly had realized he'd been about to do it—which made it even more mortifying.

"She's—she's very astute," Daniel got out. "And she doesn't miss much at all. But, sir… isn't there some way that Miriam can be protected?"

"Oh, now." The judge rose from his seat, his knees creaking so loudly that Daniel could hear them. "I can only answer the *legal* niceties of the case, Daniel. What *I* can decide is whether Ms. Singleton is entitled to even a redacted medical file. Everything else? Well, that's above my pay grade. If the law is on her side, then, yes, she gets the whole ball of wax."

"Is it, though? The safe-haven law was

designed to protect babies—and their birth mothers. It was designed to—"

"You don't have to tell me," the judge said, cutting off Daniel's words. "I remember one case where a birth mother came before me— she didn't even realize she was pregnant until very late, and then after having the unwanted baby she tried to smother it. Told me that her boyfriend had sworn you couldn't get pregnant the first time. Ruined two lives, she did, because that baby was never right. No, sir. The safe-haven law is a good one—most of the time. And I'm inclined to let it have all the teeth the legislators intended it to have. But…" He frowned, raised up the head of his walking stick and jabbed the glass globe in Daniel's direction. "You, now, you have a different quandary altogether, son."

"Sir?" Cold anxiety puddled in Daniel's stomach. What had he not thought about?

"The doctors, the paramedics, the nurses… even I as the judge on the case—all of us are sworn to never let Miriam's name pass our lips. But not you. You were just a Good Samaritan. As I read it, you aren't bound by the safe-haven law, no more than any other bystander would have been."

"What?" Daniel gaped at the judge. "That

can't be right. I mean, she came to the fire station. I was on duty at the time. She—Miriam—thought it was all official. So did I."

"No, sir, Daniel. Like I said. Maybe ethically you shouldn't say anything. But in the eyes of the law? You're the only one who can *legally* tell Ms. Singleton what she needs to know."

CHAPTER SEVENTEEN

KIMBERLY STOOD ON the narrow front porch stoop of the neat and tidy ranch-style house and pressed the doorbell again.

Again Gail Korman did not answer the door.

Kimberly chewed on the inside of her lip. She peered at the text message Gail had sent her—yes, she had the address right, and the time and date.

So where was Gail?

The retired nurse hadn't struck Kimberly as the forgetful type. No, Gail Korman had repeated the address and the appointed date and time and then offered to send it in a text message.

Kimberly surveyed the neighborhood, hoping for a nosy neighbor to appear.

But the nearby houses, almost carbon copies of the Korman house, with its redbrick veneer, white trim and black shutters, seemed abandoned. No cars stood in any of the carports or driveways, no curious eyes peered around drapes. The only noises that Kimberly could hear besides the cawing of a raucous blue jay were a low hum, like a car being vacuumed out, and the faint sound of music. She couldn't tell where they were coming from.

As she debated whether to ring the bell again, a postal delivery truck rolled to a stop in front of the house. The driver hopped out of the vehicle and trotted across thick grass in the direction of the mailbox by the front door.

"Looking for Gail?" the woman asked her as she jammed a thick stack of mail into the narrow confines of the box. "You might try in back—she's liable to be giving their camper a good cleaning. She does that when they first get back from a long trip."

"Thank you, I'll try that." Kimberly gave her a grateful smile. Then she wound her way around the house and under the attached carport that barely housed a large extended cab pickup. On the truck's dented steel bumper, to the right of a towing hitch, a bumper sticker proclaimed, If You Can Read This, I've Lost My Trailer.

The backyard was dominated by a large camper, white with green stripes. The windows and doors were thrown open, and Kimberly had solved the mystery of where the noise was coming from: faint music filtered out over the hum of a vacuum cleaner.

She pulled herself up on the metal grate that served as the camper's doorstep. An older woman was bent over a vacuum cleaner in the back of the trailer.

Kimberly rapped her knuckles against the door frame. When the woman didn't respond, she knocked again, louder.

The woman whirled around, her eyebrows sky-high on a wide forehead. The hand still gripping the vacuum's cord flew to her chest. "Oh! You gave me a fright!"

She turned and switched off the machine, then stretched over to the tiny kitchen cabinet and jabbed a button on the radio. The trailer fell silent.

"You must be Kimberly. Is it ten o'clock already? I thought for sure I could give the camper a good going-over and have time left before you got here. Oh, well."

"I didn't mean to scare you—" Kimberly began.

Gail shook her head. "No need to apologize. Harold says that when I get to cleaning, it's as though I'm on another planet. And after two weeks with this place jammed with our grandkids, I wish I *were* on another planet.

You want to go inside? Or we could just sit here."

"Here's fine. Unless you need…er, the file? I'll try not to take up too much of your time."

Gail collapsed into the cramped dining nook built into the camper, indicating that Kimberly should sit across from her. She adjusted a scarf tied in her hair, and after assuring herself that it hadn't slipped, she blew out a breath. "I did look at the file again. Pauline faxed me a copy. I wish I could share it with you, but I talked with Judge Malloy and he said that he'd have to make a ruling on it, and any copy would have to go through him."

"I know. He spoke with me this morning. He's approved it so that I can get a copy of my daughter's medical files."

"Much good that will do you," Gail muttered. "There's not a lot there, I'm afraid."

A bubble of hope popped in Kimberly's heart. "Really? I'd expected—"

"Honey, a dozen years ago we didn't even have an ob/gyn that delivered babies at this hospital—one had retired, and the other had moved that summer. So we were diverting all but emergency deliveries to other hospitals. Boy, was I glad when they finally found a couple willing to open up a local practice again."

"I don't understand. What does that have to do with Marissa's medical records?"

"Well, everything, don't you see?" Gail settled back against the banquette. "Your daughter was getting the absolute basic care—that stupid ER doctor didn't even realize there was a problem until I hounded him about it."

"A problem?" Kimberly kicked herself for sounding more like an echo chamber than an intelligent human being.

"Sure. When we did have an ob/gyn, I'd been in L and D—that's Labor and Deliveries. But when we shut down our maternity ward that spring, they moved me over to the ER and put me in as a charge nurse. I'd have rather caught babies with screaming mamas all day and all night long than have to put up with whiny contract ER docs who aren't even from around here. Worst cost-saving measure our hospital big cheese ever did, you want to know my opinion. But they didn't ask me."

Kimberly still didn't quite get the connection between the status of the hospital and the paucity of Marissa's records. She remained quiet, though, and waited for Gail to tell the story in her own way. Now that the woman had been primed, she seemed to relish reliving those times.

"So of course I knew that babies come out of their mamas bruised up. Fifteen years of catching babies, you bet I did. And I knew when something was wrong—your little girl was just covered in bruises. They looked like some sort of pox. And then her umbilical cord, which we'd stopped all the bleeding from at first, started bleeding again—"

"Oh, Gail, this is information I really needed," Kimberly interrupted, unable to stop herself. "It sounds like the medical records will help."

"No, they won't. Because all that isn't in there. It's up here." Gail tapped her salt-and-pepper hair. "That idiot doctor wouldn't believe me at first. Said I was making too big a fuss over nothing. But then the girl— whoops."

She put her fingers to her lips and said nothing at all for a beat. All Kimberly could focus on was the cobweb of cracks in Gail's dry, reddened hand as the woman considered what to say next.

When Gail did begin speaking again, her words were more circumspect with a touch of self-recrimination. "The judge warned me not to say anything about the birth mother. And here I go, a regular chatty Cathy. Anyway, suffice it to say that other developments finally got that blasted doctor to see that maybe I wasn't some hot-air know-it-all. So we transferred the baby out by helicopter."

Kimberly could pick up the story from there, based on the records of the hem/oncs Marissa had seen over the years. Most every test doctors had ordered had come back normal, and in the very first years, they had even debated whether her earlier bleeding issues had been a fluke.

But the nosebleeds and other incidents had continued—without a clear explanation until one specialist had speculated that maybe Marissa's disorder was related to a PAI-1 deficiency.

"So how old was she when you adopted her?" Gail asked instead of continuing with her story.

"Oh, Marissa was a baby—she was still in the hospital. They called me out of the blue—I was diagramming gerund phrases on the blackboard for my students, and the principal walked in and said I had an emergency phone call. The social worker wanted to know if I'd be willing to foster a baby with known health issues, that they didn't have any other foster parent willing to take her."

"And you said yes?"

"Yes. The minute they put her in my arms, I knew...she was the one. She was mine. I wouldn't have cared if she had two heads—she was my miracle baby." Kimberly blinked back stinging tears at the memory of holding Marissa for the first time.

"Oh, my, it must have been something," Gail breathed.

"You have no idea. I was in a panic. The social worker took me up to the NICU and showed me Marissa, warning me not to get my hopes up—she had been there a few days by then, and they still had no clue what was wrong with her." Kimberly fixed her eyes on the granite pattern of the Formica tabletop and clenched her fingers together. She remembered with crystal clarity the tiny bundle in the clear plastic bassinet, dwarfed by a host of mystifying equipment standing at the ready.

Gail nodded vigorously and took Kimberly's hand in a firm grip. "That NICU, it's a scary place for parents. But you stuck with her."

"I did. And she stuck with me. But Gail...I

have to find out. I have to know what's wrong. How can I help Marissa, keep her safe, if we don't have a sure diagnosis?"

"You said they might have one?"

Kimberly recapped the possibility of PAI-1, and when she got to the bit about the insurance company not being willing to pay for a German lab to do the DNA testing, Gail blew a raspberry of disgust.

"Insurance companies! Telling us what we can and can't do for patients. Ties doctors' hands, I tell you, because they work for the hospital, and the hospital has to keep its doors open. Oh, hon, I wish I could help you. I wish I could tell you all you need to know. You need to find that birth mama. You *need* to. That would answer so many of your questions. Why, I'll bet—" Here she bit off her words again and shook her head regretfully. "All these rules and regulations, I know they're there for a purpose, but…"

For a moment, Kimberly dared to hope that Gail would toss caution to the wind and blurt out what she knew.

She didn't, though. Biting her lip, Gail remained silent, giving Kimberly a regretful shake of her head. "I can't. The judge was really, really clear. Right now, the only thing I can talk about is your little girl."

"Do you—do you think if I requested the birth mother's records, Judge Malloy would release them?"

"Now, that, well, I don't know. You'd have to file a petition, I think. And they'd have to run a notice in the paper—wherever they had good cause to think the birth mother would be. And that still doesn't give you any guarantee that the judge would rule your way. He's a stickler for these things. Follows the law."

Kimberly swallowed. It nearly tore her apart to know that once again, a person sitting across from her had vital information that could help her daughter.

She recalled how Tim had thrown her a crumb about the tow-truck driver.

"Is there…anything you could tell me? Did…did anyone visit the baby while she was at the hospital here? Maybe if I could track them down, they'd know something and could tell me."

Gail drew her brows together in contemplation. "Hmm. That's a good question. Let's see…I do recall a few people coming in, but the girl… Whoops. Get me to talking, and I just blather on and on about things I'm not supposed to. Okay, let's put it this way—the hospital bigwigs finally weighed in and said that since it was a safe-haven surrender, Judge Malloy had said that we couldn't let anybody know who the mother of the baby was. And if the mother of the baby was still in the hospital—" she winked broadly "—well, nobody could tell any of her visitors that she'd even had a baby. So…no, there was nobody around who asked specifically to see the baby, no."

Kimberly nodded, hopes dashed. It had been a long shot.

Then Gail brightened. "Oh, wait! There was a visitor—Daniel Monroe. He came by, wanted to hold the baby. Marissa. The birth mom—well, I guess you know this, so I can say—had named her Marissa. So Daniel—gosh, he was so young back then! And just starting out with the fire department. He wanted a picture of him holding her. Most precious thing I ever did see." Gail beamed. "He was the one who delivered her, you know."

"Yes. He's showed me the picture. It's beautiful."

"Well, why hasn't he told you all this, then? I mean, good gracious!" Gail sat forward in excitement, her face wreathed in a relieved smile. "He's not bound by the safe-haven law like I am or the hospital staff is. The fire department can't take babies here in Georgia. That girl wasn't covered by the safe-haven law until she got into that ambulance. Daniel could tell you everything you need to know. Everything."

CHAPTER EIGHTEEN

Marissa yawned and stretched her free leg to work out a kink. The boards of the tree-house floor dug into her backside through the blanket she'd spread out.

"Hold still!" Taylor ordered. "Or I'll smear it."

"Aren't you almost done?" Now Marissa sat up, careful not to jostle Taylor. Her friend's blond head was still bent over Marissa's left foot, a fine-point nail-polish pen in her hand.

"Almost…but if you want it like the one you did on mine, you're going to have to give me a few more minutes. You're better at this than I am." Taylor returned her focus to the pedicure.

Marissa gazed around the leafy green confines of the tree house. She and Taylor had taken over the place, bringing up some of Ma's old blankets and cushions, really jazzing up the place. They'd also found a big plastic bin to keep their stuff out of the rain. Taylor had come up with the idea of rigging up a pulley to lift their haul—otherwise, Marissa couldn't imagine getting all that stuff up here.

To her far left, in the neighboring pasture, she could see Taylor's aunt Maegan working with a kid on the big gray mare. Something in her shriveled at the sight of a kid, way smaller than she was, and with a disability, too, on the back of that horse.

Marissa had let Daniel bring up the possibility of learning how to ride. Her mom hadn't given her an outright no…but she'd had that flat look of hers and said, "We'll see," which Marissa knew was Mom-ese for "never in a hundred years, but I don't want an argument about it right now."

She should be on that horse. All the Monroe kids knew how to ride, Daniel had said.

And she was a Monroe.

"Hey," she called over to Taylor. "You got any ideas about what I talked about? About Daniel and my mom?"

Taylor raised her arms in a *V*, causing a small spray of white droplets from the paint pen to cascade on the weathered boards. "Woo-hoo! Done! Ow! My neck!"

Marissa inspected the final artwork. Yes, the flower was a little lopsided, but it still looked pretty good for a first-timer. "Not bad," she told Taylor.

"How'd you get so good at doing nail art?" Taylor capped the pen and leaned back on her palms.

Marissa snorted. "Are you kidding? It's about the only thing my mom *will* let me do. Painting nails doesn't involve sharp objects, the risk of falls or sudden stops."

"You are so right. We've got to do something to help your mom, you know, chillax."

"Yeah. I think if we could just fix her and Daniel up…"

Taylor nodded enthusiastically. "They'd be perfect together. And that would mean you could live down here, and we could go to school together, and now that Libby Danvers has moved, we've got a spot on the cheer squad, and I could ask Coach if you—"

"Don't even bother. My mom would never, ever let me cheer. She'd swear I'd get mortally injured."

"You don't know that. I mean, you wouldn't have to be a flyer. You could be a base."

Taylor had a way of saying things that persuaded Marissa to believe, if only for an instant, that they could happen. She was so *certain*.

"Maybe," Marissa replied, still harboring doubt but wanting desperately to believe her. It would be so cool to start the school year in a place where nobody knew about her bleeding—or at least, the ones who did know didn't make such a big deal out of it.

Still, she'd learned that if you didn't wish really, really hard for something, it didn't hurt so bad if you didn't get it.

She had a long list of things she hadn't gotten because of that stupid bleeding disorder.

"So what's your plan?" Taylor asked. "Get Uncle Daniel to ask her on a date?"

"Yeah, right." Marissa rolled her eyes. "You don't know my mom. She's the queen of excuses—she can say no in a hundred different ways, believe me. If Daniel asked her out, she'd just put him off. No, I've got to figure out a way to get them together, by themselves, so they can talk. Because…"

She found herself not wanting to talk to Taylor about seeing Daniel and her mom together. There'd been a connection between them, an unvarnished honesty. It was as if her mom had felt comfortable enough to reveal her true self to Daniel—something Marissa had never seen her do with anybody.

Her mom was so strong, so independent, so we'll-get-through-this.

Plus, she'd sounded so lonely. Marissa didn't want her mom to be all alone. She wanted her to be happy. Her mom *deserved* to be happy.

"Shoot, that's easy," Taylor proclaimed. "Get Uncle Daniel to take her horseback riding—you know, to show her how gentle the horses *really* are. That's a win-win, because then maybe she'll let Aunt Maegan teach you how to ride."

"She doesn't ride, either. I don't think she'll go for that."

They sat there, the breeze rustling around them, both lost in thought.

"So is there anything she really likes to do? You know, that would tempt her?" Taylor asked.

Marissa tested the white flower on her bright pink toenail. It was dry. She eased herself into a cross-legged position and hunched forward as she considered Taylor's question. What did her mom like to do?

"She likes picnics," she said finally. "She's always after me to go on a picnic, but it's so much trouble, and then you get there and all you have are ants and no Wi-Fi for my iPod.

Mom thinks all I do with is listen to music, but you've got to have Wi-Fi for the web and text messaging and for—well, everything."

"I know, right? Why not eat at home where you can get a decent internet connection?" Taylor lifted her hands in a "duh" gesture. "And with air-conditioning. Grown-ups… they like to think about the old days, I guess."

Something about Taylor's words sparked a lightbulb moment for Marissa. She snapped her fingers. "That old mill house! Is that a good place for a picnic?"

Taylor shrugged her shoulders. "I guess. We've done it—taken a sack lunch and gone down there for the day to fish. The millstone makes a pretty good table, and you can prop your poles out the open windows while you eat. It's got big old oak trees with lots of Spanish moss over the millpond. I guess it could be, you know, romantic. It's not the Eiffel Tower or anything, but…yeah. I could see it."

"What if…" Marissa hopped up and paced around the confines of the tree house.

"You are *so* like Uncle Daniel. He has to pace around when he needs to think out a problem, too."

Marissa grinned at Taylor. "You think so? Am I like him?"

"Hey, cuz, you are a carbon copy of all the Monroe kids, twisty elbows and all."

"Yeah, but you don't have the bleeding disorder," Marissa muttered.

"Yeah, but *you* get to eat corn chips—and Krispy Kreme doughnuts."

"Yeah, but Ma cooks you homemade doughnuts."

"All right, you win. Ma's doughnuts *are* pretty great. So what was your idea?"

"Okay, so I ask Daniel to take us on a picnic, and tell him that I want to see the old mill house. He'll feel bad, right? Because I didn't get to go with you on the four-wheeler. And so he'll say yes and he'll ask Mom."

"And your mom will looove the idea of a picnic, so she's in, and then…wait. You'll be there." Taylor frowned. "That sort of defeats the whole getting-them-alone part."

"No, see, that's the cool part. It's too far to walk, right? Especially with the picnic basket. That's why you said we needed to take the four-wheeler. So Mom will freak about me being on a four-wheeler, and I'll back out, but then I'll tell her *she* needs to go and tell me all about it."

Taylor's eyebrows skyrocketed. "You. Are.

So. Devious. Don't ever let me make you mad," she commented admiringly.

Pleasure at the compliment surged through Marissa. She waggled her fingers toward her chest and preened. "What can I say? Mom is always telling me that I just have to look for the work-around solution. Who knew? Sometimes even Mom has the right idea."

KIMBERLY SAW THE Indiana number flash up on her screen and grabbed the phone. "Hello?" The raucous noise from the kids in the pool made hearing almost impossible until she stuck a finger in her ear. Only then was she able to make out the voice on the other end.

"Hi, I'm trying to reach Kimberly Singleton. This is Martina Parrish, with Dr.—"

"Oh, yes! Thank you for calling me back so soon. I wasn't expecting it."

"Dr. Fischer is very interested in your daughter's case. We, ah, were sort of expecting to hear from you sooner."

"Well, yes…" Kimberly sank down on Ma's back porch swing, grateful for the shade from the heat of the day—even after six, the sun showed no inclination to go down and it was still blisteringly hot and muggy. "Can you hear me okay? The kids are all in the pool, and I hate to leave them and go in where it's quieter."

"Not a problem. Yes, I can hear you. So about these medical records you faxed over to us… These are her neonatal records?"

"Yes, if you remember, I adopted her, and by then she'd been transferred from the hospital where she was born—"

"Yes, yes, I do remember that. Well, I have to tell you, these records don't give us many more pieces of the puzzle. If we had the birth mom's records… Because PAI-1 does seem to run in families. It has a definite genetic heritability, you know."

Kimberly ground her teeth. "I'm working on that. It looks as though I'm going to have to file a court order to get them—and there's no guarantee."

"Hmm…" Kimberly heard the sound of something like a ballpoint pen being rapidly clicked. "So you have no contact with the birth mother? Is there any other option available? Maybe one of the birth mother's relatives that could act as a go-between? Or a family friend?"

Daniel immediately came to mind, which made Kimberly want to gnash her teeth even more. "I'm pursuing that possibility, too."

"Dr. Fischer is ready to work her into the schedule anytime this summer—but you know, as August approaches, we'll have a lot less flexibility. In fact, the last two weeks are already booked solid. We have one of those awful early-start school dates here—I'm not sure about Georgia?"

Kimberly groaned in commiseration. "We do, too. First week of August—and that's when students come back. I have to report for pre-planning the last week of July."

"Wow! That's coming like a freight train, isn't it?" Martina said. More clicking emanated over the line. "Dr. Fischer has jotted some notes down on the file..."

"Dr. Fischer herself has reviewed them?" A warm feeling of gratitude buzzed through Kimberly.

"Oh, yes. Like I said, she's very interested in the case. She doesn't want to horn in on another doctor's patient, but your hem/onc has actually called her on this one."

"I really appreciate your interest. And we are planning on coming out," Kimberly assured her. "I had hoped to have more information."

"More information is always better. I do wish that we could have gotten her in the study we did a few years ago—Dr. Fischer received funding to do DNA testing."

"Oh! Any plans for any additional studies? I have scoured the web, but…"

"There's not a lot of interest in PAI-1 deficiency, is there?" Martina's chuckle was kind but knowing. "It's a really rare disease—especially outside of groups with close kinship, like the Amish here in Indiana. And as for studies, DNA testing is expensive, and we haven't secured any additional funding yet. But never say never."

"So I have, what, a couple of weeks, maybe three, before Dr. Fischer's schedule gets crazy?" Kimberly asked, bringing the topic back to the calendar crunch.

"Yes, since Dr. Fischer won't be leaving town for the Fourth. Or you could wait until September or October, later in the fall. But…"

Kimberly immediately picked up on Martina's concern. "But what?"

"Well, it's only that I see from the file that your daughter is nearly twelve. She's going to hit puberty very soon, if she's typical, in the next year or so. And puberty is a very, very dangerous time for PAI-1 deficient girls."

A chill tingled its way down Kimberly's spine. "I know. I've read a few medical journal reports on bleeding disorders in women. So you're suggesting sooner rather than later?"

"Yes. If Dr. Fischer can come to a more definite conclusion about whether this is PAI-1—and keep in mind, she can't really do that without family history or a genetic DNA study—we really need to get a plan in place for your daughter's first period. I can't stress the seriousness of this, Kimberly."

"I should come now, then." Kimberly had risen to her feet, unconsciously moving toward the door, her suitcases and a hasty departure.

"Well…" Martina hedged. "Can you get *any* more information before you come? The mother's medical records from Marissa's birth would be so helpful to Dr. Fischer."

Kimberly dropped back down on the swing and put her head into her free hand. The shrieks of laughter from the pool echoed through the phone, but they seemed a million miles away from her current problem. Despite all the noise the kids were making, Martina's message had come through loud and clear: dig, but dig faster.

CHAPTER NINETEEN

KIMBERLY ENDED THE conversation with a promise to fax any new information to the doctor and to set up an appointment as soon as possible. She laid the phone aside and rubbed her eyes in frustration.

The screen door to the kitchen banged shut. Kimberly looked up to see Ma coming back out with yet another pan of peas to shell.

"Well, now, you don't look at all happy," Ma remarked. She dragged a bucket for the hulls around to her favorite chair and sat down. "Bad news? Or none of my business?"

Ma's eyes crinkled in a way that reminded Kimberly of Daniel's when he lost some of his solemnity. Kimberly couldn't help but smile back. "Not bad news, not exactly. Just... stressful." She repeated her conversation with Martina.

Ma listened intently as Kimberly explained the situation. She paused before flicking a long purple pea shell into the bucket. "That does make things a mite complicated," she observed. "Daniel can't help you?"

Kimberly steepled her fingers. "He says not. *He* says that the law won't allow him to."

Ma's fingers zipped through another pea, splitting the hull neatly. Kimberly watched as the peas dropped—*thunk, thunk, thunk*—into her aluminum dishpan. She wished that the solution to her problem would fall into her lap as easily as those peas.

Then Ma said something that surprised her. "You don't believe that, though, do you?"

"Well...I believe that *Daniel* believes that." Kimberly tried to carefully frame her answer... After all, what woman would want to hear that someone thought her son guilty of bending the truth to suit his purposes?

And what *was* his purpose? What on earth could be so soul shattering that Daniel had to protect the identity of Marissa's birth mother? To her annoyance, Kimberly found herself cracking her knuckles, a habit she thought she'd kicked.

It didn't escape Ma's notice, either. "Your hands need something to keep them busy so that your mind can think. Want to help me a spell with these peas? They're easier than the butter beans."

"Sure…but aren't you fishing for more free labor?" Kimberly teased.

"I wouldn't turn down that, no. But I have to admit, I've solved some mighty gnarly problems over a pan of peas." Again, Ma's face was warm with such gentle wisdom.

Kimberly didn't argue. She made the trek to the laundry room and retrieved another dishpan. Back on the porch, she joined Ma in her shelling.

The peas were easier. And Ma had been right. She could think a lot more clearly as she went about the monotonous work. It helped, too, that Ma didn't try to fix this problem for her, just let her attempt to work it out in her own way.

They shelled in companionable silence as the evening finally began to cool and the kids' shrieks gentled to tired laughs, the water making lapping noises against the side of the pool. Kimberly's mind turned this way and that as she considered one approach and then another.

When she'd first adopted Marissa, she'd been selfishly glad that the adoption was a "closed" one. It meant that Kimberly didn't have to risk Marissa's birth mother coming back and saying, "I changed my mind."

As the years had passed, though, she desperately wished that she could hand Marissa, when she was older and ready, a piece of paper with her birth mother's name and contact information on it.

Kimberly hadn't simply wanted the information for Marissa's medical needs—she'd wanted it for Marissa's peace of mind. She, of all people, knew what it was to feel as if she was in the way, as if she was a ball and chain hooked to her mother's ankle, dragging her down.

She recalled what her mother had said when she had shared her plans of being a foster parent and eventually adopting. "Oh, sugar. You don't want to do that. Kids are noisy and messy and expensive, and they tie you down."

Kimberly had stared at her mother in shock. "Well, gee, Mom. I wish I had the money to pay you back for every mouthful I ate, or a trip around the world to pay you back for all the times I kept you at home."

"Well…" Her mother had drawn her brows together, considering. "You could keep the trip around the world, but I'd sure take the money."

And she hadn't been joking.

Why couldn't Mom be more like Ma? Kimberly cast a sidelong glance in the older woman's direction. She was everything her own mother wasn't: kind, gentle, patient.

But wishing for that was like Marissa wishing to be free of her bleeding disorder—a complete waste of time and mental energy.

Wet feet and giggles approached them. Kimberly paused in her shelling to see Marissa and Taylor trekking across the deck, swimsuits dripping, no towels in sight.

"I hope you don't think you're going in the house that wet," Kimberly told Marissa.

"No, we're going to walk around, dry off outside."

"I can't believe you two are giving up the pool to everyone else. I figured you'd be the last ones out."

Taylor shook her head. "They can have it. I'm all pruny. Stick a fork in me. I am *done*."

Ma laughed. "I've got supper in the oven. Is your mom planning on staying when she comes in from work? I made enough for her."

"Ma, you always make enough for Pharaoh's army. I'll eat, even if she doesn't. You cook better than her."

"Much to my despair. I tried to teach that child how to cook when she was your age. All she had her mind set on was brownies and the rest she swore she could get at McDonald's."

Taylor did a fair impression of Ma as she clucked her tongue. "Didn't figure on having a kid with food allergies, now, did she?"

Ma swatted at Taylor's bare leg with a pea shell. "No, ma'am, and that's why you should show a little interest in the kitchen, too, young lady."

But the rebuke was without sting, and Taylor let it slide off her. "Can we go for a few minutes, then? And I promise, after we get back from the tree house, I'll set the table and I'll—"

"Tree house?" Kimberly's gaze snapped up from the pan where she'd been searching for errant unshelled peas. "What tree house?"

Marissa couldn't hold back a groan. "Now you've done it," she muttered and glowered in Taylor's direction.

Taylor had the grace to look shamefaced. "Uh, you know—the, uh—" She stumbled to a stop.

"You said tree house." Kimberly set her pan aside on the swing. She hated the way her voice had taken on a steely edge.

Ma spoke up. "It's a tree house the boys and their dad built when the kids were young—

about Taylor and Marissa's age, I'd guess. You didn't want Marissa going up the tree house?" She tapped her cheek with her open palm and answered her own question. "You're worried about her being safe, what with her bleeding disorder. I should have thought of that and asked you. Land sakes. I do apologize."

"Marissa, you know better than to climb a tree—" Kimberly began.

Taylor interrupted. "No, ma'am, we've got a rope ladder and everything, and it's real safe, not even very high off the ground—and Uncle Daniel checked it out and took Marissa up first. Made sure the rope wasn't rotten or the railing loose."

"Did he?" Kimberly replied grimly. "Why doesn't that surprise me?"

"Yes, ma'am, he did, and he even showed her how to climb the ladder so she'd be safer—"

"Taylor!" Marissa protested. "You are *not* helping."

"Oh, no. I disagree," Kimberly responded tartly. "She's being way more cooperative than you. I am extremely disappointed in you, Marissa. You knew how I'd feel about this, and you still did it. And us three—"

"Hours away from Atlanta and my stupid

doctors! You won't let me ride a four-wheeler, you won't let me ride even the gentlest old nag and now you're saying you don't want me to climb any higher than a blade of grass!"

Taylor skulked backward, looking extremely uncomfortable and guilty. "It's real safe, Ms. Kimberly—Uncle Daniel wouldn't let us go up if weren't completely safe—"

Ma interjected with a calm smoothness. "Taylor, honey. Ms. Kimberly has the right to tell Marissa what she can and cannot do. And if she doesn't want Marissa up in the tree house, then I expect you girls can find somewhere else to play."

"We're not playing!" Taylor exploded. "We're almost twelve! We don't *play* anymore."

Ma shot a warning glance at her granddaughter, and instantly Taylor's face softened. "I'm sorry, Ma. I didn't mean to— What do you call it? Bow up at you?"

"Like a rattlesnake, you did. Thank you for the apology. Now extend the same courtesy to Ms. Kimberly."

Taylor shuffled her feet. "I'm sorry, Ms. Kimberly. I didn't know it would get Marissa in trouble."

"But Marissa did." Kimberly shot a pointed

look at her daughter, who showed none of the softening that Taylor had.

Just then, the sound of Daniel's truck door slammed, and Kimberly realized with a start that she *could* pick that sound out from any other vehicle that pulled up at Ma's. In less than a minute, he was taking the porch steps two at a time, his face split with a broad smile.

It nearly undid her anger. But she held on to it. He was a responsible grown-up who had seen dozens, if not hundreds, of serious accidents to people who *didn't* have anything wrong with them. He, of all people, should have known better.

She would not let whatever she felt for him interfere with giving him a piece of her mind.

His grin faltered. "Something wrong?" he asked, his eyes going around the somber circle.

"My mom's wigging out over the *tree house* now," Marissa said in a nearly inaudible tone.

"I'm surprised at you, Daniel," Kimberly said. "I thought you'd see the potential for injury and steer Marissa away from places as unsafe as a tree house."

Daniel burst out laughing. "Unsafe? Six kids and almost a dozen grandkids have played in that tree house, and what's the worst that's happened? A broken arm? Yeah, Rob double-dog-dared me to jump out when I was ten, and I broke my arm and my collarbone." He flexed his arm. "See? Good as new."

"Yes, but *you* didn't have a bleeding disorder," Kimberly pointed out. She was proud of the way she hadn't lost her cool, even if her words carried a sharp edge.

Daniel's face blanched. "I—I didn't think about that. She just needed a place to think. And that's the Monroe kids' thinking tree."

"I want that ladder taken down," Kimberly persisted. "And, Marissa, you are not, under any circumstances, to use that tree house again. Am I clear?"

Now Taylor and Marissa let out near howls of anguish. Marissa was the first to put her protest in intelligible words. "It's not fair to keep the other kids from it, Mom! They'll hate me!"

Ma made another one of her dips into the conversation. "Now, Marissa, they won't hate you. And there's plenty of other places on the farm to play…uh, to hang out. Isn't that what you kids say when you're nearly all grown-up?" She winked, and Kimberly saw Marissa's face sink into resignation.

"Can I be excused?" Marissa asked. "I swear. I won't go in the tree house or climb higher than a blamed blade of grass."

Kimberly decided to cut her losses. "Go on."

With that, Marissa dashed off, with Taylor in hot pursuit. Kimberly sighed. "Marissa's right—she was using it as a leverage point, hoping I'd cave, but she was right. It's not fair for me to demand the ladder be taken down. We should leave and get our hotel room in town. Although—" and here she glowered at Daniel "—you could have just as easily broken your fool neck as your good as new arm and collarbone."

"Which is why I didn't do it again," he popped back.

"Daniel," Ma interjected. "Go on. Take the ladder down. You can put it back up after Kimberly and Marissa are gone—and, Kimberly, I won't hear of you wasting your hard-earned money on a cramped little shoebox in town. You stay right here. Daniel will take the ladder down."

"Ma!" Daniel protested, sounding more like Marissa. "Kimberly's told her not to go near it. That ought to do."

Ma arched an eyebrow. "Obviously, you've

never had kids, and your memory is a wee bit fuzzy on all the times I told you not to do something and you did it anyway. A few days without that ladder won't kill anybody," Ma asserted. "And it will give Kimberly some peace of mind."

Daniel gawked at Kimberly. "Climbing is *good* for Marissa. She needs exercise and fresh air and core strength. You keep telling her no and she's going to rebel big-time, you mark my—"

"Daniel." Ma said his name in a crisp, cool way that brought him to heel. "Kimberly has to raise her child the way she sees fit. She knows the risks that Marissa can take better than me or you—like DeeDee had to teach us what foods were safe for Taylor. Now, am I going to have to ask Rob or Andrew to take that ladder down?"

"No, ma'am. But it's pointless." Daniel waved his hand. "Forget it. I can see I'm wasting my breath." He stalked off in the direction of the barn and its storehouse of tools.

Tension drained from Kimberly, and she realized just how taut she'd been holding herself. "Thank you," she told Ma. "I really appreciate the way you backed me up."

"Ahem." Ma had gone back to shelling

peas. "I don't pick favorites. When my own do something out of line, I call it like I see it. Like I said. It's your right to raise your child as you see fit."

Something in Ma's words niggled at Kimberly. She ran her fingers through the shelled peas in her pan, searching for any unshelled ones she'd missed.

"You...you don't agree?"

"Are you asking me? For advice?" Ma fixed her with eyes that were as blue as Daniel's.

"Well...yeah. I mean, yes, ma'am. You—" Kimberly's throat clogged up with unexpected emotion. "I wish my own mother were more like you. You're so calm and patient and—and *wise*."

Ma chuckled and shook her head. "I'm like a duck, darlin'. I'm paddling like mad underneath. But...well, I *have* raised six kids. So I guess I've gotten to understand a few things."

"Like?"

Ma weighed her words. "Daniel didn't put it very tactfully, but you might want to look at ways you can say yes to Marissa more often. I know, I know. We deal with it with Taylor. They don't want to be different. They think they're ten feet tall and bulletproof.

But, honey, you have to look ahead—in six years, where will Marissa be?"

Kimberly gulped. "I don't even want to *think* about college, Ma. I'm busy praying I can get her to graduation safe and sound."

"Kimberly." Now Ma set aside her pan and grasped Kimberly's hands in her own. "I raised six kids. Lost a husband to a fire. Saw all three of my boys bent on following in his footsteps and, despite all my worry, being firefighters. I see Taylor go out every day, knowing...*knowing* that someone could hand her something to eat that could make her drop dead of anaphylactic shock before we could even fumble for her EpiPen. I know a thing or two about wanting to get somebody to graduation safe and sound."

"Then you should understand—"

Ma shushed her with another gentle squeeze to her fingers. "But, honey, Kimberly, when all you're doing is praying to crawl from rock A to rock B by sunset, that's not living. That's *surviving*. I'm not saying throw caution to the wind. I'm saying..." She closed her eyes, drew in a deep breath. Then she fixed that Daniel-blue gaze back on Kimberly. "Say yes when you can. If my Maegan can keep a cerebral palsy patient safe in the saddle, she can keep *your* baby safe, too. It will give Marissa a sense of independence, and right now, that's what she needs. Plus…you need some help. You've toted this load alone for far too long. It's too much for one person, Kimberly. Way too much."

Kimberly burst into tears, allowing herself to be folded into Ma's arms, sobbing against her shoulder. She pulled back and wiped at her eyes. "I'm sorry. I'm not usually like this. I can't understand what you Monroes do to me. I've cried more since I've been here than I have…ever."

Ma patted her on the hand. "Maybe that's part of your problem. A good cry isn't a sign of weakness. It's like the wash cycle. Cleans your insides up."

"Oh, Ma, I love you!"

"And I feel the same. Daniel accuses me of adopting every stray that comes to my door, but…you're special. Daniel thinks so, and I do, too. Maybe it's because of Marissa and how Daniel…well." She stared off, not speaking. Then she turned back and added, "But I think…no, I know—even if I weren't in the business of adopting strays, I'd take you in. In a heartbeat."

Kimberly felt a wave of pleasure pulse

through her at Ma's words. Then, inexplicably, pain trailed in its wake. This whole Monroe family was worming its way into her heart—Ma, and Daniel, and even scrappy Taylor. But, she reminded herself, they *weren't* her family—she and Marissa had to go back home, and soon.

And that would leave the both of them feeling even more scared and alone than if they'd never found this oasis in the first place.

CHAPTER TWENTY

Daniel spied Marissa scrunched up next to Rufus's soft brown body at the bottom of the oak tree as he bent over the eye hooks that held the ladder in place.

"You don't have to take it down," she told him. Her voice was doleful and low, the words barely making the ascent to the tree house. She stroked the dog's ears and Rufus uttered a grunt of approval. "It's not fair to the other kids. I won't go up it. It's stupid, but I'll listen to my mom."

With feet as slow and heavy as his heart, Daniel clambered down the ladder and dropped to the ground. He crouched on the balls of his feet in front of her.

"Marissa, I told your mom I would take it down. And a Monroe says what he means, and *does* what he says. I couldn't look your mom in the eye if I told her a barefaced lie."

What about a not-so-barefaced lie? his conscience poked back in response. *You heard what the judge told you. You're not le-gally bound to keep Marissa's identity a se-cret.*

But he was *ethically* bound. After all, he was a Monroe. Marissa stabbed at the soft dirt in the fork of the gnarled roots of the oak. Startled, Rufus sat up, shaking his head. "It's just not *fair,*" she said.

He ruffled her hair. "I know, kiddo. Life stinks sometimes."

"Can't I—can't I move down here with you and Ma and Taylor? I could work, you know. I could earn my keep. I'm really good with the babies."

"Oh, Marissa." He sat back on the soft moss-covered ground. What could he say to her? "Your mom loves you, you know that. You love your mom. And you'd get bored of life down here pretty quick, I assure you. This place is no Atlanta."

She stabbed harder at the dirt, churning up the soil with a vengeance. "I wouldn't. I hate it up there. I hate the school—I don't even get to do PE, because the stupid coach is afraid I'll get hurt and bleed to death. And they gave me *safety* scissors in home ec—like I was little kid. Plus…I couldn't even use the sewing machine. I really wanted to learn how to sew."

"Okay..." He blinked and drew in a breath. "So school is pretty tough. But you have friends, right?"

"Who wants to hang out with a freak like me? They all gather around me and ask stupid questions. Like...if I cut you, how quick would you bleed to death?" The stick broke under her fierce attack, and she tossed it away. "I hate it. I wish I didn't have to ever go back. If my mom would let me, I'd do homeschool."

"Your mom..." Maybe he didn't agree with Kimberly's decisions when it came to Marissa, but Ma was right. Kimberly was in a better position to know what was safe for her daughter. He should have realized the danger the tree house posed. "She's in a tough spot, too, you know. She needs to keep you safe."

"It's just... If I *knew*, you know, that it would be over. That I'd maybe outgrow this. That I could get big enough, old enough, to finally *do* things." Marissa shook her head. "I know that doesn't make any sense, but I...I can't figure out a better way to say it."

Daniel remembered the awful days after he'd lost his father, how the prospect of the years ahead without him had yawned like an endless chasm. He understood how something that seemed never ending was a worse torment than something with a clear and definite end.

He fumbled for words to let her know he understood how she felt—and maybe even why—but couldn't figure out how to do it in a way that didn't condescend.

As he stared at the gathering dusk, two flashes lit up the ground where the wide oak limbs bent low.

"See there?" He pointed in the direction of the flashes. Marissa followed his finger. Sure enough, another pair of spectral lights glowed briefly.

She gasped with pure, unadulterated pleasure. "Ooh…are those lightning bugs?" she asked. "I've never seen real, actual lightning bugs before. They're *awesome*."

"You ain't seen nothin' yet, 'Rissa. You watch. In a few minutes, we'll have quite a show. But you know why a lightning bug makes such a splash?"

She shook her head. "No. Why?"

"Because it's dark enough that we can see them. In the daylight, even if they shone their hearts out, they wouldn't show up.

Sometimes…sometimes we have to have a little darkness and gloom to appreciate a lightning bug."

Okay, so his attempt at philosophy was corny, and she'd probably roll her eyes—

But then he felt her hand grip his arm, and she turned those green eyes up to his. They were shiny with tears, glowing in the twilight with almost as much impact as the lightning bugs. "Don't give up, Daniel. *Please.* I'm a Monroe, right? You said it. I'm a Monroe kid. So don't give up on me. Mom really will listen to you and Ma if you tell her to let me try things. I know it. I just *know* it."

Daniel couldn't keep back the scoff. He thought of all the prickly conversations he'd had with Kimberly, how much they'd tussled over whether he should break his word to Miriam. "I think you've got that wrong. Your mom doesn't think too highly of me right now, Marissa."

"But you like her, don't you?"

The question, coming out of nowhere, startled Daniel. "Why—sure, of course, and I like you, too," he stumbled. "Your mom's really nice."

"And smart. She's really smart."

He couldn't resist ruffling her hair again.

She didn't seem to mind. "Surprising you should say that, kiddo, seeing as how in the past few minutes one of your favorite words has been *stupid.*"

Marissa blushed. "I know. I shouldn't use that word. Mom likes to point out that the only pronoun in the word *stupid* is *I.* So when you say stupid, you're really showing everybody how stupid *you* are."

Daniel raised his eyebrows. "She is smart, isn't she?" He let his mind drift to all the reasons he liked Kimberly Singleton: her drive, her compassion, the fierce protection she exhibited, how she sprang to the challenge of raising the baby girl he had brought into this world.

If only we could have met some other way. Maybe we might have had a chance.

"Will you take me fishing? If you have to take that stupid—okay, sorry—that rope ladder down, can you at least take me fishing? At the old millpond? Taylor says it's really cool."

"Well—" He hesitated. "I've learned my lesson. Let me ask your mom first."

He expected protests and groans, but all he got was a delighted grin. "Okay! Thanks!" Inexplicably, Marissa jumped up and scampered off, Rufus at her heels.

Amazing. He couldn't figure out the daughter...and he sure couldn't figure out her mom. With a sigh, he started back up the ladder in hopes that he could get it dismantled and climb down by way of the branches before darkness well and truly fell.

KIMBERLY HAD STAYED behind on the swing when the rest of the women and Daniel's brothers had filed into the house to complete the preparations for the evening meal. It seemed as if the family was drawn to this house for that meal, regardless of whether it was a weeknight or a weekend, early or late... they genuinely enjoyed each other's company.

Her excuse to Ma for staying on the porch was to finish shelling the peas, but she had really wanted a chance to talk to Daniel in private.

She'd grown impatient waiting for him. The peas had long been shelled, and now she dallied on the back porch. How long did it take to unhook a ladder after all? Her impatience nursed the embers of her earlier anger at him, and she hated how she drew strength from it.

So what? You've got to be mad at him to stand your ground. You're right, Singleton.

You *are in the right, and he is no more legally bound to keep this secret than the man in the moon.*

His work boots scraped along the porch steps as he came up them, a good deal slower than he had earlier that evening. The rope ladder was loosely coiled in one hand.

"You want to keep it?" he asked. "So you know beyond a shadow of a doubt that I didn't go behind your back and put it up again?"

She felt her face color. Did he really think her as overbearing as that? *Was* she as overbearing as that? "Don't be silly. We'll be gone before you know it and you can put it back up. I expect you think I'm an overprotective mother."

"It doesn't matter what *I* think. What matters is what *you* think."

Kimberly sat back, startled, the swing screeching a protest in the still night. "I—I—" It *did* matter to her what he thought. It mattered a great deal, she realized, and that knowledge bothered her. She'd never cared a fig for what anybody thought about how she raised Marissa. She'd done it all by herself—nobody else volunteered to help, that was for sure, so they could think what they wanted.

She did the best she could, and that would have to do.

But with Daniel…it did matter. And that scared her. Was she somehow painting him into her mind's eye as a sort of father figure for Marissa?

"I heard you got Marissa's paperwork from the hospital today," he said.

The sudden change of subject confused her. "Yes."

"Did it help?" Was that *anguish* in his voice? Something was vibrating along the edges, a pleading hopefulness.

If it was anguish, she wasn't going to let him off the hook. Maybe he'd give up a hint of information—toss those bread crumbs she so desperately needed—if he felt badly enough and knew how little use Marissa's local hospital file had been. "The doctors say not much. They still want… They at least want the birth mother's records from the hospital about the details of the labor process. It could tell them a lot, Daniel. It could help them figure out what was wrong with Marissa. They say—they say she could die."

His shoulders slumped, and the rope ladder drooped even lower, pooling on the wide painted boards of the deck. "I was hoping…"

"Hoping I wouldn't point out that the safe-haven law doesn't prevent you from telling me who Marissa's birth mother is?"

Daniel shook his head. "Maybe the letter of the law is kind of murky on that. But I'm a fireman. And I responded to an emergency on fire department property, Kimberly. What's more...I gave that girl my word. And I meant it. If I don't get to second-guess how you raise Marissa, then you don't get to second-guess how I do my job. I keep my promises. All of them. And I've learned to make only those that I *can* keep. I realize you don't understand. I realize you think it should be easy for me to blab everything I know. But I do have my reasons, and just as your reasons aren't always easy for people to understand, maybe mine aren't, either. But that doesn't mean they aren't good ones."

She put a hand to her face. "Drat it," she mumbled. "Why do you always have to *do* that?"

"Do what?" he asked.

"I get so mad with you, so ready to tear into you and give you a good telling-off... and then you go and say something so—so reasonable."

"Maybe because I'm a reasonable sort of guy?"

She leaned back, staring at the tongue-and-groove porch boards forming the high ceiling. They were in pristine condition; she could tell a fresh coat of paint had been added recently.

How nice it must be to have people look after things for you. Back home, she didn't have so much as one person to help her change a lightbulb. And pretty soon she and Marissa would be back home.

Alone.

Fatigue and exhaustion seeped into her every pore.

"Can you do me a favor?" she asked finally.

"Anything but tell you who Marissa's birth mother is."

"I got *that* loud and clear." Kimberly sat up. "Can you and Maegan teach Marissa a little about riding? On the oldest, pokiest nag you've got?"

"Sure. But you could be there, too—"

"No," she said firmly. "I can't. Call me weird and paranoid, but I'll completely freak. I can't be there, Daniel. I *can't*." Her voice broke, and she gritted her teeth to keep more of those Monroe-induced tears at bay. She would *not* cry again, if it killed her. If she exploded from holding all those tears in, so be it. She would *not* cry. "So can you help me?"

"I'd be honored. It would be my pleasure."

His words washed over her. A man telling her that it would be his pleasure to help her do something tough and scary when it came to Marissa… She could get hooked on this.

Yes. Every fiber in her being was telling her to run, and run fast, before she could get well and truly addicted to the entire Monroe clan…but especially to a man like Daniel.

CHAPTER TWENTY-ONE

TWO WEEKS LATER, Kimberly was so frustrated she was ready to tie Daniel to his precious "thinking tree" until he was willing to tell her what he knew about Marissa's birth mother.

She sat at the lady's secretary in the room Ma had given her, staring at her original list.

People who might know something:
EMTs who responded
Police who responded
Emergency room staff
Newspaper reporter
Former fire chief
The person who took the picture of Daniel and Marissa

Every single lead had been crossed off. Kimberly had combed through the old newspaper file copies until her fingers were blackened with ink the day before. The story that referenced "an unlicensed female juvenile driver" was little more than the lead paragraph on that week's police blotter, and there was absolutely no mention of a baby.

Not one word. It was if Marissa had never been born.

How could that be? She knew reporters—reporters who worked both for the smaller papers in and around Atlanta and for the *Atlanta Journal-Constitution*—and they would have never passed up a story as dramatic as an abandoned baby on the Fourth of July, at a fire station, no less.

But this report implied that the girl was merely ill and had used the car as a means to get to help. It didn't even explain why she hadn't simply dialed 911.

Maybe the town didn't have 911 a dozen years ago?

At any rate, the reporter was long gone, with no forwarding address, the former fire chief was on an extended vacation at Yosemite Park, with no contact information...and nobody at the hospital would talk to her.

Not even good ol' Pauline, Queen Bee of Information.

Judge Malloy was taking his sweet time considering Kimberly's pro se motion to release Marissa's birth mother's medical records.

She'd called his office until it had gotten to the point where his assistant instantly recognized her voice and cut her off before she got past her greeting.

"Sweetheart, he'll call you the minute, the very minute, he makes his decision."

But minutes turned into hours, and hours turned into days, and days...

Martina had called her yesterday, as well. Had she found out anything more? Had the judge ruled on her motion? Did she want to schedule the appointment?

No, no and maybe.

She thought again of the money it would cost to go to Indiana, not counting the medical expenses, which were higher there because the clinic and the doctor weren't in-network with her insurance. She'd even spent a few precious hours arguing with the insurance company, begging them to give her a waiver.

No, they said in their most official and final tone; Marissa had several in-network hem/oncs available to her. The second opinion wasn't medically necessary, in their view, and they would not waive the out-of-network fee.

They cheerfully added that she was always free to use any doctor of her choice—it would simply not be as "cost effective."

Maybe it was time to rip herself and Marissa from this warm cocoon and admit defeat. It was as plain as the nose on her face, and she might as well face facts and just deal with it.

Kimberly was never going to win over the insurance company. She was never going to find out what was wrong with Marissa by sticking with the doctors they'd already seen. She was never going to convince Daniel to tell her what he knew...and nobody else would tell her anything until the judge agreed to let her access those files.

The judge. Who, it turned out, was a dear old family friend and practically a surrogate father to Daniel after his dad had died in that fire.

No wonder he was taking his sweet time.

Frustration. It ate at the soul sometimes.

Through the wall, she heard thumps and bumps as Marissa pulled on riding boots, shin guards and her helmet in preparation for her evening riding lesson. Kimberly's stomach tightened. Was she making a mistake? Had she caved to guilt when she should have stood strong?

But Daniel had been as good as his word. He and Maegan had picked a gentle gray mare that Maegan used for her least able clients. The riding lessons took place only after Daniel got home from the station, and didn't take place at all if he had to work late—which was more frequent than Kimberly would have liked, she hated to confess.

She enjoyed having him across the table from her. Liked seeing the connection between him and Marissa. Appreciated knowing there was someone else out there who cared about Marissa's well-being. She'd ginned up the courage to watch one lesson from afar, without Marissa or Daniel or Maegan knowing. Daniel had hovered by Marissa's side, as close and as careful as Kimberly would have been. And yet Marissa's face had been wreathed in smiles, her self-confidence overflowing. She'd been attentive to what Maegan told her to do.

She hadn't seemed the least bit afraid. Kimberly, on the other hand, had been petrified.

Ma had stood by Kimberly's side and held her hand as they leaned against the back fence looking down into the hollow where Maegan kept her corral. Ma hadn't said a word, not an I-told-you-so or it-will-get-better or any other mealymouthed platitude. As they'd turned to walk to the house, Kimberly asked, "How'd you know not to say anything?"

Ma exhaled. "My older sister. She stood with me on my back porch the first day Daniel went to work with the fire department. She knew I was in a stark-raving panic, because it hadn't been that many months since she'd been right there beside me in the Augusta burn unit. With Daniel's dad. Oh, my. That was a hard day, seeing Daniel in that uniform, knowing he could be killed like his dad. Later, when Rob and Andrew followed their big brother, she stood with me again. And while she was alive—I lost her last year, you know—every big structure fire the boys were in, she'd stand with me, hold my hand. And just be there. That's what you need. Someone to climb down in that hole with you and be willing to *be there*."

"Oh, Ma! Can I keep you? Will you adopt *me*?" Kimberly joked.

The teasing question didn't make Ma smile as Kimberly had intended. She stopped, turned to Kimberly and squeezed the hand that she still held. "I'd be proud to call you my daughter. I only hope I have the chance."

Ma refused to explain her cryptic comment,

but Kimberly decided to accept it as a deep compliment.

Now, in the fading pinkish light of yet another day gone with no further clue as to who Marissa's birth mother was, Kimberly was left fingering the gold baby bracelet.

"Who are you?" she whispered to the bracelet as if it was the girl herself. "*Where* are you? You loved her enough to give her this, to have this made, so that she would always know the name you wanted her to have. I am absolutely, pulverizingly certain that if you knew how much we needed you right now, you'd come forward. If only Daniel would give us that chance."

The tiny bracelet barely fit over three of Kimberly's fingers. She recalled slipping it on Marissa's wrist when she was still a baby, and it had seemed big and clunky back then.

Now the links so deftly wrought in gold seemed incredibly delicate, the ID plate polished to a bright shine except for the carefully engraved name. A tiny tag at the bracelet's catch proclaimed it twenty-four-karat gold.

Funny how Kimberly had never noticed that, but then she seldom took out the bracelet, and she'd always assumed it was gold electroplate.

But no. It was pure twenty-four-karat gold. She hefted the tiny wristlet, estimated its weight as at least an ounce despite its small size. In today's market, an ounce of gold was worth nearly a thousand dollars.

How would a sixteen-year-old girl afford that?

The thought came like a lightning bolt out of the blue. With quick, trembling fingertips, she tapped a query into her phone's browser: the price of gold in 2003.

The answer popped up promptly.

Three hundred sixty-three dollars was the average price.

Whoa. Even if it wasn't a thousand bucks, it was nearly four hundred. Still a pretty penny for a teenager to get hold of. How had Marissa's birth mother done it?

Maybe the better question, she thought with another flash of insight, *is* where?

ONCE MARISSA HAD heard that jewelry stores were on Kimberly's list, wild horses—or even Maegan's old gray mare—couldn't keep her on the farm the next morning.

"I love jewelry, Mom! You know I do! And this is my bracelet after all! But I don't understand…why couldn't I mention it to

Daniel? He might have known some of the jewelers in town."

Exactly, thought Kimberly. *For once I don't want Daniel to have a head start and talk to the people I need information from.*

The first jewelry store was a chain that hadn't even been open in 2003. But they had helpfully directed her to a downtown jeweler who'd "been in business forever," the clerk had said.

Kimberly felt as though she'd stepped back in time as she pushed through a slightly grimy door with faded metallic cursive proclaiming it to be Sullivan's Fine Jewelry.

A small bell jangled, echoing across the deserted store. The dim interior housed a U shape of glass display cases filled with twinkling gold and silver and diamonds. The right side was a trifle shorter to allow for a linen-covered table loaded down with various china plates. A closer look revealed discreet embossed cards declaring that various happy couples had chosen that particular pattern of formal china and flatware.

With a leap of her heart, Kimberly realized that she'd also given up simple joys like picking out china and flatware when she'd decided against marriage.

It had seemed infinitely sensible. She didn't need a man to have a baby, not when the state was so eager to have foster parents that they would accept single women into the program. Back then, she'd been jaded and cynical about men—the only ones she'd known were the trash her mother had dragged home from bars and the callow college guys who had their minds on the short-term physical, not the long-term emotional aspects of a relationship.

Wouldn't it be nice to have it all? she thought now.

"Hey, look, Mom! Here are some bracelets kind of like mine!"

Marissa's excitement pulled her back from her musing, one that she was ashamed to admit had Daniel lurking at the edges.

"You're right," Kimberly agreed, coming closer to the slightly dusty revolving display case. The glass case creaked when she turned it to see all of the bracelets and tiny baby necklaces. Yes, the bracelet could well have come from here.

A white-haired old man hobbled out on a quad-based walking stick, a watchmaker's glass pushed up on his forehead. "How do you do. I'm Hiram Sullivan. Can I interest you in one of our baby bracelets or necklaces? I do free engraving with every purchase. That's eighteen-karat gold that you're looking at right there, mind you, but if you'd like something less expensive, I could show you our sterling silver. It's quite appropriate."

Kimberly noticed the worn carpet beneath her feet. The entire jewelry store looked more than a little down at the heels, but in a genteel, can't-be-bothered sort of fashion. It felt more inviting to her than the slick newer store in the mall.

"We *are* interested in your baby bracelets, but not to buy one. We're hoping you sold this one about a dozen years ago." She briefly explained why they were interested as she handed over Marissa's baby bracelet.

The man promptly flipped down his watchmaker's glass and carefully inspected the bracelet. "Ahem." He looked up at her, the one eye strangely frog-like through the magnifying lens. "My eyes aren't what they once were. Do you mind if I take this back to the light? You can step back with me if you'd like."

With that, he flipped up a section of the counter and opened a half door. Mr. Sullivan gestured for them to follow him. "Ordinarily

I don't let folks I don't know back here…but you look like the honest type. If you cosh me over the head, be gentle," he said with a wink.

If the front of the store was slightly dusty, the back was a mishmash of organized chaos. Broken watch pieces were strung out over velvet-covered workbenches, while tiny jeweler's tools and soldering equipment took up every nook and cranny of the custom-built racks. Clear plastic chests, the drawers crammed with tiny parts, stood dusty but at the ready. A vise held a man's wedding band in worn, scratched gold.

Now Mr. Sullivan pulled a gooseneck work light over another, bigger magnifying glass on its own stand and stuck the bracelet under it for his inspection. Kimberly and Marissa waited as he uttered a series of "ehs" and "hmms" and "tsks."

Then he held the bracelet up and nodded. "That's my work, yes, ma'am. I'd recognize that engraving anywhere. That's my own font. But that chain needs repairing. If you'd like, I can fix it for you. Won't take two seconds."

"Well, sure," she said. Maybe if she paid for a minor repair, he'd be more inclined to hunt up the information from the original sale. The shop's dusty, keep-everything-forever appearance made it a good bet, at least to Kimberly's way of thinking, that he still had a record of the sale.

With a deft twist of a pair of needle-nose pliers, the old man adjusted the gold links. He handed the bracelet back to Kimberly. "That's the problem with twenty-four-karat gold," the jeweler observed. "It's soft, so links can get stretched. If that catch chain had worked itself loose when the baby wore it, then, oops—that's a thousand dollars gone in today's market."

"How much do I owe you?"

"Pshaw. T'weren't nothing. On the house."

"Are you sure? I'd be glad to pay for it," Kimberly pressed.

Hiram Sullivan shook his head. "Maybe one day you'll come back and buy a graduation gift for your daughter here. I sell a lovely string of pearls that would be perfect for her."

Kimberly had to admire the man's sales approach. Yes, she'd rather buy pearls from him than any of the Atlanta shops she'd ever been in.

"Now what can I tell you about this here bracelet?" he asked.

"Well…I know it was bought between July 4, 2003, and…hmm…August 15, 2003, because I was already teaching my classes when they called to let me know about Marissa," Kimberly said. "And the social worker had the bracelet then. Do you… Is it possible that you still have bills of sale or receipts that far back?"

Hiram Sullivan threw back his full head of white hair and laughed, his jeweler's glass shaking along with his hint of a potbelly that stretched his starched white dress shirt. He fingered his bow tie. "Ma'am, my wife fusses at me because I still keep the very first receipt from our very first day—and that was in 1964. I only wish she was here today—I've always told her someday my pack-rat habits would come in handy. Pity she had to go get her hair fixed."

He hobbled along to a row of boxes that looked extremely similar to an old-fashioned library card catalog. "Back before the chain stores—and all their cheap imported jewelry— it was important for us to keep detailed records, because we had repeat customers and they'd bring the pieces in for repair. My wife came up with our system. Smart woman, she is. Like I said, pity she isn't here."

He allowed gnarled fingers to glide over the stacks of drawers. A label in neat handwritten script stated 1964, with each subsequent column moving closer to the current date. She noticed that the script for 2015's label was a good deal shakier than the earlier ones.

"Ah, here we are. July, 2003, you say?" He didn't look up as his fingers began painfully flipping through the index cards. "Engagement ring—sad, that couple is divorced now, didn't even make it two years. Golden anniversary ring…lasted ten more years, and then died twenty-four hours apart, those folks did. Good people." He muttered his way through a remarkable history of the people who had bought items twelve years ago. Kimberly held her breath, hoping he would be equally as informative about the person who had purchased that baby bracelet.

She could imagine the day: a strawberry blond girl, features strangely obscured in Kimberly's mind's eye, scurrying into that careworn jewelry shop, hoping to be unnoticed, exchanging a messy wad of bills she had saved up over time for the baby bracelet. Maybe Hiram Sullivan would know her parents or even the girl herself.

Girl. No, she'd be a woman now, twenty-eight. Had she gone to college? Gotten married? Did Marissa have a baby sister or brother out there somewhere?

"Ah-ha! Here it is! And I have the satisfaction of telling my wife 'I told you so.' I don't often get that pleasure, I might add." There was a twinkle in the old jeweler's eye.

Kimberly's heart thumped madly in her chest. She couldn't help but glance Marissa's way, and saw that she, too, was breathless with excitement.

Hiram Sullivan put the card down and stared at it for a moment. "And that explains why I don't remember selling the bracelet," he murmured, tapping the card. "Had me worried, when I couldn't recall it. Thought my memory was slipping, but no, my wife sold it, and the buyer left it to be engraved. Came by and picked it up a week later. You were right, my dear. It was bought in late July of 2003."

"By a girl? A teenage girl?" Kimberly prompted.

He frowned. "Why, no." He glanced again at the card and read it once more. "No, a young man, and one from a fine local family. Pity about his father. He was an excellent fire chief. Very sad the way he got killed in that warehouse fire. And then it turned out to be arson. They never caught the scoundrel who started it."

Kimberly's mouth went dry. "Wh-who?" she stuttered.

Hiram Sullivan handed her the card. There it was, in a feminine script in faded blue ink.

The buyer was listed as one Daniel Monroe.

CHAPTER TWENTY-TWO

DANIEL SCANNED THE meeting's brief agenda. "Well, guys, that's all I have. I tried to keep things short, because you know how I hate meetings. What about y'all? Anything on your mind?" He sent his gaze around the semicircle assembled in his cramped office: his fire captains and his brother Rob, the county's arson investigator.

A captain from another fire station shifted in his chair. "My guys are getting pretty restless, Dan…I mean, Chief." He cast an apologetic grin toward Daniel. "All we've had for three weeks now have been pretty much minor calls, and not really much before that. Nothing big. You know what a superstitious lot firefighters can be."

Daniel felt his mouth quirk in amusement. "Can't be any worse than a team of baseball players, but yeah, I see that around here. I know they've got a lot of bottled-up energy, even if I have been working my guys into the ground. I was thinking about maybe a training burn—the county's considering burning two old houses that it condemned and then had to take back on a tax lien. Maybe that would help the crew a bit. But it won't be until next week before I find out definitely," he warned.

The men nodded in agreement. Their crews needed to keep their skills sharp, and a controlled burn was a good way to do that.

With nothing else offered up as a concern, Daniel released the group with a wave of dismissal. Chairs scraped against concrete, the room filled with jokes about which station's crew would beat the others at the upcoming baseball tournament. Daniel ignored it all and bent over paperwork that needed his attention.

At the sound of someone clearing his throat, Daniel looked up to see Rob still standing in front of his desk.

"Yeah?" Daniel halfway expected his brother to start teasing him about Kimberly—he'd gotten more than a few nudges and winks the past couple of times Rob had joined them for supper at Ma's.

"I'm reopening the investigation of the warehouse fire, Daniel."

Confused, Daniel leaned back, scratched

his head. "What warehouse fire? There was that one last year, the one caused by the lightning strike—"

"No. Dad's fire."

It was a wallop to Daniel's gut. He compressed his lips, tried to think what to say to his little brother. "Rob…it's done. It's over with. Some punk kid started that fire, and he's long gone now. That arrogant wannabe chief Rick Perdue—now, *that's* who killed Dad."

Rob scowled and leaned a hand against the back of a folding chair. "No, you got that wrong. Some punk kid *did* start that fire—well, at least someone did. I don't know if it was a kid. But that's why Dad was there that day—and yeah, I agree. Perdue was a sorry excuse of a fireman, but if that fire hadn't been started in the first place, Dad wouldn't have ever been in harm's way."

"You got so much time on your hands that you can kick a dead horse? How many hours were sunk into that investigation when it was fresh, huh? And they didn't come up with anything solid then."

Rob didn't say anything for a minute, and Daniel thought maybe he'd put this crazy obsession of Rob's down, at least for the time being. He waited for Rob to agree.

His brother tapped out a staccato rhythm on the back of the chair with the pen he held between his thumb and forefinger. Then he set his shoulders and straightened up, but his words weren't what Daniel had been hoping for.

"Science has changed things, Daniel. You know I try to keep up with the science—I get heckled out of every training class I attend by old-timers who still want to believe that sagging bedsprings and spalling in concrete are sure signs of arson, but science *can* help us find out who did this. And I want to chase that punk kid down and put him behind bars for murder."

"Fat chance—I hate to say it, Rob, but you've got a goose egg's chance of finding out the truth, even with the most current science." *Not this again*, Daniel thought, not when he had his plate full already with Kimberly and Marissa. "Besides, all the investigation in the world isn't going to bring him back. The only thing it will do is hurt Ma, dredge up old memories. You know that."

"It nearly killed her, Daniel. You weren't there when they came to tell her. She wound up on the kitchen floor, on her knees, screaming. I can still hear those screams…"

Daniel clenched his jaw. Guilt from being away, chasing a foolish dream, when his mother had needed him the most, gnawed at him. "It had to be hard on you kids, I know that—"

"Hard? Hard!" Rob scoffed. "Ma deserves the truth. I don't plan on shouting from the rooftops about what I'm doing—I don't want to get her hopes up, for one thing. But I just wanted you to know that every spare minute I have, I'm going to be reviewing that fire. So…I may need to talk to some of your men."

"You mean Dad's men. The ones that were here when Dad was chief." Daniel shook his head, wanted to snap in two the pencil he held in his hand to relieve his pent-up irritation at his brother. "And you seriously think it won't get back to Ma?"

Rob swallowed, doubt eroding his confident expression for the first time. He averted his glance. "I've got to try, Daniel. Fresh eyes… What can it hurt?"

"It better not hurt Ma, that's for sure," Daniel growled. "She's just getting back to her old self, so do what you gotta do—you're a stubborn cuss, and you're going to do it anyway, but…tread lightly, okay?"

Without a word, Rob moved for the door. Daniel heaved a sigh and tried to turn his attention back to the paperwork in front of him. But the door didn't slam closed.

Instead, it swung open, and in marched Kimberly, her eyes dark and thunderous. Marissa trailed after her mother.

"I want to know why you bought Marissa her gold baby bracelet…and then lied about it," Kimberly demanded.

If Rob's news had been lobbed like a grenade, Kimberly's question completed the ambush. He couldn't answer her at first.

"Well, don't just sit there gaping at me," she added. "You lied, Daniel Monroe, you who are so big on truth and integrity—*you lied*."

That blasted away some of his paralysis. He shot back, "I did no such thing—"

"Oh, yeah? Maybe not overtly. But you stood on your mother's front porch and held that bracelet in your hands and never told either of us that it was you who bought and paid for it. And you did it again in my hotel room. I think—no, I *know* you owe us an explanation."

Daniel swore inwardly. He'd thought it a

harmless misunderstanding that first day and then again when he'd helped Kimberly find the bracelet—who was he to burst Marissa's idea that the bracelet was from her birth mother?

"What does it matter?" he asked. "And how did you find out? I never told anybody."

"The jeweler who engraved it. He still has a bill of sale for it, by the way. You didn't figure on that, now, did you?"

"Kimberly—" He stared past her to Marissa, afraid of how she might be taking the discovery. Strangely, Marissa didn't seem even a quarter as upset as her mother. Instead, a beatific little grin played at the corners of her mouth—it was almost, if he didn't know any better, an I-told-you-so smile.

He turned his attention back to Kimberly, who showed no signs of cooling off anytime soon. "Yes. I bought the bracelet. But it was Marissa's birth mom's wish—well, not exactly the bracelet. She made me promise to do what I could to get Marissa's adoptive parents to keep the name she'd chosen for her."

Kimberly quirked a brow. "And you always keep your word, don't you, Daniel?"

Anger torched through him, but he held its full force back. Instead, he growled, "I try.

To the best of my ability. I do try to be a man of my word."

"You lied, though. You told the social worker that it was a gift from Marissa's birth mother."

"No," he said heavily. "I didn't. I called that blasted woman and left at least a dozen messages on her voice mail. I told her I had a bracelet for Marissa—tried to explain it as best, as honestly as I could, given what I could and could not say about, well…the whole deal—"

"And you can't say a lot, even though we both know you're under no *legal* obligation—"

"Kimberly!" he snapped. "I have my reasons."

"Right. You and your precious reasons are going to—" Kimberly clamped her mouth shut in midsentence and darted a glance at Marissa.

Her daughter had that same little grin, watching the two of them as if she was a spectator at Wimbledon. She shrugged her shoulders. "I get it. The kid should leave so she's not scarred by grown-ups disagreeing. Better stop before she should actually ever see conflict resolution play out."

With that, she ambled out, letting the door slam behind her.

Well, thought Daniel, *Marissa's wrong about one thing. From the way Kimberly is looking, there won't be any resolution to this conflict anytime soon.*

He gestured to one of the empty chairs. "You might as well sit down. This is going to take some explaining."

Kimberly didn't immediately sit. It was as if she was afraid she was giving up hotly contested ground if she did. But finally she sank into the chair. Some of her earlier anger dissipated. "I'm sorry for screaming at you like a fishmonger's wife, Daniel. But you have to understand. It was… Marissa— I thought it was Marissa's one link to her birth mother."

"I never, ever, in a million years meant to hurt you or Marissa. When you first said it was left to her by her birth mother, I debated then on telling you the truth," he admitted. "But what did it matter who actually bought and paid for the bracelet? It served its purpose, right? You kept Marissa's name."

Kimberly shook her head. "You don't get it, do you, Daniel? It's not the blasted bracelet that I care about. It's what it symbolized. For years, I've told Marissa over and over that bracelet meant her birth mother loved her and cared for her and wanted to keep her, but couldn't. It was part of her adoption story. I don't expect you to understand…but it was all Marissa had from her birth mother—that bracelet and the name engraved on it."

"I—I get that. Now." He hung his head and breathed out to clear his churning thoughts. "And all I can say is that I'm sorry. How upset is Marissa?"

Kimberly's eyebrows skyrocketed. "I can't figure her out, to be honest. I thought she'd be devastated. But…it's like water off a duck's back."

"Guess we should be thankful for small miracles?" he ventured.

"Yeah, I guess." Her conciliatory tone evaporated a second later. "Still—think about it, Daniel. It was my last lead. You have to tell me what you know, because there's no one else left for me to ask."

Her pleading eyes nearly undid him. Miriam's name was once again on the tip of his tongue. To escape the power of Kimberly's eyes, he stared at the clutter on his desk.

There, off to the side, was a framed studio shot of his father, in full dress uniform. It had been taken not six weeks before his death—

and in fact, the finished photographs had come in right before the funeral. His mom had chosen the big eight-by-ten version to stand by the casket—the closed casket, because his dad's body was in no shape for an open casket service.

Keep your word, Danny, keep your word, no matter the cost.

"I would if I could, Kimberly. I would if I could," he told her.

Without a word, she stalked from his office.

CHAPTER TWENTY-THREE

"So? WHAT HAPPENED?" Taylor exploded the minute she and Marissa were out of earshot of the house and the grown-ups gathered on the back porch. "You sent me that text and then it was radio silence. I couldn't get anything else out of you!"

"Didn't have Wi-Fi for one thing, plus my mom is hovering really bad now, worried that I'm going to freak because I found out..." Marissa grinned at Taylor as they headed for the oak tree.

"What? Are you *trying* to drive me up the wall, cuz? You know, you are *such* a drama queen when you want to be."

"Can't help it. I like to keep you in suspense."

She liked it so much, in fact, that she made Taylor help her spread out the blanket they'd brought under the low boughs of the oak tree before saying another word.

Maybe it wasn't only the power she held over Taylor at that moment. Maybe instead it was the sure knowledge, deep in her heart, that Daniel Monroe was most definitely her dad.

He had bought that bracelet for her. When she was a tiny baby, he had been the one to lean over that counter and turn that display case, choosing her very first gift. Maybe even the whole thing about her birth mom wanting her to be named Marissa was complete hooey. Maybe Daniel—*her dad*—had picked out her name.

Marissa Emily Monroe. It even sounded right. She was a Monroe. She belonged.

As she and Taylor collapsed onto the blanket, the hard warm ground biting into her even through the layers of thickness, she wished for the thousandth time that her mom wasn't a complete freakazoid about her bleeding disorder. What would it hurt to climb up to the tree house? Sure, it could be dangerous. But so could anything, right?

But she had promised her mom…and moreover, she'd promised her *dad*, too. Marissa hugged herself, holding that secret close to her for a moment or two longer before she could share it with Taylor. Once she told it, maybe it would break the magical feeling it had cast over her.

Taylor pulled a big plastic jug of Ma's homemade lemonade and waggled it in Marissa's direction. "I will drink *all* of this in front of you and not offer you a single sip if you don't spill, and *this minute*," she threatened. "What happened?"

So Marissa spilled. Over Ma's lemonade and a stash of leftover chocolate-chip cookies, Marissa mumbled out the events of the morning, trying not to forget a single detail.

"Your mom hasn't figured it out? That Uncle Daniel's just got to be your dad?" Taylor stuffed yet another cookie in her mouth. "Is she totally dense or what? I mean, it's as plain as the nose on your face—or should I say, the cleft in your chin?"

"I think she was too mad about him lying to really get it. Honest, I had to keep my expression poker-faced because she seemed to think I should be all sad. I mean, what difference does it make? My birth mom must not have really wanted me—but Daniel did. He wanted to keep me all along. He said so." The knowledge warmed Marissa, and she pulled it closer to her as if it was a blanket on a chilly day.

"After you left them alone in Uncle Daniel's office, could you hear anything? I mean, maybe he told her then."

Marissa shook her head and reached for the jug of lemonade. "They were through yelling, and they got all quiet. Well, until the last, when Mom came storming out. I don't think he told her the truth. My mom would have been completely shell-shocked by that news, and she wasn't, believe me. She was mad as all get-out on the way home—well, here, because this isn't really home."

Taylor giggled. "*Yet* anyway."

"Yet. You are so right." Marissa set her red plastic cup carefully on the blanket and lay back on the soft cotton patchwork to stare up at the bottom of the tree house way above her head. Huh. From here, it *did* look pretty high.

"You do have a problem, though," Taylor pointed out. "If they're blazing-hot mad at each other, how are you ever going to get them to go on a picnic with you—a picnic that you plan on ditching at the last minute? Whenever my mom gets on the outs with my dad—which isn't often, ya know, but it happens—the last thing she wants is alone time with him before she has a chance to cool off."

"I know. I thought about that." Marissa

twisted around and propped on an elbow. "Are there any more cookies left?"

Taylor poked around in the bag. "Oops. No. Ma's got more in the kitchen. I think. Unless I ate more than I thought."

"You've got to have a tapeworm inside you. If I ate like you, I'd weigh a ton."

"Cheering." Taylor licked an errant smudge of chocolate off her upper lip. "I highly recommend it—it melts the pounds off you if you have a coach like ours. Just wait. She runs you. In. The. Ground. Planks and laps and push-ups—boy push-ups, not girl push-ups. When you get on the squad, you'll be eating your head off, too."

"I don't know, Taylor. I mean, honestly..." Marissa let her doubts get the better of her. "My mom has a teaching contract in our old school, so even if I did get them together before we have to leave for me to get poked and prodded by those new doctors in Indiana, she can't quit, at least not for this school year."

"So?" Taylor slurped up the last of her lemonade. "It's only, what, three hours away. Maybe your mom will let you start the school year here and she can go teach until, say, she finds a substitute. Teachers do leave in the middle of the year. My art teacher did last year. Of course, she probably had to because of all the practical jokes some of the boys in my class did to her. Man, they were *nasty*. Dad said they should have been expelled."

"My mom would never leave in the middle of the year, not if she signed a contract. She's like Daniel when it comes to doing what she says, and saying what she means. She won't go back on a promise, even if it nearly kills her. And you have *got* to be the most *majorly* optimistic person in the entire *world* if you think for a second Mom will let me stay three hours away from her, even with Ma, and she's nuts about Ma."

"But once she knows that Uncle Daniel is, you know, your *dad*, then it will be okay, right? I mean, my mom has to go out of town sometimes and she doesn't freak about leaving me with my dad."

"Your mom and my mom?" Marissa snorted. "They are two completely different animals."

"Then, we've *got* to get her and Uncle Daniel together and so absolutely in love that she can't bear to be away from him."

"Which means…" Marissa blew out a breath. "I have to figure out a way to get her over being so mad at him that she spits every time she says his name."

"Spits?"

"Spits," Marissa confirmed. "But she wouldn't get so mad if she didn't really love him, right? Because, honestly, I've never seen anybody push my mom's buttons like Daniel does—not even my stupid doctors."

"Yeah. It's like that in all the movies. First they hate each other, and then they can't bear to be apart."

Marissa frowned. "You reckon real love is really like that? Like in the movies? Wouldn't it be easier to skip the hating part?"

"I think it must be some sort of natural law, like, you know, you always find romance in Paris," Taylor said in that knowing voice that told Marissa she really didn't know any more than Marissa did.

That, of course, triggered Taylor's favorite subject, about how one day she was going to get rich enough to go to Paris and live there and walk in the rain and find her true love under the Eiffel Tower.

Marissa couldn't understand it. Who needed Paris when right here was the closest thing to paradise anybody could ask for? Taylor had *so* much to be thankful for, and she sometimes took it all for granted. She had a mom and a dad, Ma, good friends at school, a place on the cheer squad, family who didn't freak if she wanted to do *normal* things, like ride a four-wheeler or climb up into a tree house.

Taylor, though, thought all this stuff was pretty humdrum and that Paris was her destiny. She went on about it. All. The. Time.

And her fixation on *that* subject meant only one thing to Marissa. She'd have to get this deal with Daniel and her mom done pretty much on her own.

"HEY, MOM! IT'S for you!" Marissa hustled Kimberly's cell phone over to Kimberly as she pored over Marissa's medical records. Then, just as quickly, her daughter melted away into another part of the house.

"Hello?" Kimberly said breathlessly into the phone. "Is this Judge Malloy?"

"Uh, no. This is Daniel, Kimberly."

Opposing emotions dueled for dominance: one, that hateful instantaneous jolt of happiness that bubbled through her at the sound of Daniel's voice…and two, anger that he could continue to sit on information she needed for Marissa.

"Hello, Daniel," she replied in as careful a tone as she could muster.

"You haven't heard from the judge? It's been, what, a week?"

As if you didn't know. As if you aren't probably lobbying him hard to rule against me. "Nearly two," she said. "I can't wait much longer before we have to head to Indiana. I have to get out there and get back before pre-planning starts, and I can't afford to fly."

"That's an awfully long drive to do alone," he said.

Well, I might not have *to make it if you'd tell me what you know,* she thought uncharitably. Aloud, she observed, "I'm used to doing things by myself. Marissa and I will be fine."

Silence filled the line—Kimberly's thoughts consumed with what a painful wrench it would be for both her and Marissa to leave this town. She could see it every day, the hold it had taken, especially on Marissa. She shouldn't have allowed it. She should have stuck to her plan to come here for a day or two, three at the most, and then head on to Indiana.

"Uh, well, the reason I'm calling is that— well, you've been avoiding me."

He was right on that score. It had been too painful to be around him after she'd found out about the bracelet. He'd led her down a dead end, allowed her to believe, for so many years, a story that wasn't true.

And the truth? Well, it made her doubt everything she thought she knew about Marissa's birth mom. Maybe the girl hadn't cared about Marissa. Maybe, even if Kimberly could find her, she wouldn't want to help a daughter she'd tossed away like trash.

"I've been busy." True enough, but she'd been busy *trying* to avoid Daniel. "And I guess we've missed each other."

Daniel's response was derisive, as if he knew she was lying. "If you hadn't been avoiding me, I could have asked you this in person. We do share a roof, you know."

"Temporarily," she added primly. "What was it you wanted?"

"Marissa asked me to do something...and I told her I'd have to get your permission first."

Gratitude and surprise flooded Kimberly. There, he'd done it again, snuffed out her anger with such calm and reasoned consideration that she felt like a ninny for being mad in the first place. "Thank you. I really appreciate you telling her that. What does she want you to do?"

"She wants me to take her fishing—and have a picnic. The picnic was very important to her. And she asked if I minded if you went along."

"Huh?" The request floored her. "Marissa hates picnics. She's carped incessantly every minute of any picnic I've ever forced her to go on. You'd think I was forcing the child to do hard labor, and she's miserable without a router and a Wi-Fi signal."

Daniel's rumble of laughter vibrated through the phone line. "We may be turning her into a country girl after all…or…it could be that this is her way of apologizing to you."

Now that made more sense. Marissa did have a big heart, one that strove to make peace and soothe injured feelings. Even as a small child, she'd always drawn 'I'm Sorry' cards whenever she'd been disobedient.

"Where…where would this picnic be? And I've never been fishing—for that matter, neither has Marissa. Are you sure she wanted to go fishing?"

"Hey, she's a Monroe kid now. All of us love to fish, so maybe she wants to give it a whirl, see what it's like. We've got an old mill house on the edge of our property line. Perfect for fishing because the fish like to swim around the raised piers under the mill house—and it's safe," he hastened to add. "Built from heart pine and we make sure it stays in good repair. It's nothing fancy, now—more like a covered bridge than anything else—but it keeps the sun off you in weather like this."

"That's the place she wanted to see with Taylor…" Kimberly recalled. "When we got into that awful fight over the four-wheeler."

"I hope Taylor hasn't made it out to be more than it really is. Taylor has a talent for spinning tales—not lying, exactly, more like being a hopeless optimist and dreaming big. But it is one of the prettiest spots on our entire tract—big old oak trees in the water, Spanish moss everywhere. It's where Dad took us to fish."

"It sounds wonderful," she found herself saying. "When did you want to take us?"

"You'll go, then?" His voice bubbled with pleasure that he didn't bother to hide. "I was afraid…after the blowup over the bracelet…"

The reminder soured her joy, but she made a Herculean effort to banish her anger. "Of course I'll go. I'm not going to deny Marissa her chance at fishing because…" She didn't want to say, "I acted like a snit," or "You did, too," so instead she trailed off, letting him think what he would.

"Of course." His reply was cool, and instantly she realized she'd wounded him without meaning to.

"Besides," she heard herself add, "I adore picnics."

Mentally she kicked herself. Now, why had she told him that?

CHAPTER TWENTY-FOUR

SATURDAY MORNING, THE day Daniel had planned to take Marissa and Kimberly on their fishing trip, dawned hot and humid. Ma's central unit could barely keep up, running constantly even as the breakfast dishes were cleared and Ma supervised the assembly of the picnic basket.

Kimberly had expected Marissa to be brimming with excitement at the prospect of their trip. She wasn't, though. She dragged from the refrigerator to the counter, from the counter to the pantry. It put Kimberly in mind of all the previous picnic junkets she'd asked Marissa to go on.

And for some reason, Marissa kept baiting her. It was as if she wanted to start a fight. Ma had picked up on it, too, casting a knowing glance Kimberly's way a couple of times. It was as if she was telegraphing, "Don't worry. All kids are like this. Marissa's just a normal kid."

Oh, how Kimberly wished for that, for Marissa to be just a normal kid.

"Don't fill it too full," Kimberly warned Ma. "We'll never be able to tote it, and you've got so much food in there already, we'll be lucky to eat even half of it."

Ma wrinkled her brow. "But Daniel said—" Abruptly she about-faced and put her hands on her hips, her head turning as she gazed over at Marissa near the screen door and then back to the window over the sink.

"Oh, wait!" Kimberly snapped her fingers. "I forgot sunblock. Let me go back and get it now."

It was as she was coming back down the hall to the kitchen that she heard the buzz of a motorcycle or…maybe a chain saw? This early in the morning? And in the heat of the summer? Who'd need firewood at this time of year?

"Kimberly? Daniel's ready for y'all," Ma called.

She froze as she crossed the kitchen's threshold and saw the big black four-wheel utility vehicle through the window. Daniel stood by it and waved a hand toward it theatrically.

"What on earth…?"

Did he honestly expect her to let her child bounce through the woods on that—that monster? If he did, he had another think coming. She stomped out the door, sunscreen still in hand.

"You like it? I borrowed it from our neighbor up the road. I've actually been thinking of trading in one of our four-wheelers and getting one of these babies," Daniel said as he patted the camouflage-patterned hood.

He thought she'd be pleased?

"Daniel—"

"See? It seats four, and...voilà!" He bent over and pulled up the webbed strap of a seat belt. "Much safer than a regular four-wheeler."

Kimberly felt her resolve faltering as he went through all the safety features point by point. As energetically as he hawked the contraption, he could have been a salesperson.

"You've obviously put a lot of thought into this." Her words sounded hollow, even to her.

"I did. I tried to put myself in your shoes, tried to think, if I was Kimberly, how would I keep my daughter safe?"

Her heart swelled with emotion. She had to turn away for a moment so that he couldn't see the tears in her eyes. How could he be such two entirely different people? On the one hand, so kind and considerate and thoughtful when it came to the little things…and on the other?

Obstinate, bullheaded and totally uncooperative about sharing what he knows about Marissa's birth mom.

"So?" Daniel laid a hand on her arm. "Does it pass inspection?"

She gazed up at him and saw…was it fear? Yes, it was fear that she'd reject his attempt. All at once, she could imagine him as a little boy, toting a bouquet of scraggly wildflowers to Ma.

And knowing Ma, she'd probably take them even if they were all goldenrod and ragweed and made her sneeze her fool head off, Kimberly thought. "Yes. Yes, it definitely passes inspection. You have totally earned the Helicopter Mom's seal of approval with this particular choice."

Daniel whooped with pleasure and pumped his fist, letting a loud "Yeees!" split the quiet morning air.

Behind her the screen door banged shut. "Mom?"

Kimberly turned back to see Marissa drooping against the doorjamb. "Yes, honey?"

"I don't think I want to go after all. I don't think I feel…up to it."

Disappointment shot through Kimberly and right behind it that familiar black cloud of worry.

She crossed to the porch steps and laid a hand on Marissa's forehead. No, not a fever. "Honey? What's wrong?"

Daniel stood behind her, and she could feel his concern, too, emanating in waves. "What hurts?" he asked bluntly.

"Nothing *hurts*," Marissa grouched. "I don't feel good, that's all."

Kimberly turned toward Daniel and bumped him in the shoulder. She attempted a light-hearted tone to disguise the worry still nagging at her. "Now, what was that about her turning into a country girl? I told you she didn't like picnics *or* fishing."

"It's not *that*, either." Marissa fixed her gaze on her clenched fists. "I'm tired, okay? Maybe another time."

"Honey, we may not *have* another time. Depending on when your appointment in Indiana is, we may have to leave before Daniel has another day off. And here he has gone to the trouble of borrowing a vehicle that's safe for you—"

"I *know*, Mom. I'm a brat and ungrateful and I should be grounded for a month."

Kimberly stepped back, dropped her hands by her sides. She was at a complete loss as to what had come over Marissa. "Are you sure you're not sick? Your stomach's not hurting? You don't have an earache or a sore throat? Because you usually only get this grouchy when you're coming down with something."

"I'm not sick," Marissa insisted. "I just don't…"

"Feel good. You said that." Kimberly threw up her hands. "I give up." She turned to Daniel again. "I am so sorry, Daniel. I guess we aren't going after all."

Ma spoke from the far side of the screen. "No reason for you folks not to go on. I'll keep a look out for Marissa. I suspect, young lady—" Ma's voice turned a bit crisper than usual "—you stayed up late texting Taylor. That right?"

Marissa dropped her head a fraction of an inch lower. "Yes, ma'am."

"Marissa!" Kimberly shook her head in disbelief. "When you knew Daniel was planning a special day—that you asked for, mind you. And after I've told you no texting after ten o'clock."

"I'm sorry I've spoiled everything. It was stupid," Marissa said. "But Ma's right. Y'all go on."

Marissa's casual use of *y'all* blew Kimberly away. Her baby *was* turning into a country girl—and one who could apologize when she knew she was in the wrong.

Still, Kimberly hesitated. "I don't know..."

"Here's the picnic basket all packed up. Don't want that food to go to waste, now, do we?" Ma asked. "Marissa, honey, move out of the way, please, so Daniel can load it. It's a mite heavy for me."

Quick as a rabbit, Marissa scooted out of the doorway, and Ma promptly handed the basket to Daniel. "Thank you, son," she said. "Kimberly might have been right about me packing too much. Shoo-ee, but that basket is heavy."

She came out to join them on the deck. With a hand on Kimberly's shoulder, she said, "Go on, now. Enjoy your day. Bring me some fish for supper. A nap will put Miss Sleepyhead here to rights, and if something goes wrong, well, you're a few minutes away, and I can call you on your cell phone, now, can't I?"

"I'll bet you Monroes could have made levitation sound like a reasonable thing," Kimberly marveled. "You could probably sell ice cream to a polar bear. I can't believe I'm letting myself get talked into this."

"I'd listen to Ma, if I were you—and that advice is born of long experience of finding out what happens after *not* listening," Daniel quipped. He gestured toward the utility vehicle. "Madam? Your chariot—and all its safety features—awaits."

As Daniel put more distance between the house and the utility vehicle, Kimberly's mood lightened. Maybe Ma was right, and all Marissa needed was a good nap. One late night wouldn't hurt her. After all, Kimberly had been allowed to stay up as late as she'd wanted to and as often as she'd wanted to as a kid, mostly because her mom had done the same. But still—it proved that one late night was survivable. She'd deal with the texting issue when she got back, but she suspected Marissa having to bail out on this trip was punishment enough.

"Marissa's really missing something nice!" she told Daniel over the thrum of the engine and the bounce of the wide tires across the dips and washouts in the rough dirt track.

"Bet she'll be sad she stayed behind when I tell her all about it."

He grinned and downshifted as he approached a rise through a thicket of young pines. "We planted these about ten years ago—amazing how fast pines grow, isn't it?"

"You plant them in rows? Just like carrots?"

Daniel chuckled. "They're more like carrots than you know—pine trees have a great big tap root, just like a carrot. When the big winds come, you'll see piles of huge oaks and hardwoods crashed down, but the flimsiest of pines will bend whichever way the winds blow."

Now they were through the young pines, trundling past larger trees with thicker trunks and gnarled branches, their needles casting a dense shade over the track. "Loblolly pines— Hey, look! A redheaded woodpecker!" Daniel pointed up.

Sure enough, a huge white bird with a scarlet head was banging away at a tall pine. He didn't even bother to look around at the noise of the vehicle.

"Gee, wonder if that guy's head hurts at the end of a day?" Kimberly asked. "I feel like him sometimes, banging my head against a wall."

"Hey…" Daniel shrugged, his hands gripping the wheel as he rounded a hillock of exposed roots. "That's how he gets his supper—he goes after juicy bugs and worms. Sometimes the wall gives if you bang on it hard enough and long enough."

Kimberly restrained herself from asking how many times she'd have to knock heads with Daniel before, like the insects in that pine tree, he'd surrender.

On they went through the wooded forest, Daniel pointing out different birds and animals and plants. She saw a deer hightail it through the woods, and once Daniel had to stop and turn off the engine because an opossum had laid itself out in the middle of the track, pretending to be dead.

He put his finger to his lips. "Shh. Give it a minute, and the old guy will pick himself up and haul out for the woods. Don't know what he's doing keeping daylight hours. That's about the first time I've seen one out this late in the morning."

Sure enough, once the forest had returned to its customary chirping, creaking noises, the critter toddled off to the cover of the trees.

Kimberly could see now that oaks and hardwoods had choked out the pines, Spanish moss trailing from every branch. Birds flitted through the dappled canopy the close-knit limbs created. The air felt heavier, slower somehow, and she sensed they were approaching water.

The track sloped downhill and around a curve, then forked into a wider, smoother road of pale white sand studded with brown pebbles. "This used to be the old access road to the mill," Daniel explained as he speeded up. "The county closed it, oh, had to be thirty years ago. Now the only way to get here is through our land. The mill house is up ahead."

And it was—weathered gray boards on a structure that looked remarkably like the covered bridges she'd seen in magazines, but with a big wooden waterwheel still attached to the side. Daniel slowed to a stop at the edge of the mill house and switched off the vehicle. "See? Told you it wasn't much."

"Oh, it's beautiful! So peaceful!"

"You won't say that after you've been swatting mosquitos for a while—come to think of it, you'd better spray yourself with this." He tossed her a can of insect repellent. "And by all means, don't play in the Spanish moss or you'll take home a nice crop of chiggers."

"I don't believe I know what a chigger looks like." Kimberly didn't argue but liberally sprayed the repellent over herself.

"It's not what they look like, it's how bad they itch. Yow."

He hefted the picnic basket out of the back of the vehicle and grabbed up a big plastic carton. "Bait," he said slyly. "You're not afraid of worms, by chance, are you?"

"Spiders, yes. Worms? Nah. I dissected my share of them in college."

"Good to know I won't have to bait your hook, ma'am." He tipped his head toward her and started for the mill house.

"Wait!" Kimberly called. "Where are the poles?"

He motioned at the mill house, still walking backward toward it. "We keep some spinners locked up in here so we don't have to fool with bringing them every time."

The basket stowed in the shadiest, coolest part of the mill house, Daniel gave her a quick tour, showing her the massive millstone that had ground wheat and rye and corn in decades past.

"I'm surprised you let Taylor come down here," she commented, "since she's allergic to corn."

"Ah…but she couldn't come here, not before Rob and Andrew and I scrubbed that millstone and every speck of every surface in this place with a bleach-and-water mix," Daniel said. "I rigged up a siphon hose for water from the millpond, and we used that. Had the place spic and span in no time."

Her surprise must have revealed itself. "Hey," he protested. "When I know what has to be done, I do it. But I admit…about that tree house, well, I had a failure of the imagination. I am sorry, Kimberly."

Impulsively she blurted out, "Let's not talk about that, or Marissa's birth mom or…or anything serious today. Right now, I want to play hooky and pretend the real world won't jump on me with all four claws extended when we turn your neighbor's cart around and head back to Ma's."

He took her hands in his. "Ah, Kimberly." His voice grew husky. "You need a day to play hooky, that's for sure. But don't make any promises you can't keep. I know how hard they are, how much they tie a person down."

He was talking about his promise to Marissa's birth mom, of course. This trip had been perfect so far—well, except for Marissa. Kimberly didn't want to cast a pall over it.

So she told him, "Teach me to fish, Daniel."

And he did. He set her up at one of the wide, deep windows overlooking the mill-pond, with its lush oak canopy, and tried to show her how to cast the spinner's line between the big trees standing on hulking roots in the water.

Kimberly didn't prove to be a natural at casting. Maybe it was *because* of Daniel's nearness more than in spite of him.

It was incredibly difficult for her to concentrate on the proper casting technique when she felt his strong, warm body against her, his arms around her, attempting to guide her hands. As if that wasn't enough to completely distract her, the barest hint of stubble grazed her cheek, and the scent of him—clean soap, nothing fancy—finished the job.

"Whoa!" he hollered as she cast yet another line into the trees. "That one is a goner, too." He pulled out his pocketknife and clipped the line.

Kimberly watched his nimble fingers restring the rod for a third time. "Let's face it. I'm hopeless at this."

"Nah." He deftly tied the finishing knot and stood her rod up against the rough-sawn timber wall of the mill house. "It'll take you a while, but you'll get the hang of it. Shoot, my dad didn't give up on me, and I sank the hook straight into his backside. That was *after* I'd cast into about four trees and tangled our lines twice."

"You miss him, don't you?" she asked.

Daniel didn't say anything in the time it took him to carefully stow his spool of line back into his tackle box, then still more slowly bait Kimberly's hook and cast it out into the water. He propped the pole in a notch carved into the wide window ledge. "Yeah," he said finally. "There's not a day that goes by that I don't wish he were here."

"I wonder what it feels like to be Marissa," Kimberly mused. "I mean, I know what it's like to not have a dad, but I at least knew who my dad was. She never had a dad at all. Not until... Daniel, I—I want to say how much I've really loved watching you with Marissa these past few weeks. You're so patient with her, so good with her. I think you've really filled a void in her life, a void that I didn't fully realize was so big. Thank you. I mean that."

He fixed his gaze out on the calm sun-dappled waters of the pond, where a pair of dragonflies were chasing each other in slow lazy circles. "You don't know how much that means to me to hear you say that. I've screwed up so much—no, I know that, Kimberly." He forestalled her protest even before she could form the words. "First not being as honest as I could be about that bracelet and then about the tree house. You talk about being hopeless at casting… I was beginning to feel hopeless about this father-figure business."

She let her fingers slide along his tanned forearm, relishing the feel of taut muscles, solidity, all the things that made him so rocklike and reliable. "You are far from hopeless. You're too good, in fact. Marissa's going to miss you when we leave."

He captured her hand in his and pressed her palm to his lips, then folded her fingers in an intimate clasp. "What about you, Kimberly? Will *you* miss me?"

Without thinking, she leaned up and pressed her lips to his. It was supposed to be the briefest of kisses, but he caught her up in his arms and didn't let her go. The kiss continued, sweet and beguiling. It was Daniel who finally broke their embrace. "Man, oh, man, Kimberly Singleton. You really know how to take a guy fishing."

She blushed. "Maybe we should try some

of Ma's lunch if we have such strong appetites, huh?"

He exhaled. "I think that's a very wise idea—but then, Marissa told me you were really smart."

The mention of her daughter's name helped ground Kimberly in the here and now, not the fuzzy, romantic land of *maybe* or *if only*.

"Ha," she replied shakily, smoothing her hair and hoping Daniel didn't see her fingers tremble. "Marissa's sure got you fooled. She was angling for something. Usually I'm one of the most ignorant creatures on the planet, didn't you know that?"

He turned to her, his eyes dark with an emotion she couldn't quite read—pain, maybe?

"I don't believe that at all. Not to me. I wish—I wish things could be different, Kimberly." His voice was harsh with emotion.

Daniel didn't elaborate on what those things would be, didn't wait for her to ask. He walked out into the brilliant sunshine and tossed rocks hard and far into the millpond.

The ripples went wide, spreading quickly from a small concentric ring where each stone sank to ever-larger rings that crossed into the ripples from previous rocks. Kimberly couldn't help noticing how they crashed into one another, getting in the way of each other, canceling out the energy each had been imbued with.

Hesitantly, she walked out to join him. "Daniel…"

He threw another half-dozen rocks before he acknowledged her presence. Dusting off his hand, he met her eyes. "Can we not talk about this? I just—I just can't. When I'm with you, I want to tell you…everything. Every last detail. Especially after…well, after…" Setting his jaw, he started back toward the mill house, determination in every line and crease of his face. "I promised. And I intend to keep that promise, at least until I'm released from it. And nothing—not even the sweetest kisses in the world—is going to change that fact. You have no idea how much I wish it could."

CHAPTER TWENTY-FIVE

DANIEL FOUND HIMSELF perversely glad that he'd planned to work at the station on Sunday morning. It gave him an excuse not to see Kimberly.

His crew, however, was not as pleased to have him there.

"Whoa, Chief, wake up on the wrong side of the bed this morning?" one firefighter asked after Daniel snapped at him.

Another made the mistake of asking if the county had approved the training fire. "Is the county office open today?" Daniel growled. "No? I didn't think so. When I know, you'll know."

Even Daniel cringed at the rough tone he'd used. Before he could apologize, the firefighter had raised both hands and backed away.

It wasn't the crew's fault. They were restless. Too many calls that could be handled by a couple of them with one hand tied behind their backs. Too many days of stepping on toes, bumping into each other during the long shifts with nothing much to do except mindless cleaning and straightening and prepping. Too much proximity.

Proximity. The feel of Kimberly in his arms rushed back to him, making every nerve ending tingle. He'd had way too much proximity with Kimberly the day before, and that was his problem—not the guys, not being fire chief.

He squared his shoulders and renewed his determination to be more like his dad. His father had hardly ever carried work home—at least not that he let slip to Daniel and the rest of the kids when they were young—or taken problems from home to work. Keep it separate—do your job at the station and then do your duty at home. That had been his philosophy.

Daniel hoped that one day it would come to him as naturally as it had to his dad.

He walked into the day room, ready to burn off some of his own bottled-up energy. What he needed to do was stop mooning over Kimberly. He needed to challenge a few of the guys to cut out the video games and instead try to beat him at push-ups.

They never could—for some reason, Daniel had always found it amazingly easy to rip out a long string of uninterrupted push-ups. It didn't mean he could bench-press more than some of his guys, but it was a sure way to bait them away from their current couch-potato status.

But before he could crank out even ten pushups, the buzzer reverberated through the building. Daniel froze, barely suspended above the ground, the concrete floor biting into his knuckles.

Structure fire. A big, fast one from the sound of it. A restaurant on the south side of town. Possible electrical fire. Wires down, power still on.

Daniel remembered the place: it prided itself on churning out authentic Southern fried chicken deep-fried in 100 percent pure lard, and who cared about your arteries when you tasted their chicken?

A hand reached down to yank him up. It was the crewmember who had backed away from him earlier when Daniel had practically bitten his head off.

"Guess we won't be needing that training fire after all, huh, Chief," the man said, his eyes somber. "I don't like the sound of this one."

As Daniel hustled for his turnout gear and

watched his captain supervise the organized chaos of both engines gearing up and heading out, a lump formed in his throat.

Pride. These men and women knew what they were doing—and they didn't have to turn to him for direction. His department, after months of struggle, looked a lot like his dad's well-oiled machine so many years ago.

He hauled himself into the cab of his captain's truck, slamming the door as Hank peeled out behind the second engine.

His captain didn't take his eyes off the road as he asked, "Chief, you think they're a little trigger-happy on this one? You think it's as big as they say?"

"Hmm." Daniel looked toward the south side, saw a huge billowing cloud of black smoke suddenly belch up from behind the steeple of the First Christian Church.

That restaurant was cheek-to-jowl with four churches, one of which had been standing in that spot for nearly a hundred years. On a Sunday morning, every one of those churches would be filled with a congregation.

A shiver ran down his spine. For the first time in a long time, pure, cold fear pooled in his gut at the prospect of a fire. Suddenly he craved one more shot at a morning with Kimberly and Marissa. A slice of toast and Marissa's fresh-out-of-bed grouchiness. Kimberly's breathless laugh during awkward moments when she wasn't sure exactly what to say.

Had his dad thought something similar riding to that warehouse fire? He tried hard to push the superstitious idea from his head.

"Nope," he said in a grim voice. "We're probably going to wish they had it wrong, but I think they called it right, Hank. I think this one will be an all-hands-on-deck deal. Let's just hope it doesn't turn out to be a killer."

KIMBERLY AND MA were in the kitchen, elbow-deep in putting up a bumper picking of Ma's tomatoes, when the call came in. Ma had asked Marissa to grab the phone for her.

"What?" Marissa's strangled cry instantly got Kimberly's attention. Her daughter was gripping the phone, her face a pasty gray-white, her eyes wide.

She stuck the phone out toward Ma. "Y-you'd better take this," she said, her breath coming in short gasps. "This lady says it's a fire. A *big* fire."

Ma's paring knife clattered to the floor. For once, she didn't automatically bend down to pick up what she'd dropped. She stepped over it and extended a trembling hand for the cordless.

"There's been a fire?" she asked into the handset, collapsing into one of the kitchen table's ladder-back chairs.

Kimberly abandoned the tomatoes, wiped her hands on a towel and crossed to her daughter. She wrapped her arms around Marissa, who laid her head against Kimberly's chest. "Marissa? Honey? What did they say?"

"Oh, Mom! It's a big one—every engine. Bobbi told me once they never call out every engine unless it's a killer fire. A-and Daniel— Daniel's hurt."

Kimberly's breath caught in her chest. *Breathe*, she ordered herself. *You can't think if you don't breathe.* Her lungs obeyed, dragging in a choking inhalation. She licked her suddenly parched lips and swallowed. Staring past Marissa, she scrutinized Ma for any clue as to Daniel's condition.

And I waited for him to leave this morning before I came into the kitchen. The thought tore through her like the ripping action of a serrated knife. *Oh, please...don't let the last time I see him be his back through my bedroom window.*

Ma was nodding, her hand to her mouth,

her own breath coming in quick little pants. "I understand. And Rob? And Andrew? They're okay?"

She wobbled to a standing position, pushing the chair back with a nails-on-chalkboard screech. "Yes, yes, I have someone to drive me." She looked at Kimberly, a desperate appeal in her eyes. When Kimberly nodded, Ma spoke hurriedly into the phone. "We'll be at the hospital quick as we can."

SOMEONE HAD MOVED the hospital five miles farther down the road and placed every slowpoke car in front of her to boot, Kimberly was certain. How else could a ten-minute trip seem to last an eternity?

In the backseat, Marissa was trying—and failing—to hold back choking sobs. "Go faster, Mom!" she pleaded.

Kimberly darted a peek to check on her, tried to telegraph some calm and peace. "We'll get there, Marissa."

With one hand, Kimberly gripped the wheel, but with the other, she held Ma's hand, their fingers intertwined. Ma's short nails dug into Kimberly's palm, but she didn't care. She knew what it was like to fear for your child—

if it had been Marissa, she would have been all to pieces.

She was barely holding it together as it was.

Glancing down, she saw that she'd left the house in such a hurry she hadn't even taken off her tomato-speckled apron. Ma, too, still wore hers. "Marissa," she began, more in an attempt to distract her daughter than concern about how they looked, "can you untie Ma's apron at the neck?"

"Land sakes," Ma exclaimed, a hand to the flowered apron. "Why, I just left everything, didn't I? Oh, my! Did I turn the stove off? Daniel will be the laughingstock of the department if the house burns down because I forgot the stove."

"I did, Ma." Marissa was calmer now, her fingers busy untying the bow at Ma's nape. "While you and Mom went for your purses. And I picked up the knife, too. I didn't know what exactly to do with the tomatoes, though."

A jolt of pleased surprise ran through Kimberly. She wouldn't have guessed that Marissa would have had the foresight and maturity to act calm in a crisis. She'd put Kimberly to shame.

"Thank you," Kimberly told Marissa as she felt fingers on her own neck and the apron strings fall away. "I really appreciate you remembering, and I know Ma does, too."

"Those tomatoes will be fine just like they are, or we'll throw the whole mess out if they sour," Ma stated in an uncharacteristic departure from her careful, frugal ways. Now she moved around in the seat, untying the back apron string as well and balling up the cloth. "And, Kimberly, I guess I forgot—you don't know the ropes of being in a firefighter's family. That was Louise Dubberly on the phone—Hank Dubberly's wife. Hank's a captain at the station. If it had been…" Ma trailed off, but picked right back up again, injecting a determinedly positive note in her voice. "If it had been real bad, they would have come to the house and got us. They always do. Now, that's not to say he's not hurt, but…it's probably not real bad."

Kimberly braked behind a slow-moving pickup and used the chance to study Ma for signs and clues, as much as she had earlier. Daniel's mother had clasped her hands together until the knuckles were taut and white, and she'd focused unmoving eyes on the road ahead of her. She didn't look as though she really believed her own words.

"What could she tell you?" Kimberly willed

the pickup to move faster. "Louise Dubberly, I mean?"

"It was that fried-chicken place off Grady Street—no, I forget, you probably don't know it. Anyway, it caught fire, and what with all that grease…" She drew in a deep, noisy breath.

Finally the truck turned off, and Kimberly could once again speed up. "And Daniel?" she prompted.

"He was working with a rookie—a young fellow— Oh, my, I didn't even think to ask how he was. I should have called his mama. Look at me, I've lost my fool mind," Ma murmured. "That kid— What possessed him, I don't know, and Louise could have it all wrong, she was going off what she'd heard. He'd climbed up into the suspended ceiling and got his BA—that's his breathing apparatus—caught."

"And of course Daniel went up after him." Kimberly had the sudden urge to throttle Daniel if he was alive enough to feel it when she got to the hospital.

And there was the hospital. She yanked the wheel toward the ER entrance, pulled up and parked. Ma was out the door and around the car before Kimberly even turned off the engine.

But then Ma froze.

Kimberly yanked her apron from her waist and tossed it into the car. Following Ma, she saw the clusters of firefighters in various degrees of turnout gear gathered around the ER entrance. She realized that the older woman had seen something that made her fear the worst.

"Ma?" She came up on one side of Daniel's mother while Marissa flanked her on the other.

Ma captured both Kimberly's and Marissa's hands. "Oh, girls. I'm so glad you're with me."

The firefighters parted ways so the three of them could move through the dense throng. Kimberly could hear scraps of tales that were suddenly cut off as the women approached.

"—had to cut Chris's airline to get him out—shared one mask all the way out, and they were—"

"—hot as the devil's kitchen in there—"

"—and pure lakes of fire. They can say all they want that lard has a flashpoint of six hundred degrees, but man o'mighty, I ain't never seen it just explode into flames—"

"—I swear, thought Chief was sure a goner,

climbing up after Chris in that ceiling when the whole roof was about to collapse on both of 'em—"

"—years of grease built up in that ceiling, fire burning from every direction and the *smoke*—couldn't see my hand in front of my face—"

"—who's that with Ma? Is that—"

"—girlfriend—"

"—hear tell maybe it's his daughter—"

But as they passed, the firefighters descended into silence, except for a few brave ones who managed to almost look Ma in the eye and say, "Hey, Ma, you holdin' up?" before dipping their heads respectfully in Kimberly and Marissa's direction.

The throng continued until they made it into the ER proper. It was almost a blessed relief when Kimberly found herself, Ma and Marissa ushered behind the door to the treatment areas, away from Daniel's firefighters. The sight of doctors and nurses and medical equipment—now, that was familiar to her, scary, but a known quantity. She knew the territory.

Out there? Something about all those somber-faced firefighters scared her to her core.

"Hey, Mrs. Monroe!" one of the nurses called. "You'll want to see Daniel, I'll expect."

The woman came around the nurse's station. "Now, don't be alarmed. We've got him in trauma room two. It's not too bad, but I think the doctor will probably admit him at least overnight."

"And the other boy?" Ma's face was tense as she waited for word.

"He's okay, too—got more smoke than Daniel, but he's breathing on his own."

"Glory be!" Ma let out a shaky breath. Kimberly thought the older woman might fold up in a heap on the floor as the tension went out of her.

The moment passed, and Ma straightened her back, following briskly behind the nurse. Kimberly and Marissa trailed after them.

The door to the trauma room was blocked by a doctor reviewing something on the screen of a small tablet. He looked up at their approach. "You told me your family would be here lickety-split," he said to someone inside the room.

And then she spotted Daniel, laid out on the gurney, his white T-shirt grimy with soot. The plastic tubing of an oxygen mask cut grooves into his cheeks, as smudged and blackened as his undershirt.

When he caught sight of them, he struggled to sit up and swing his feet off the bed, pushing the mask away from his mouth.

Ma rushed to one side and gently manhandled him back against the pillows. "You know the drill, Daniel," she decreed as she replaced the mask. "You sit back and listen to what these doctors tell you. I raised you better than that."

"Dad!" The word tore from Marissa and she barreled into his arms. Kimberly saw him hold on to her tightly, burying her face in the crook of his neck, smoothing her hair, his eyes closed as though he was soaking up the very substance of her. A tear snaked a path through the soot on Daniel's face.

"Kiddo," he said huskily. "I'm okay. No worries. What? You think one kitchen fire's gonna do me in? Even if it was a mongo-giant economy-size one?" He waved a hand to indicate they should all gather in for one big hug.

Kimberly fell into that embrace, not bothering to stop the flow of tears that poured down her cheeks.

At first, it was enough to know that Daniel was alive and well and they could chalk up the experience to a near miss. Then her relief and her tears vaporized into fierce anger. She pulled back.

"What?" he protested, the words garbled by the mask and a sudden coughing fit.

"How could you? They said you crawled up into the ceiling—of a burning building! And with the roof about to cave in! You're a fire chief, Daniel, not a—a superhero! You didn't even have to go into work today."

Daniel shrugged. "I wasn't trying to be a superhero. If I was—" He stopped to cough again and drew in a ragged breath. "Maybe I could have put that fire out with my X-ray ice vision, now, couldn't I? Chris thought maybe there was another fire starting up in the ceiling—and he was right, by the way. All that grease from all those years of frying chicken had coated the framing up there. It went up like a torch." The long speech set off a hacking cough that shook him. "Maybe he should have waited on me, because climbing up there by himself wasn't the world's smartest idea," he choked out.

"And climbing up after him, into a ceiling that could collapse at any minute under the weight of one man, much less *two*—how smart was that?" She folded her arms across her chest as she waited for his reply.

"Well, it seemed like the thing to do at the time," he quipped.

"Are you serious? Daniel Monroe!"

Daniel turned doleful eyes toward Ma in an apparent appeal for backup as he continued to cough in a way that sounded to Kimberly like a pack-a-day smoker.

Ma patted his back, but nodded in Kimberly's direction. "Preach on, Kimberly, you just preach on," she said. She scowled at her son. "Scare us to death and then expect us to let you off the hook? When you've told us you'll be careful?"

"Sure, I was careful," Daniel insisted, a crooked grin spilling out from beneath his oxygen mask. "Careful doesn't mean risk-free. It means what it says—to be full of care. I climbed up in that ceiling *full* of care for my backside, that's for sure." He coughed yet again.

"Careful?" Kimberly exploded. "Daniel— Daniel, please *promise* me you won't take a chance like that again," she begged, taking his hand in hers.

Whatever amusement he had shown moments ago faded. "I can't make you that promise, Kimberly. I can't, because I've already given my firefighters my word that I won't leave them behind. A man was down, don't you understand? Chris needed me. And I'd do it all over again in a heartbeat."

"Daniel—" She averted her face so he couldn't see her tears. "Don't we count?" she finally choked out in a low voice. "I mean, where do we fit in? You give away your promises to everyone else. Where does that leave us?"

His finger tipped her head back around, and he pulled her down on the edge of the gurney. "You count. I swear. It may not seem like it. But all I could think about—" He shook his head, coughed some more. "I promise this— I won't take an *unnecessary* risk. Because you do count." He squeezed her fingers in his, pulled her down against his chest. "All of you. You count more than you know. But I have to keep my word, or what kind of man would I be?"

As she lay there, hearing the thump of his heart against her chest, breathing in the sooty, ashy smell coming off him in wave after wave, Kimberly wept.

She loved him. Somewhere in these past few weeks, she had fallen in love with this stubborn, obstinate man who took idiot risks and ran into burning buildings and wouldn't break a foolish promise he'd made over a decade ago. And she knew, deep in her soul, that all it could ever lead to was anger and heartache and coming last in line to his precious promises.

It was only then that she realized what Marissa had called him when she'd first laid eyes on him in the ER.

Dad.

Marissa had called him Dad.

It made Kimberly weep all the harder, because worse than any pain she might go through herself was seeing her daughter go through that same pain—and being helpless to do anything about it.

CHAPTER TWENTY-SIX

A WEEK AFTER the big fire found Daniel standing in the same spot he'd delivered Marissa exactly twelve years before. The summer sun bore down on him as hotly as it had that July Fourth, the patch of grass in front of the fire station still as lush and green.

Her birthday. Today was Marissa's birthday.

He'd had a lot of time to think while he'd been laid up in the hospital. The doctors hadn't been satisfied until he'd had clear lung films for two days straight, so he'd spent countless hours staring at a muted television screen.

Thinking.

He could have died. He very nearly had, though that was a secret that he and Chris would take to their graves. Nobody need know just how close the two of them had come to punching their tickets. No, Kimberly was mad enough already, and she had no idea what had really gone on inside that inferno of a kitchen.

It had been Kimberly and Marissa's faces that had come to him in that smoky darkness. He'd realized then with a startling clarity that if he didn't make it out, he might take with him one of the few sure means Marissa ever had to find Miriam.

In the hospital, in between visitors and flower deliveries and him shooing Ma and Kimberly home, Daniel had turned the quandary over and over in his mind. Now, finally back at work, standing at the very spot where all of it had started, he still was trying to figure out what to do.

If it had been any other fireman besides him, would they have revealed Miriam's identity already? Would his dad have told Kimberly? What was the right thing to do?

He'd searched online for Miriam's name. But an Amish girl who was determined to hide wasn't so very easy to find. He'd spent a rainy afternoon using the hospital's Wi-Fi to check out every possible lead.

Uriel Hostetler was still alive, still full of acid-tongued hate for the English—or anybody who might question his authority.

His son, Marissa's birth father, wasn't.

A short newspaper article in an Indiana weekly turned up scant details about the farming accident that had taken his life. Daniel's heart softened for old Uriel as he read the article. He knew a thing or two about loss, but he couldn't imagine how it would be to lose your own child.

He'd searched for an obituary, and as he read the brief account of the services, he recognized the name of the town. It was the settlement Hostetler had left to come to Georgia after a split in the church.

Apparently Hostetler had smoothed things over.

Yesterday, Daniel had given up on the internet and started dialing numbers to the town's few non-Amish businesses. Someone somewhere had to know what had happened to Miriam.

And they had. The woman at a local florist had revealed the information in hushed tones, as though she was afraid of being overheard, and only after she'd called the fire station's number.

It was a slim lead—the name of a community college across the Indiana state line in Kentucky. And that led him to a friendly alumni-affairs director who miraculously was in her office the day before a holiday, and who happily told him that, yes, Miriam was still on their alumni rolls, married now and living in Chattanooga, Tennessee.

Which brought him here. On Marissa's birthday. To this patch of lawn where he'd wrapped her as a wet and squalling newborn in his T-shirt and gazed at her with wonder.

He gathered his courage and dialed the number the woman at the college had given him.

"Hello? If this is a telemarketer, I—"

"Miriam? Miriam Graber?"

"Who is this?" she hissed, every bit of warmth draining from her voice. "How did you find me?"

"I don't know if you remember my name, but I'm Daniel Monroe—I'm the fireman who helped you with your baby. Marissa."

Silence filled the line, and Daniel thought she might have hung up on him. Then, in a low voice, she said, "I remember you. You helped me. I could have never gotten away if you hadn't helped me."

"Look," he began, digging his toe into the thick thatch of grass and jamming his free hand into his pants pocket. "I wouldn't call, but it's about Marissa. She's sick, Miriam. She needs your help."

"I—I can't help her. I can't. That's why I gave her up. So someone else could."

He ignored her words and pressed on. "Her adoptive mom—she's really good, Miriam. I know you'd like her. But Marissa has this rare bleeding disorder and she needs your medical history. You could call her adoptive mom, you don't even have to come back to Georgia—"

"No! No! My husband—he doesn't know I had a baby, and I can't tell him. Because—because—" Miriam began sobbing into the phone. "I can't have a baby now. Not after—They had to do a hysterectomy. And if he knew... I just can't."

"He doesn't have to know." Only desperation would have made Daniel say this, encourage deception. "You could fax it here to the fire station, and nobody would be the wiser. You wouldn't have to put your name down—"

"No, I can't." Her tears had ended, and she was preternaturally calm on the other end of the line. "It's not only Billy I'm worried about. How did you find me? If you can find me, Uriel can find me, and he knows—he knows about the baby. And he wants her now, the baby, and he'll fight custody. I know him. After he lost his son, he got even meaner.

He'll take Marissa away from the only family she's ever known, and he won't think twice about it. And I will *not* let her go through that—I will *not* let him have her. I don't want to know anything about her except that she's safe. What I don't know, Uriel can't make me tell."

"You don't seriously think—"

"I do. There was this guy in North Carolina who was able to get his daughter back years later—and he'd signed papers terminating his parental rights. I saw it on the news. They took it all the way up to the Supreme Court. Uriel Hostetler will stop at nothing—he'd probably kidnap her and skip the courts altogether. Either way, Marissa would be gone. And you can't let that animal have her. You can't, Daniel, please. You promised me you'd keep her safe. You *promised*."

He could dismiss the immature fears and requests for secrecy from a sixteen-year-old girl, but now Miriam was a grown woman of twenty-seven or twenty-eight and was asking the same thing.

Keeping him bound to that promise.

He closed his eyes. Tried one more time. "I haven't told them about you. But they need your medical information. That's all."

"You know that's not all. If you tell them, they'll figure it out. They'll want more. And if they find out I was Amish, and where I came from, they'll go looking. Uriel—Uriel will still be there. After he's dead, then I can, Daniel. But not while he draws a breath. You have to understand."

In the background, he heard a man greet Miriam with a "Hi, honey, I got the hot-dog buns you wanted. Now, why do they sell ten hot dogs in a package and eight buns?"

Miriam came back on the phone, hushed and hurried. "I've gotta go. Don't call back, and, please, don't tell anyone. Think of Marissa, and keep your promise."

KIMBERLY HUNG UP her phone and sank down on the porch steps, weary from the late-afternoon heat bearing down on her. She put her head in her hands.

She hadn't expected Judge Malloy to call her on the Fourth, especially not as late as four o'clock in the afternoon. He'd been kind...but final. He could not release Marissa's birth mom's records, not even with identifying demographics redacted, not without the woman's permission.

Which kind of meant Kimberly needed to know the woman's name.

Which kind of meant she needed the woman's medical records.

Talk about a vicious circle.

What a great Fourth of July present, she thought sourly. The news seemed even worse coming on Marissa's birthday.

Something landed on the ground by her feet with a *thunk*, and a soft brown nose pushed up through her hair, snuffling gently. She peered down to see the Monroes' old chocolate Labrador shooting his biggest, roundest puppy-dog eyes at her.

Now that he'd captured her attention, he nudged the battered tennis ball at her feet. "Oh, Rufus... You miss Daniel, don't you? You got used to him hanging around while he was off work, throwing you balls to retrieve."

Getting to her feet, she threw the ball into the pasture and watched as Rufus loped off after it. If only she could send Rufus to fetch Marissa's birth mother. He wouldn't give up. He'd hunt until he found her.

Well. There was nothing left to do but pack up and head to Indiana. She'd let Marissa have one more day here—Ma had secretly baked a huge birthday cake for Marissa to serve at the cookout tonight, and Marissa was pumped about going to the fireworks at the park afterward.

But tomorrow—tomorrow they needed to start the drive to Indiana. There was nothing left for them here.

Her heart protested that. She knew it to be true, though. Even if it felt as though she were ripping out a part of herself to leave the Monroes behind—*leave Daniel*, her heart whispered—Kimberly had to remind herself that Daniel, if he wanted, could stop her.

All he had to do was say the word.

Since that day in the ER, they'd been stiff around each other, nervous and formal. Whenever she'd been near him, Daniel would stare at her, *through* her.

Maybe he was regretting what they'd said to each other. Maybe he thought she was some clingy woman who fell in love too quickly.

As for her, common sense told her that the last person her paranoid, übercautious self should be involved in was a firefighter.

She'd get over Daniel. She'd get used to being alone again.

She had to.

Rufus dutifully brought the worn tennis ball back to her. Kimberly just as dutifully tossed it out into the pasture. As she shielded her eyes to watch the way Rufus's brown coat gleamed in the late-afternoon sun, she spied Daniel's truck coming up the long driveway.

He saw her, too. She could tell he was a man on a mission the way he jumped out of the cab and barreled toward her.

"What's wrong?" Kimberly asked.

"I wanted you to know—I asked, Kimberly," he blurted out. "I tried to explain about Marissa and how she needed the medical records, and that you didn't even need the name, only the information."

"If you're talking about Judge Malloy, I got off the phone with him a few minutes ago. He's not releasing the records detailing Marissa's delivery or the birth mom's care after she got to the hospital."

Daniel frowned, his eyes squinting in concentration. "Huh?"

"He turned me down. Your wonderful family friend, the judge, called me and told me, sorry, no can do."

Daniel swore softly and put his hand to his mouth.

"Don't act so surprised," she said with more bitterness than she should have. "Isn't this what you wanted?"

"What I wanted? You make it sound like I'm part of some sort of grand conspiracy to keep you from finding out. All I ever wanted was to be able to follow the law and keep my word!" Daniel retorted.

"Well, now..." She ticked off the items one by one on her fingers. "You blocked me with Tim. You blocked me with Pax. You *would* have blocked me with Hiram Sullivan if you'd thought about it. You blocked me with Judge Malloy—which meant you effectively blocked me with Gail, who was *there*, Daniel. She could tell me what we needed to know."

"What if we'd given you the info, huh? What if we blabbed every little detail, and it still didn't help? What if it still didn't give doctors what they needed to figure out what Marissa has? What then?" he bellowed. "We'd have broken the law and our promise—"

"Don't you talk about the law. You aren't bound by—"

"I'm bound by a *higher* law!" His words rang out, sharp and steely.

She shook her head in despair. "You don't get it, do you? You will never get it."

"No, you don't get it. That girl has reasons— good reasons. She is *afraid*, Kimberly, in a full-blown panic. And you would be, too. I've thought about it and thought about it—"

Something in what he said caught Kimberly's attention. Disbelief mingled with white-hot anger. "Wait. You've *talked* with her?" She took a step closer to him. "Daniel Monroe, you have talked with Marissa's birth mother?"

"That's what I was telling you. I called her. I tried to explain, tried to get her to see—"

"Explain what? How we needed family medical history? Then, why don't you give *me* the chance to explain it to her, huh? What right do you have deciding whether or not we can contact her?"

Daniel laid a hand on her shoulder in a move to calm her down, but she jerked away.

"Kimberly—she's worried. You have to see it from her perspective. She was in a terrible situation, with nobody to stand up for her—not her parents, not that sorry excuse of a boyfriend, even if he is cold and dead in the ground now. She's afraid that there might be a custody dispute—"

"You talked with her. About me. But you don't give me the common courtesy of at least asking her to talk with me," Kimberly stormed, not wanting to hear all the excuses he had.

Behind them, the screen door creaked in protest. "Stop!" Marissa yelled. "Just…stop."

They both wheeled around to see Marissa standing on the steps, fists clenching and unclenching by her sides.

"Honey—" But when Kimberly would have stepped toward her, Marissa slashed through the air with her fist.

She didn't even look at Kimberly. Instead, she stared at Daniel. Her eyes shone with tears.

"You're not my dad?"

Pain tore across Daniel's face, twisting his mouth. "Marissa, I—"

"Answer the question. Yes or no. Are. You. My. Dad."

He ran a hand through his hair, glanced sideways at Kimberly. "No. No, I'm not your biological father."

A wrenching sob racked through Marissa. "I'm not a Monroe? You said—you said I was a Monroe kid. You said— I thought I *belonged*."

"I—I meant, you know…" Daniel closed his eyes, swallowed. Kimberly looked first at him, then Marissa, with the helpless feeling a person has watching a head-on collision.

"And my dad—my real dad—he's dead?"

Daniel pressed his lips into a thin line. After a beat of hesitation, he nodded curtly.

"Marissa—" Kimberly took another step toward her.

But Marissa glared at her. "I hate you! I hate you both! I never want to see either of you again!" she shrieked.

And with that she blew past them, running across the pasture, past the big oak tree and disappearing into the thick pine woods.

CHAPTER TWENTY-SEVEN

DANIEL PARKED THE four-wheeler inside the barn and pocketed the key. He took in the dim expanse of the barn's interior, the shadowy hayloft. Could she be here?

"Marissa?" he shouted. "Marissa! Come on, now. Your mom's worried about you."

Empty silence was the only response. Still, he climbed up in the hayloft and checked one more time.

Nope. No sign of her.

After Marissa had run off, he'd urged Kimberly to let the girl cool off. "She needs some space," he'd told her. "Let her run off some steam in the woods. She'll be back."

For once, Kimberly hadn't argued with him, though he could tell she wanted to. Instead, she'd nodded slowly. "Yeah. I guess you're right."

Then, as she'd turned back in the house, her face awash with misery, she'd spun on her heel. "Daniel—I didn't know she thought that about you. I had no idea."

He hadn't, either. The idea that Marissa had believed—had wanted a dad so badly that she'd fashion him into one...

The thought ate at him as he stepped back out into the darkening evening. As dusk had crept closer, even he'd gotten worried when Marissa hadn't turned up, wearing her usual sheepish expression after a blowup.

And Kimberly—Kimberly was out of her mind with worry.

He'd sent Rob and Andrew out looking for Marissa, with orders for Kimberly to stay put at the house and call them the minute Marissa turned up. They'd divvied up the property and looked everywhere they could think: at DeeDee's to see if Marissa had gone to ground with Taylor, the tree house, even Maegan's stable.

But Taylor hadn't heard a word from her—and she was worried, too, because Marissa wasn't answering any of her texts.

In a moment of desperation, Daniel had taken the four-wheeler down to the mill house to see if maybe Marissa had gone there.

But the mill house had been deserted—

empty of everything except for the bitter-sweet memories of his day with Kimberly.

"Where *are* you?" he asked aloud.

The lonely sound of a whip-poor-will was his only answer.

He started across the pasture toward the house, his feet heavy. Facing Kimberly, telling her that he'd struck out at the last place he could possibly think of, was not on his top-ten list.

Rufus ambled out from under the low branches of the oak to join him, falling into step beside Daniel. The Labrador carried his favorite tennis ball in his mouth and a hopeful expression in his soulful brown eyes.

"Hey, buddy." Daniel stopped to stroke the dog's massive brown head, then scratched him under the chin. "You got your ball for me, huh? Sorry, fella. I don't feel much like playing catch."

Rufus's tail slowed to a dispirited wag as he apparently gathered that even his most dependable human couldn't be conned into throwing a ball. As Daniel approached the house, he realized that the dog had stopped.

He called over his shoulder and clapped his hand on his thigh. "C'mon, Rufus. I'll get you some supper."

But the magic words didn't work. Rufus didn't come. Instead, he wobbled his head first toward Daniel and the house, then toward the oak. His decision made, the dog moseyed back to the oak. With a sigh Daniel could hear from halfway across the field, Rufus flopped down at the base of the old tree.

Daniel frowned. It wasn't like Rufus to ignore his supper.

The dog's tail fanned the sandy soil as Daniel neared him. But Daniel didn't take too much notice. Instead, he gazed straight up at the floorboards of the tree house.

The barest flicker of movement gave Marissa away.

Relief surged through Daniel. She must have doubled back and hid up here after he'd checked earlier. Hoisting himself up on the lower branches, he began the slow, awkward climb to the tree house, the rough bark stinging his palms, and the ache in his thighs telling him loud and clear that he wasn't ten anymore. Carefully, he pulled himself over the railing.

Marissa greeted him with a sour, "So I guess I'm grounded for a month— Oh, wait. I forgot. You're not my dad."

The remark cut, exactly as she'd intended it to. Daniel kneeled down in front of her, took in her swollen, tearstained face. His heart ached.

"I may not be your biological dad, Marissa, but, if I were, I'd be proud to call you my daughter."

She sniffled and wiped her nose with the back of her hand. "My real dad wasn't. He left me, Daniel. And my real mom—she dumped me out and forgot about me. I don't belong *anywhere*."

"Your *real* mom is at the house, going out of her head, wondering where you might be. She may not be blood kin, but she was the one who got up in the middle of the night to check on you, who cooked you supper, washed your clothes and—"

He broke off when he saw her head droop all the lower.

"I know," she whispered. "I meant my biological mom. I—I wanted to be a Monroe kid so *bad*, Daniel. I wanted—I wanted to fit in. I wanted *you* to be my dad."

"Hmm...someone told me just a few hours ago that she hated me and she never wanted to see me again. Apparently I stink at this dad business."

She shrugged one shoulder. "It takes some practice. But you'd get the hang of it."

"Would I?" His insides ached for the chance. It wasn't going to happen, though. Kimberly was going to pack her and Marissa up and head back to Atlanta and forget all about him.

Maybe that was for the best, because she couldn't seem to wrap her head around why he couldn't talk about Miriam. Maybe once she left, he could kill off this hope that something would happen to magically fix Marissa's health problems so that Miriam could stay lurking in the shadows.

He knew that wouldn't happen, and even if it did, Kimberly couldn't forget that he knew who Marissa's birth mother was—he knew and wouldn't tell her. It simply wasn't in her nature to forget.

"You really aren't my dad?" Marissa asked him again.

"I'm really not. But if I could pick any kid to have as mine, it would be you."

"Taylor—Taylor was sure I was a Monroe. I mean, I've got the cleft in my chin, and the light eyes, and even the twisty elbows." She demonstrated her double-jointedness.

"Huh, you do have twisty elbows," he commented.

"But if you say I'm not... I guess I've got to go back to Atlanta, huh?"

"That's where your mom will be." The thought ripped through him. He didn't want to contemplate how empty and quiet the house would be with just him and Ma and Maegan rattling around, without Kimberly and Marissa there.

He didn't want to contemplate how empty his *heart* would be.

"You sure I can't live with you and Ma?" Marissa pleaded. "And go to school here? I'd work hard—I'd earn my keep. I know how to shell butter beans fast now."

Daniel couldn't stop his hand from ruffling her strawberry blond hair. "Wouldn't you miss your mom?"

"Maybe she'd miss *me* enough to move down here," she replied.

"I don't think that's an option right now. She's got a job and a house. People can't just up and move."

"Yeah, that's what I figured." Marissa fiddled with a branch, stripping it of its tender green leaves and shredding them into bits.

"But it was worth a shot, right? Because… because it's not that you don't *want* me."

His heart twisted as if she was squeezing it in her hands. "We all want you. Me, and Taylor and Ma and Maegan and everybody. But especially your mom. She really loves you, you know."

Marissa sniffled again. "I know. I love her, too. She can be all…Helicopter Mom and all, but I love her. She kept me. When nobody else wanted me, she kept me. You think she'll forgive me for being such a brat? I know it was wrong, what I said. But it—it hurt so *bad*."

"She's already forgiven you. And you'll come back and visit us, right? Maybe next summer? After all, Maegan's gotten used to you helping her exercise the horses, and Ma could always use help with the beans."

He could see hope flood her face, and then the instant she squashed it deep down inside her. "Yeah. Maybe. But it won't be the same."

"Hey, it's getting dark. If you don't hurry, you'll miss your cookout."

"It's for the Fourth, not for me."

"Best I recall, today's your birthday, kiddo. And I think I happened to see Ma baking a cake for you."

"Really? For me?" Her eyes shone. "She made a cake for me? After I was such a brat?"

"I think she'd started it earlier. She sure was bent on finishing it. She was certain no girl would want to miss her birthday. Still..." He shook his finger at her in mock solemnity. "It won't be long before we have to head out for the fireworks, and you know Ma's rule—no dessert if you don't try at least everything on your plate. And that even counts for birthday cake for birthday girls."

Marissa scrambled to her feet. "What color is it? What flavor?"

He lifted his hands. "How should I know? I'm a guy. Cake is cake to me. I do know she had Rob churning the ice cream to go with it."

Marissa clambered over the railing, intent on skittering down the tree. "I'll bet it's strawberry! I told her strawberry was my favorite—"

"Wait, Marissa! Let me go—"

Before he could get out the word *first*, her foot had slipped in the darkening twilight. With a screech, she scrabbled for a hold.

He saw it unfold in slow motion, his hands reaching out and touching nothing but air as he tried to catch her. She slid down the main trunk, landing with a thud on her belly at the base of the tree.

Daniel was down beside her in an instant, Rufus butting in and nosing her.

"Uhh," she groaned. "And I thought the sand would be soft."

"You okay? Are you hurt? How many fingers am I holding up?"

"Two...wait—" She squinted. "Three now. What are you trying to do, trick me? Make up your mind, will you?"

He laughed, sick with relief. "Wait, let me check you out."

Quickly he ran through a neuro and vital signs check and had her wiggle her arms and legs, fingers and toes.

"Amazing. When I took a tumble out of that tree, I broke my collarbone and my arm," he told her. "I can't believe you just got the wind knocked out of you."

She gripped his wrist. "Please—don't tell Mom. She'll worry, and I've already worried her enough. She'll be sure to make me miss the fireworks and maybe even the cookout, and it's our last night here. It's my *birthday*, Daniel. Please?"

He pressed his lips together, considering. "I don't know—"

"Please? As long as I'm okay? I mean, sure, if I get sick or something, but I *won't*, I know I won't. And promise me you won't tell Mom I was up here. You know I'll be in such hot water."

He sat back on his heels. "You're sure you're okay?"

"Absolutely positive." To ram her point home, she rose to her feet and made a big show out of dusting herself off.

Daniel's gut didn't sit well with keeping this from Kimberly—but Marissa was right. Kimberly had worried enough, and Marissa seemed no worse for wear.

"All right. Here's the deal," he said. "I won't say anything…unless something starts hurting. But if you feel anything—any little twinge, any dizziness, any nausea or headache or numbness or tingling—we have to tell her, deal?" He extended his hand. "Can we shake on that?"

She gripped his hand and pumped up and down. "Deal. Now let's go find out what flavor my birthday cake is."

A BOISTEROUS COOKOUT was the last place Kimberly wanted to be. For one thing, she didn't feel like celebrating, not with Marissa gone.

Kimberly had tried to tell herself that everyone was right: Marissa needed time to cool off. She'd be back. She couldn't have gone far.

That worked as long as Kimberly put out of her mind all the things that could harm Marissa—poisonous snakes, a rabid raccoon, a black widow spider, the murky water of the millpond.

Ma seemed to understand. Even so, it amazed Kimberly how she could calmly complete the final details on the three-layer birthday cake she'd made for Marissa. "I'm not trying to condescend or to downplay your concern." She'd focused on piping a big fluffy rose onto the cake. "I know Marissa has her issues. But, Kimberly, I raised six kids myself on this farm, and none of 'em came to harm—nothing that couldn't be fixed. Besides, they'll find her, or she'll come back— I feel that in my bones. Stressing over it isn't going to get her back here one second sooner—and all it's going to do is cloud your mind so you can't think of other places to tell the boys to look."

It made sense, what Ma said, even if Kimberly couldn't completely follow her advice. Ma had seen that and put her to work.

"I promise—it will help. Keep your phone with you, check in with them all you want, but keep your hands busy, Kimberly. Take it for what it's worth from a woman with three grown boys who run *into* burning buildings when everybody else has the good sense to run *out*."

Now Kimberly wandered down the long picnic table, clad in its red-checked table-cloth, making sure the plates and napkins and everything else needed for the cookout were there. So what if she had to count everything twice because she kept losing track?

Already off-duty firefighters and their families and other friends of the Monroes were showing up. There was Pax, holding court over by the grill, telling horror stories of EMS runs while he flipped burgers. Tim, off tonight from the police department, was there, too, helping set out folding chairs and card tables.

Ma came out with a huge platter of lettuce, tomatoes and onions. "Still no word?" she asked Kimberly. When Kimberly could manage only a curt shake of her head, Ma frowned, set the platter down on the table and shaded her eyes with her hand. She stared out across the pastures. "Now, where could that girl be?"

"Daniel went to check the mill house… Wait, wait! There they are!" Kimberly clapped her hand to her mouth as she spotted them coming down the rise from the far pasture. She pushed through a crowd of people and ran to meet them.

She buried Marissa in a bear hug, then, as she had with Daniel after the fire, her anger got the better of her. She held her daughter at arm's length. "I've been worried sick! Where were you?"

Marissa's eyes flickered up to Daniel's, and Kimberly detected an unspoken message telegraphed between them. It made the gratitude she'd felt toward Daniel curdle in her belly. "Lots of places. I just kept running."

"Where'd you find her?" she demanded.

Daniel didn't quite meet her eyes. "I found her up in the far pasture, near the fence," he said.

She could tell he was holding something back. Before she could launch into him, Taylor came galloping up the rise to meet them. "Hey, Uncle Daniel, Ma says come quick, because Pax is going to turn the burgers into charcoal! Hey, Marissa! Everybody's been looking for you! Wow! How'd you get so dirty? Want to go in and change? Did you know Ma made a birthday cake for you?"

With that, still talking a mile a minute, Taylor yanked Marissa toward the house and clean clothes, and Daniel headed over to rescue the burgers. Kimberly stood alone in the pasture, feeling forgotten and overlooked.

And lied to. Obviously Daniel must have extended another one of his famous promises to Marissa.

Swallowing her anger, she told herself that this was the last night she'd have to put up with him. Tomorrow she and Marissa would be gone, and she could begin the hard job of getting on with her life and forgetting about Daniel. He didn't really care about her. Regardless of what he'd said in that ER, she didn't count—not if he couldn't see how, when you gave away a promise to someone, you were closing off communication with everyone else.

Back at the cookout, she plastered a smile on her face and gritted her teeth. Staying here for her birthday was what Marissa had asked for—so Kimberly would do that. She could endure anything for a few hours.

The burgers were heaped on platters, and people around her were laughing and settling down on the long bench seats of the picnic table and at the card tables Tim had finished setting up. The night air was thick and humid, punctuated by tiki torches to keep the mosquitos away.

"Hey, where's the birthday girl?" Maegan asked. "I didn't know if we were doing presents, but I got her something small."

Kimberly looked around. Where were Marissa and Taylor? They'd been holed up in the house for ages, and now it was almost time to eat. If they didn't hurry, they'd miss the fireworks. Already, she could see Daniel glancing at his watch. As fire chief, he had to head in and be on hand where the fireworks firm was shooting off the explosives.

Then over the hubbub of laughter and small talk, another sound ripped through the night: the slamming of a screen door, followed by Taylor's agonized voice.

"Help! Somebody help! Marissa's real bad sick! You've got to come help!"

CHAPTER TWENTY-EIGHT

MARISSA LAY DOUBLED over on Ma's wedding-ring quilt, her face a grayish pale, sweat beading on her forehead. Pax straightened up from his quick assessment. "Pulse is tachy. She's going into shock. We've got to get a bus here now."

Without waiting, he yanked his phone off his belt, punched at the keypad, then barked at the person on the other end, identifying himself and ordering them to send an ambulance ASAP.

Hanging up, he bent back over Marissa. "Marissa? You're not allergic to anything, are you? Not like Taylor? This isn't anaphylaxis, is it?"

She shook her head, unable to speak.

"She has a bleeding disorder," Kimberly answered for her. "Is she hurt? Is she bleeding? Marissa, you've got to tell us what happened! When did you get sick?"

She whirled around to Taylor. "What happened?"

"I—I don't know… She got real tired, and sick and then she said she felt like she was gonna faint. I got her to the bed, and she told me not to get you, that you'd freak…but I was scared, Ms. Kim. I was bad scared."

Daniel pushed past Taylor and stood by Kimberly. "She fell. When I found her—she fell."

Pax narrowed his eyes. "How? How far?"

Daniel swallowed, then set his jaw. "From about halfway down the oak with the tree house. That's where I found her."

"She what?" Kimberly stared at him in disbelief. "And you didn't tell me? She could have been killed— She could die—"

"I know. She didn't want to worry you— so I told her I wouldn't say anything." Before Kimberly could light into him, he held up both hands. "I know, Kimberly, I shouldn't have. It was stupid. But she seemed fine—I checked. I ran through a neuro, checked her pulse, checked to make sure she wasn't cut— Made sure nothing was broken—" Daniel's voice cracked.

"Don't you get it?" Kimberly cried. "With a bleeding disorder, it's not the blood you *see* that you worry about—it's the blood you *can't* see!"

Meanwhile Pax had lifted up Marissa's shirt. "Sorry, honey, let me take a peek—oh. Yeah—significant bruising and guarding in the upper left quadrant. Daniel, was that there earlier?"

He lifted his hands. "I—I didn't check there. She said she wasn't hurt."

Kimberly connected the dots in a flash. "You think it's her spleen?" she asked Pax.

"Yeah, I think it's her spleen." He craned his head toward the window and peered out. "Where's that ambulance?"

Daniel shook his head. "No. She needs more than that. Doesn't she, Kimberly? Get a helicopter, Pax. Now. We've got to get her to Atlanta. To her doctors."

"Okay, but I'm not turning the bus around. I need an IV started. I don't have the supplies with me. And—what's her blood type? I should have told the EMTs to bring a couple of bags to hang. Daniel, I just don't know. Maybe we should get her stabilized here?" Pax stared first at Marissa, then at Kimberly. "It's your call."

Kimberly clasped her hands, tried to fight the urge to go down on her knees and shriek.

She had to be calm; she had to think. She had to be like Ma, because Marissa needed her now.

"Helicopter." The word was a near whisper, but her voice grew stronger. "I'll call her doctors. They know her case—the hospital here might not have the medicine she needs," Kimberly spluttered.

The next few minutes were a blur to Kimberly—lights flashing, sirens sounding, the gurney clacking over the back porch boards and across the gravel. Pax and the EMTs bent over Marissa's now-still body, rushing, rushing, rushing. And then somewhere out of the approaching darkness, Kimberly heard the *thwack-thwack-thwack* of helicopter blades so loud and close it reverberated in her chest. The aircraft dropped like a stone into Ma's pasture, Maegan's horses skittering in fear on the other side of the fence.

They wouldn't let her ride in the chopper, no matter how much she begged them. No room, they said, and against policy. She had time to squeeze Marissa's still, limp hand just once before the helicopter crew tore after the chopper and hoisted the gurney into it.

And then the huge machine rocked to and fro, lifted up and disappeared into the night sky.

Shaking and jerking, Kimberly hit her knees, sobbing, keening. She knew she had to stop, she knew she had to get hold of herself. But no matter how much she ordered herself to stay calm, she could not quiet the powerful tremors that rumbled through her.

Strong hands lifted her up—Pax and Tim. Ma was there, wrapping her in a blanket against the night air that suddenly chilled her.

And Daniel?

Daniel sat crumpled on the porch steps, his head in his hands.

The sight of him steeled her. This was his fault. He'd never taken Marissa's illness seriously. He'd undermined her and gone behind her back and now he was the one who was to blame.

"I have to go. I have to get to Atlanta." She made for the house and her keys.

Pax stepped in front of her, his hand on her arm. "Hey, Kimberly, you're not in any shape to drive ten minutes, much less three hours. Let somebody drive you—I'll bet Daniel would be glad—"

"I don't want Daniel. I don't want Daniel Monroe anywhere near my daughter," she whispered. "He's done quite enough." She shook off Pax's hand and stalked past Daniel without another word.

DANIEL SAT HUDDLED over a cup of coffee, finally alone in the kitchen. He'd run Pax out. Then he'd run Tim out. Then Rob and Andrew had come in, and he'd run them out. Maybe sometime in the next century somebody would get the message that he wasn't fit for company.

He wasn't fit to be a father, either. Kimberly's mouth had curled in contempt as she'd tossed a bag and her purse in her car and then tore down the drive. He'd tried to stop her, to tell her he was sorry. Oh, was he sorry—

He had lost them.

The screen door creaked open again, and he swore. "I *said*—"

But then he saw Ma standing there, her hands on her hips.

"Daniel Monroe. You care to explain yourself?"

"Ma, I—" He couldn't bear to meet her eyes. He tightened his fingers around the coffee cup, itching to smash it against the wall.

"I'm not talking about Marissa falling. *That* was an accident," she said. "I'm talking about you not being there for Kimberly, you not telling her about the fall."

"Ma...I promised Marissa."

"You sound as though you're about ten years old, Daniel." Sighing, she dragged out the chair across from him and peeled his fingers away from the mug. Holding them, she met his eyes. "I know your dad set a store by promises. But people can't expect you to keep them if they're going to hurt somebody. That's when a promise becomes a secret— and you know the only secrets I abide by are happy secrets."

"It doesn't matter, Ma. She was leaving anyway. I wouldn't tell her—"

"About that girl. I know. Ditto what I just said. Now, you listen to me, son. Your father, if he had the power to save someone's life, would move heaven and earth to do it. That's what he meant by keeping promises and being a man. He *died* doing that. And he would not think any less of you if you did whatever it took to do right by a child."

Something in her words shifted a heavy burden off Daniel's shoulders, one he felt as though he'd been toting forever. He saw his promise to Miriam and his refusal to tell Kimberly for what it was—an exercise in pride, at least partly, and a way to hold on to that last bit of his father.

He straightened, gripped her hands. "I shouldn't have taken no for an answer. I should have gone with her—I should have never let her drive by herself—"

"Darn tootin', you shouldn't have. Now, that's the Daniel I raised."

Tim barreled through the back door. "Daniel—one of my officers pulled Kimberly over for speeding. She was going nearly eighty in a fifty-five. You want me to drive her up to Atlanta?"

Daniel looked at Ma and shook his head. "No. I want you to call that buddy of yours with the airplane and tell him we need to fly to Atlanta. Eighty's not nearly fast enough."

KIMBERLY WAITED IMPATIENTLY for the police officer to come back in the room. The woman had taken her keys and put her in the back of the squad car, then driven her in the opposite direction from the interstate. Now she was penned up in an interrogation room, waiting for Tim to come and spring her. If she had to pay a thousand-dollar fine and a tow bill to match, it would be worth it—she'd pay anything, just later. Later, after she'd seen Marissa.

But where was he? Were they arresting her? They couldn't keep her—she had to get to Atlanta.

In the quiet of the cramped, airless room, the image of Marissa, so pale and limp and lifeless, flooded back to her.

She'd fallen out of the oak tree. Kimberly shuddered at the imagined impact. Marissa had been up in that tree house, after Kimberly had ordered her not to go there. She'd even told Daniel to take down the ladder—

He'd taken down the ladder.

And that was why Marissa had fallen.

Because there was no ladder.

And Kimberly had never let Marissa learn how to climb a tree.

A wrenching sob tore through her and she collapsed back into the hard plastic chair. Her fault. It was her fault.

The door opened, but Kimberly couldn't lift her face from her hands.

"Kimberly?"

She choked out a laugh as she recognized who it was. "Man, Daniel Monroe, do you have this town wired or what? What sort of favors did you call in to get me pulled over, huh?"

He kneeled down in front of her. "I did

wrong. I made a bad decision, and I regret it. But are you going to waste time yelling at me, or are you going to come with me to the plane Tim's got waiting for us? And by the way, if you know anybody who could pick us up at the airport in Atlanta, you can tell them we'll be there in about thirty minutes."

IT WAS CLOSER to forty-five minutes by the time they were actually on the ground and in the car of the one friend she could find who hadn't left town for the Fourth. She hadn't been able to speak in that entire forty-five minutes, just prayed and hoped. They seemed to be landing as quick as they'd taken off.

Daniel hadn't offered any conversation, either. He'd been quiet in the plane, looking more than a little green around the gills. In the car, he was as quiet as she was.

Kimberly could barely look at him—not because she blamed him, but because she blamed herself. If she'd listened to him in the first place, Marissa would have had a ladder to get down from that tree house—a ladder she had safely climbed before.

At the hospital, they were ushered to a surgery waiting room. Marissa's hem/onc found them and sat down across from them.

"She's being prepped for surgery as we speak," the doctor told her. "But all we can do is fly by the seat of our pants here, Kimberly. There's a lot we don't know. I know you've been looking for the birth mother—have you found *anything*?"

Kimberly hung her head to hide the tears. She shook her head. "No. I tried—I really, really tried, but a judge wouldn't let me have the records—"

"Sir." It was Daniel, his voice crisp. "I think I can help you. If you'll hold on for a moment, there's someone I'm hoping will be able to fill in some gaps."

She lifted her head, not daring to hope. Yes, he was dialing a number. His jaw was set as he waited for the phone to ring.

"Miriam? It's Daniel again. I have the doctor here, like I said I would when I called before. He needs to talk to you. I know you're scared, but I swear, I would not ask this if there were any other way. You trusted me back then to keep her safe—you made me *promise* to keep her safe. And this is the best way I know to save her life."

Miriam. Her baby's birth mother's name was Miriam.

And then, miracle of miracles, Daniel stood

and extended the phone to the doctor, who began asking detailed questions. Kimberly stared at Daniel, not bothering to even attempt to quell the tears running down her face.

"You broke your promise," she whispered.

His eyes were dark and stormy, a far cry from the blue they usually were. "No. I kept it. Maybe not like I thought I should—thought I needed to, but I *am* keeping that promise. I'm sorry it took me so long to figure that out. She could die— She could die—" Daniel's face crumpled. "And it's all my fault."

Kimberly wrapped her arms around him. "No. It was me, Daniel. I told you to take that ladder down. Yeah, you should have told me about the fall. Yeah, Marissa shouldn't have been in that blasted tree house to begin with, but I smothered her. You would have taught her how to climb a tree."

"I will. I will teach her how to climb a tree," he said fiercely. "And if you'll have me, I'll take care of you both and never ever promise anything to anybody that will stop me from keeping either of you safe. I promise."

Kimberly laughed, a painful laugh that made her cry all the harder. "Ma says—Ma says I can take what you say to the bank…and I know how you are. But, Daniel—"

The doctor cleared his throat, drawing them apart. He was smiling, relief wreathing his face. "Marissa's birth mother has PAI-1 deficiency, so it's a good bet that she does, too. Lots of questions got answered just now, Kimberly. I've got to tell the trauma surgeon what protocol he needs to follow, and we'll be in touch with Dr. Fischer in Indiana. It will be a long road to recovery, but we can save her."

Daniel closed his eyes, then opened them. "It's her birthday. July Fourth. I delivered her myself. Could you please, please bring her back to me?"

The doctor leaned over, shook his hand. "Sir, I will do my level best. A nurse will keep you posted throughout the surgery. Don't worry. Marissa's in excellent hands, and I'm confident about our approach now."

He was out the door, leaving them alone. Kimberly sagged onto the chair. Daniel squatted down beside her.

"You didn't exactly answer my question. Will you and Marissa have me?"

"Are you sure? Absolutely sure that this isn't because of tonight and you'll regret it later? I mean—I'm *me*, Daniel," Kimberly told him. "And I can't change overnight. Plus, I've got to come back and teach—"

"Hey. We'll figure it out. I'll buy a plane if I have to," he joked. In a more serious tone, he said, "I'm not losing you. I gave up Marissa twelve years ago today when I wanted to keep her. But I had to let her go—so you could find her and then you could find me. I'll learn, I'll give it my all to learn how to be a good and careful father."

"Oh, Daniel—you *are* a good and careful father. *You* are a good and careful man. And yes—yes, I'll try, too. No." Kimberly pressed her lips to his, then pulled back and looked him straight in the eye. "I'll do one better. *I'll* promise."

* * * * *

Visit THE GEORGIA MONROES *again, coming in the fall of 2015 from acclaimed author Cynthia Reese.*

LARGER-PRINT BOOKS!

**GET 2 FREE
LARGER-PRINT NOVELS
PLUS 2 FREE
MYSTERY GIFTS**

Love Inspired

Larger-print novels are now available...

LARGER-PRINT BOOKS!

GET 2 FREE
LARGER-PRINT NOVELS
PLUS 2 FREE
MYSTERY GIFTS

Love Inspired® SUSPENSE

RIVETING INSPIRATIONAL ROMANCE

Larger-print novels are now available...

LISLPDIR13R